DEEP FURY

BOOKS BY DAVID FREED

THE CORDELL LOGAN MYSTERIES
Flat Spin
Fangs Out
Voodoo Ridge
The Three-Nine Line
Hot Start
The Kill Circle
Deep Fury

NONFICTION
Dear Ernest and Julio

DAVID FREED

DEEP FURY

· A CORDELL LOGAN MYSTERY ·

BLACK STONE
PUBLISHING

Copyright © 2024 by David Freed
Published in 2024 by Blackstone Publishing
Cover and book design by Candice Edwards

All rights reserved. This book or any portion
thereof may not be reproduced or used in any manner
whatsoever without the express written permission
of the publisher except for the use of brief quotations
in a book review.

The characters and events in this book are fictitious.
Any similarity to real persons, living or dead, is coincidental
and not intended by the author.

Printed in the United States of America

First edition: 2024
ISBN 979-8-212-17945-4
Fiction / Mystery & Detective / General

Version 1

Blackstone Publishing
31 Mistletoe Rd.
Ashland, OR 97520

www.BlackstonePublishing.com

To Marty and Judith Shepard, for giving me a chance

"A pilot lives in a world of perfection.
Or nothing at all."

—Unknown

Long after the naked man plummeted from the night sky and exploded like a bomb through the roof of Walt and Lena Rizzo's double-wide mobile home in the Sun Country RV and Trailer Park, Walt couldn't decide if it was the dog or divine providence that had saved his wife's life.

It was after supper. The elderly couple were watching Dancing with the Stars *with the sound turned way up when their miniature schnauzer, Rambo, who also answered to "Rambie" and "Ram-Ram," began pawing at the door so he could go do his business outside. Walt's knees were acting up again—all those years laying tile for all those rich snobs up in Knob Hill and Pacific Heights—but he willed himself out of his recliner anyway to let the dog out because he didn't want Lena missing a minute of her favorite show. Sixty-one years together, and she was the most beautiful woman Walt had ever seen.*

"Sit," she said loudly.

"What?"

"I said sit. I'll take him out."

They were both about as hard of hearing as one might expect

of two people in their late eighties. Lena pointed animatedly to herself, then to the dog, then to Walt, then to Walt's chair.

"You sure, doll? I don't mind."

"It's a rerun, honey. We've seen it before. Relax."

Walt eased himself back down into his chair as Lena slid her feet into her fuzzy slippers and took her time getting off the couch gingerly on her one good hip. She'd taken no more than three steps toward the door when the trailer seemed to go sideways with a violent, deafening crash.

Windows shattered. Photos of the grandkids flew off the walls. The Rizzos toppled like bowling pins.

They thought at first it was The Big One, the long-dreaded giant earthquake that would finally send California floating off toward Japan. Only after they scraped themselves off the floor with hearts pounding did they notice the gaping hole in the roof of the living room and the mangled body of the man who'd fallen through it.

"A darned miracle," Walt told the firefighters afterward as he stood outside with Lena, clutching their dog in one arm and her in the other. "If it hadn't been for Ram-Ram telling us he needed to go pee so bad, that guy in there, he would've landed right on top of her and that would've been it. Lights out. Sayonara. A miracle, I'm telling ya."

"It's like he knew," Lena said, kissing the dog on his head.

The three firefighters were buff and square-jawed as if each had stepped from the pages of one of those station house calendars, posing shirtless in their suspenders.

"Probably a skydiver," one of them speculated.

"With no parachute? Doubtful," another said.

The third firefighter suppressed a wry smile. "Hey, if at first you don't succeed, jumping out of airplanes may not be for you."

The others tried not to smile, too. With no flames to put out, there wasn't much for them to do but stand around looking studly in their helmets and yellow turnout gear, waiting for the Santa Isabella County Medical Examiner's Office to cart the body away. When the coroner's van finally arrived two hours later, Walt and Lena were still shaking.

No one could determine at first who the dead man was or where he'd come from other than out of the night sky. Naked means no clothes. No clothes means no pockets. No pockets means no driver's license or other ID. What wasn't hard to figure out was that a human being falling at terminal velocity is not compatible with the half-inch plywood roof of a mobile home. His skull had burst open like a watermelon. Blood splattered everywhere.

The pathologist assigned to conduct an autopsy was an Englishman by birth who looked like he made a habit of sleeping in his clothes. Everybody called him Dr. Yorkie. Not because he happened to have been born in Yorkshire, which he had, but because he was a small man with a carefully groomed beard who bore an uncanny resemblance to a terrier. His preliminary examination of the body established no obvious signs of foul play, though it was hard to tell given the extent of the injuries. Digital fingerprints and what could be gained through partial dental impressions of the decedent's fractured jawbones were run through national crime databases. The initial results would come back NOR—nothing on record. Toxicological samples were subsequently shipped on ice to a forensic lab in San Jose. It would take more than a week for those results to come back.

Then there were the tattoos inked on the man's left shoulder, two small lightning bolts. On his right forearm was the number 84. Dr. Yorkie discovered online that in the coded parlance of right-wing political extremism, 8 and 4 stood for H and D— the initials of Colonel Heinrich Dietz, among Adolf Hitler's most brutal SS commanders. Twin lightning bolts were, of course, the *common insignia of* der Führer's *storm troopers. Yorkie speculated that the man who'd fallen from the sky might have been some sort of neo-Nazi.*

I knew otherwise. The man's tattoos meant none of that. He was a patriot, as fearless a pilot as I'd ever known, who'd died trying to stop the world from blowing itself to pieces before it was too late.

ONE

"Rancho Bonita Tower, Skyhawk Four Charlie Lima is ready at One-Seven Left."

"Skyhawk Four Charlie Lima, wind one eight zero at twelve, gusting to sixteen. Cleared for takeoff, runway One-Seven Left."

I glanced over at Mrs. Schmulowitz, my ninety-year-old landlady, who was belted into the left seat of my ancient Cessna 172, also known as the *Ruptured Duck*. She was decked out like Cecil B. DeMille's vision of a Roaring Twenties aviatrix, right down to the leather flying jacket and white silk scarf, the jodhpurs and riding boots. All she would've needed to complete the look were a pair of goggles and one of those old-timey leather flying helmets, but that would've interfered with the noise-canceling headset clamped like mouse ears over a frizz of dyed ginger hair that looked like it belonged on someone else's head.

"OK, Mrs. Schmulowitz," I said, "I'll line us up on the runway and handle the throttle. When you hear me say 'Rotate,' I want you to start pulling back on the yoke. Nice and easy, nothing radical, OK?"

"The steering wheel, you mean?"

"It's not a steering wheel, Mrs. Schmulowitz. In an airplane, it's called a yoke."

"Yoke, schmoke. Whatever. Do you know who I'm feeling a little bit like right now? Amelia Earhart. OK, granted, things didn't work out too good for that poor lady, may she rest in peace, but still. I can't believe you're letting me fly this thing! To tell you the truth, bubby, I've got a bit of the *shpilkes*."

"Don't be nervous, Mrs. Schmulowitz. You're gonna do fine. Just relax and have fun, OK?"

She nodded toward the floor of the plane. "What about those thingies down there?"

"Those are the rudder pedals. I'll handle those, too." I double-checked to make sure her seat belt and shoulder restraint were good and snug. "You ready?"

"Bubby, I'm from Bensonhurst, USA. I was born ready."

I confirmed our takeoff clearance with the tower and taxied the *Duck* toward the hold-short line. "OK, Mrs. Schmulowitz, here we go. Just remember: Don't start pulling back until I tell you, OK?"

"Roger-wilco. That's pilot lingo, right?"

"Close enough."

A good flight instructor knows the value of instilling confidence in any new student pilot, even one born during the Great Depression. If you're interested in paying the bills, your goal is to persuade that student to keep coming back, to assure them that with patience and training, anyone can learn to fly an airplane. Of course, any good flight instructor also knows that's a lie. You can usually tell right off when somebody has the wrong stuff. They lack depth perception or the necessary hand-eye coordination, or the fundamental pluck required to challenge gravity in a flimsy aluminum flying machine. Others never surmount aviation's basic learning curve—that if you can't properly focus and demonstrate sound judgment at every second, an airplane will kill you faster than anything. Then there are those students, like my four-foot-something, eighty-nine-pound, cataracts-afflicted landlady, who decide regardless of age that they need more adventure in their lives, even if they can't see over the instrument panel.

Who was I to say no?

The *Duck* began rolling down the runway, picking up speed. Forty-five knots showed on the airspeed indicator.

"You want I should start pulling back now?"

"Not yet, Mrs. Schmulowitz."

Fifty knots indicated.

"Now?"

"Not yet, Mrs. Schmulowitz," I said, working the right rudder and keeping us on the centerline while scanning the *Duck*'s engine gauges to make sure all systems were in the green.

Fifty-five knots. Sixty knots.

"OK, up we go. Let's do some flying, Mrs. Schmulowitz. Rotate."

She gently pulled back on the yoke as instructed. The *Duck*'s nose sniffed the air, and just like that, we were airborne, climbing out over the beach at eight hundred feet per minute. Not bad for an old bird steering an old bird for the first time.

"Whoo-eee! Bubby, this is fantastic!"

"Just like we know what we're doing," I said.

And then, just like that, I had no idea what we were doing.

My ancient landlady in her exuberance hauled back on the yoke with both hands like she was reining in a runaway horse. Instantly, the *Duck* pitched up at a grotesquely high angle of attack, shuddered as if we were driving over a washboard road, then stalled and pitched over steeply on the right wing. Suddenly, the Pacific Ocean filled the entire windscreen.

We were headed straight down.

"I have the plane," I shouted over the stall warning horn, grabbing the yoke, chopping the power, and leveling the ailerons all at once. I kicked in full opposite rudder to break the start of a spin, then jammed the nose down even steeper to break the stall, shoving the throttle to the firewall to regain airspeed. Only then did I begin pulling up. How we didn't go into the water, I'll never know. My air force training explained part of it. Luck certainly explained the rest. Had we been a foot lower when the *Duck* stalled, or had less headwind to work with, or been a few pounds heavier, carrying more fuel, we would've become one with the fishes. But, as a wise person once said, it's better to be lucky than good.

"Holy moly," Mrs. Schmulowitz said, "that was just like riding the Cyclone at Coney Island, only about ten times more fun."

She seemed not the least bit flustered by our near-death experience. I wasn't surprised. When you've spent your career teaching physical education to inner-city school kids in New York, survived cancer, and been widowed four times, as my ancient landlady had, there's not much left in this world to unnerve you.

"I've gotta be honest with you, Mrs. Schmulowitz, I don't think you're a natural-born flier. This is gonna take some work."

She patted my knee reassuringly. "You know what? My first husband, may he rest in peace, said the very same thing when I decided to try out for the Rockettes. Talk about work. You have no idea. And I would've made it, too, had I not pulled a hammy on opening night. All that crazy kicking without proper stretching."

"You never told me you tried out for the Rockettes, Mrs. Schmulowitz."

"You had to have the legs, bubby, and I did back then, believe you me."

"You've still got the legs, Mrs. Schmulowitz."

I let her fly the plane after we got back up to altitude and were safely out over the water, where we couldn't hurt anybody. Mrs. Schmulowitz was all over the sky. Up, down, down, up. Zooming south one minute and banking north the next, having a ball. Our radar ground track must've looked like a Rorschach test.

Mechanic Larry Kropf was balanced atop a step stool in his cavernous, World War II–era hangar, repairing the wing of a Cessna Centurion dented by a bird strike.

"I refilled your fire extinguisher," he said. "I forgot to put it back under the seat after your last hundred-hour inspection. Don't judge, Logan. I'm getting old."

"How about fifty bucks off this month's rent and we'll call it even," I said as I walked in off the flight line with Mrs. Schmulowitz.

"How about forget it," Larry said.

For the past few years, I've rented a cramped, windowless storeroom in Larry's hangar that I furnished with a government surplus desk and had the chutzpah to call a flight school. Larry's a big furry man with a big black beard and black-frame glasses with lenses so thick, you could fry ants with them. Many people express their inner selves these days by visiting a tattoo parlor. Larry preferred the scowl he was born with and expressive T-shirts. The one he was wearing said, "I'm not sure how many problems I have because math is one of them."

"How'd it go up there?" he asked, climbing down off the stool.

"As much fun as you can have with your underwear on," Mrs. Schmulowitz said.

"She did great," I said.

"Oh, horsefeathers." Mrs. Schmulowitz furrowed her already deeply furrowed brow. "I screwed the pooch. Let's face it: I'm an airborne menace. Flying the Paris route for Pan Am will just have to wait. But guess what? That's OK because I've got other plans. *Big* plans."

"Lemme guess." Larry tossed me the fire extinguisher, which was normally stowed under the *Duck*'s pilot's seat. "You're off to run with the bulls?"

"Did that on my seventy-fifth birthday. No, this is much more important. Lemme borrow your stool, Lawrence."

"What're you doing, Mrs. Schmulowitz? Please get down from there," I said. "You're gonna hurt yourself."

"Relax, bubby. I was balance beam champion back at PS 247."

Larry looked over at me with one black caterpillar eyebrow cocked. "Balance beam?" he said under his breath. "Are you kidding me? They hadn't even invented *wood* back then."

Mrs. Schmulowitz stood on the stool with her arms outstretched like she was Eva Perón. "To my fellow citizens, Mr. and Ms. America, and all the ships at sea. Ask not what your country can do for you, so on and so forth. Today, I, Mrs. Schmulowitz, stand humbly before you to announce my candidacy for the Rancho Bonita City Council."

Larry looked over at me this time with both eyebrows raised.

"Well, this *is* a surprise," I said. "When, if I may ask, did you decide to seek elective office, Mrs. Schmulowitz?"

"When? I'll tell you when, bubby. When I finally got around to opening my eyes and realized this beautiful city's going to H-E double toothpicks, that's when. The roads are one giant pothole. There's garbage everywhere. And the cost of housing? *Oy gevalt*. Somebody's gotta fix things. So, I figure, why not me? I got oodles of time on my hands these days. I haven't lost *all* my marbles just yet, and I got something to say. All I need is a good campaign slogan. Any ideas? Go."

Larry stroked his beard. "I got it: 'Tippecanoe and Mrs. Schmulowitz, too.'"

"Political gobbledygook," Mrs. Schmulowitz said.

"'She may be small, but she can do it all,'" I offered.

Mrs. Schmulowitz made a face like she'd taken a bite of a bad knish. "This is the problem. All these schlemiels get elected promising things everybody knows they can't deliver. But not this time. No, sir, and no, madam. Mrs. Schmulowitz stands for nothing less than total honesty."

I snapped my fingers. "What about, 'Give Mrs. Schmulowitz a shot. She'll do the best she can, but no guarantees'?"

"Catchy," she said. "OK, bubby, what say you be my campaign manager?"

"That would be a *very* bad idea, Mrs. Schmulowitz."

I was too impolitic for politics, I told her, too blunt. Besides, I already had my hands full, what with my flight school (which at that moment had a student population of exactly zero) and the private investigative agency I was trying to get off the ground with my new significant other, Layne Sterling.

"It's not that I don't appreciate the offer, Mrs. Schmulowitz. I just think you could do much better with somebody more familiar with politics and campaigning."

"What the hell; I'll do it," Larry said. "I'm all about politics."

I looked over at him. "Since when?"

"Since I got elected to my condo board, that's when."

"Being in politics requires diplomacy, Larry. Your notion of diplomacy involves repeated swift kicks to the head."

"Look who's talking," Larry said.

"Boys, please, let's dispense with the bickering," Mrs. Schmulowitz said, slowly climbing down off the stool. "OK,

Larry, let's see what you can do. The election's in November. That's not even two months away. Time is of the essence. Let's go. Chop-chop."

I left them to their strategizing. It seemed like a disaster in the making.

An even bigger one was waiting for me when I got home.

———

Full disclosure: I've lived for years in a converted garage apartment that I rent from Mrs. Schmulowitz, along with my roommate, an orange blimp of an intellectually challenged cat named Kiddiot. The garage was all I could afford after leaving my covert job with Uncle Sugar, and Rancho Bonita seemed like the ideal place to escape the violence of my employment history. With its world-class restaurants and beaches and nearly always perfect weather, Rancho Bonita—"the American Riviera" and "California's Monaco" as the city's chamber of commerce likes to call it—is an oasis from the world's ills. But serenity doesn't come cheap. The town is home to billionaire hedge-fund managers, pampered movie stars, owners of professional sports teams, and even a disaffected member or two of British royalty. Taking up residence in a converted garage, I figured, was a small sacrifice if it meant getting to live in paradise. Then I met Layne Sterling.

"We should find a nicer place," she announced a week after moving in.

"What's wrong with this place?"

"Are you serious?" The cat joined her in giving me one of those you-must-be-kidding-me looks. "Logan, I realize that home is where the heart is, but home in this case is a windowless structure built to keep two cars out of the rain. The floor is concrete. There's no light. I mean, I've interrogated prisoners who lived more lavishly in maximum security."

"And your point is what?"

"My *point?*" The cutest dimple formed in her left cheek as she shook her head sadly. "My point, baby, is that you could do a lot better at this stage of life. You *deserve* a lot better. We both do."

I'd made the mistake of telling her that if she could find a better place for us to live without breaking the bank, to go for it, even if I personally had zero interest in moving. My dilemma was that I didn't want her to leave me, like so many others had before her. Women like Layne Sterling didn't come along every day. Princeton literature major. Voracious reader. A brilliant, achingly beautiful former CIA case officer of Eurasian descent and an IQ topping 160, with eyes the color of freshly mown grass, and legs from here to next Tuesday. Keep a woman like that happy and she'll return the favor for the rest of your life. The problem was that her we-need-a-better-place-to-live juggernaut was gaining momentum, and there didn't seem to be much I could do about it without forcing the issue.

She was sitting with a woman I didn't recognize and sipping iced tea at the picnic table under the oak tree in Mrs. Schmulowitz's tiny but tidy backyard. Layne looked up at me and smiled as I walked in through the back gate. "How'd it go with Amelia Earhart?"

"Great," I said, leaning down and kissing her the way new couples do when they've been apart for any more than three hours. "We practiced aerobatics."

The other woman was as bald as a baby's bottom and stout, decked out in a sleeveless black spandex bodysuit that showed off weight lifter's biceps and overdeveloped thighs. The tattoo of a grinning skull clutching a rose in its teeth took up much of her left deltoid.

"Cordell Logan, say hello to Dee Espinoza. Dee's my new spinning instructor. She also sells real estate. She was just telling me about a condo for lease over near City College with an option to purchase. Sounds like a super deal."

"Hey, Dee. Nice to meet you."

Dee stood and extended her hand. "Pleasure's mine." Her grip was as solid as a bear trap. "It won't be on the market long, not at the price they're asking," she said. "Only two blocks from the beach. Needs some sprucing up, but that shouldn't be a problem for you two. Layne tells me you're quite the handyman."

"Only when it comes to airplanes," I said.

Kiddiot was napping in his usual spot high up in the oak tree. Part of me wanted to climb up there with him. It's not that living in a converted garage had been my first choice, or even my second. But in an overpriced resort town like Rancho Bonita, it's hard to make ends meet on a government pension check and the meager income from a struggling flight school. Mrs. Schmulowitz had been kind enough to rent me her garage for next to nothing when I was making next to nothing. There was little question I could've afforded something a little more swanky now that I had Layne to split the rent with, but the notion of moving out on my landlady felt somehow disloyal.

"I'm not talking about going and signing a lease or anything like that," Layne assured me. "I just want to take a peek, that's all. Do you think we could at least do that?" The earnest expression on her exquisite face was impossible to say no to.

"Sure," I said.

Dee slapped the table. "Excellent. I'll make the arrangements. You two lovebirds enjoy the rest of this beautiful California afternoon. And, Layne, I'll see you tomorrow morning in the gym, six A.M. sharp. Don't forget, it's legs day."

"Can't wait."

After Dee left, Layne said, "She knows the local real estate market like the back of her hand."

"Impressive thighs," I said. "She must do a ton of leg lifts."

"That's a very sexist thing to say, Logan, wouldn't you agree?"

"Probably."

She smirked as I sat. "Look, I know you've lived here a long time, babe. I get that. And I get that change can be hard sometimes for most people. I don't mean to be a nag. Honestly, I don't. But you're not twenty years old anymore."

"Can we please not talk about this right now, Layne?"

She started to say something but didn't. She reached out instead and took my hand like a priest granting salvation.

"Of course."

Like I said, Layne Sterling was a keeper. I closed my eyes and raised my face to the sun, relishing being fortunate enough to find myself in the presence of such a woman.

"When you were flying A-10s," she asked, "what squadron were you with?"

"That's a rather personal question, don't you think? We hardly know each other."

"Can you *please* be serious, Logan, for just this once?"

"The 74th. The famous Flying Tigers."

"That's what I thought."

"Why do you ask?"

"I got a call from an old friend while you were out flying with Mrs. Schmulowitz. An air force OSI agent. We worked a few security violation cases together when I was with the company. She did a little digging for me before I agreed to go out with you." Layne smiled. "Just to confirm you were the real deal."

"You had the air force Office of Special Investigations pull my records for you?"

"Hey, you can't be too careful these days. What if you were a complete weirdo?"

"As opposed to what, a partial weirdo?"

Layne tilted her head, her eyes locked on mine—one of those distinctly female expressions telegraphing that what's coming next won't be pleasant. "Remember that naked guy who died up in Santa Isabella a couple of days ago, the one who fell out of the sky and landed on the trailer?"

"How could I forget? It was all over the news. And, by the way, it wasn't the fall that killed him. It was the sudden stop."

Layne drew a breath and hesitated. "I'm afraid I have some bad news, Logan. They identified the guy. His name was Peter Hostetler."

I made her repeat it. The shock hit me like a thunderclap.

Pete Hostetler.

My old wingman.

TWO

Every fighter jock is given a unique nickname by their fellow pilots early in their flying career—their permanent "call sign" in military parlance. The name unfortunately is never of the pilot's choosing. As we all did, Pete Hostetler aspired to something badass like "Maverick" or "Iceman." What he got instead was "Chocks." Anxious to take off on his first combat mission during Desert Shield, he nearly burned out the engines on his A-10 Thunderbolt II while still parked in the hardstand, not realizing his ground guys had yet to pull the wooden blocks holding the jet's wheels in place. I smiled at the memory, as Chocks himself would later, but the smile didn't last long. I couldn't believe he was dead.

"We played football together at the academy," I told Layne. "He went to Vance for primary training after we graduated. I went down to Texas. We both wound up getting A-10s and forward-deploying to Saudi after Saddam took Kuwait."

"When was the last time you saw him?"

I honestly couldn't remember the last time. "Had to have been after they diagnosed my knee, after I got grounded and they transferred me to Alpha. I should've looked him up a long time ago and stayed in touch. He was a helluva guy, Pete was."

Layne was still holding my hand across the table. Her long, elegant fingers felt like soft, comforting silk.

"He was a fine pilot. A fine human being. High-speed intellect, low-drag ego." I wanted to say more, but the words caught in my throat. I thought about Chivas Regal, Chocks's preferred choice in scotch as well as mine. Had I still been drinking, I would've poured myself a double.

The TV news stations went public that night with Chocks's identity. They described him as a decorated air force veteran who'd spent twenty-two years flying for Delta Airlines before retiring and becoming chief operating officer of Electrogenics, a Santa Isabella–based company specializing in the manufacture of animated children's toys. Authorities were actively investigating his death as a homicide. Chocks was said to be survived by his wife and many friends. The news made no mention of children. The public was asked to contact the Santa Isabella County Sheriff's Department with any tips regarding anyone who might've wished him harm.

I couldn't imagine anyone wishing Chocks harm. The man made friends wherever he went. As the Buddha said, making a hundred friends is not a miracle. The miracle is making a single friend who will stand with you when hundreds are against you. For me, Chocks was always that friend. Loyal. Selfless to a fault. That he'd been living little more than an hour and a half by car north of Rancho Bonita only compounded my grief at his passing. I should've kept in touch with him after I left government service. I should've let him know more often how much I appreciated all he'd done for me, both on the football field and in combat. Now it was too late.

"I'm so sorry, Logan," Layne said.

Not as sorry as I was.

———

I hardly slept that night. It didn't help that Layne and Kiddiot were both cuddlers; I felt like I was in a sarcophagus, sandwiched between them as I stared up at the ceiling. But that accounted for only part of my insomnia. How was it possible that a distinguished graduate of the United States Air Force Academy, a decorated combat pilot, my old battle buddy, could end up falling to his death under the most bizarre and mysterious of circumstances?

Quietly, so as not to disturb either of my bedmates, I maneuvered out from under the sheets, sat down at the folding table that served as my dining room and home office, and opened my laptop.

I found plenty of references to him online. Photos, too: Chocks receiving a fundraising award at a Santa Isabella Lions Club pancake breakfast. Chocks pacing the sidelines, coaching youth soccer. Chocks riding shotgun in a yellow Corvette convertible on Veterans Day, waving to parade spectators through downtown Santa Isabella. He appeared to have hardly changed physically from the man I remembered. A few more pounds. A little less hair. The same gap-toothed, little-boy grin. The same dark, sad eyes. I found his home address and the name of his widow, Miranda, and decided I would fly up to Santa Isabella in the morning to pay her my respects. It was the least I could do.

After Layne woke up, I cooked us a chile verde omelet. She cleaned her plate like she hadn't eaten in a week, which I took as high praise given her mostly vegetarian preferences. Kiddiot, meanwhile, sniffed the forkful I left in his bowl like I was trying to poison him, squeaked his disapproval, and left through his rubberized pet door.

"How is it that that cat never eats anything you give him, but is still so . . . *sizable?*" Layne asked, sitting back with her coffee and the blissful look of someone who wouldn't be eating again anytime that day.

"The universe is full of mysteries," I said, finishing the dishes. "As well as the fact that Mrs. Schmulowitz cooks him chicken recipes from the Sunday *New York Times.*"

I hung the dish towel on the magnetic hook stuck to the purple refrigerator next to the purple kitchen sink, both of which, along with the purple toilet and tub, Mrs. Schmulowitz had picked up cheap at a rock star's remodeling sale when she'd decided to convert her garage to the apartment that Layne had recently decided to share with me. Rancho Bonita was less than two hours from Los Angeles and loaded with big-name celebrities. Many had vastly more money than taste.

I promised Layne I'd be back that afternoon, then leaned down and kissed her. She smelled of lavender, and even unshowered, her long copper hair a mess, wearing one of my old air force T-shirts and little else, she glowed like a million bucks before taxes. I would've scrubbed the flight to Santa Isabella and persuaded her to come back to bed with me had it been anyone other than Chocks Hostetler. Layne said she understood without me having to explain it.

Talk about a keeper.

Larry's hangar doors were closed. Rancho Bonita was fogged in. Overcast at three hundred feet with two miles visibility, according to the latest ATIS. With the propeller turning, the fire extinguisher safely tucked under my seat, and the *Duck*'s engine warming up, I dialed in the frequency for Clearance Delivery on my Number One radio.

"Clearance, good morning, Skyhawk Four Charlie Lima with information Tango. We're a Cessna 172 slant Golf. We'd like TEC routing to Santa Isabella, please."

My passenger manifest that morning included only me. Don't ask why I used "we." It's just what pilots say. After a few seconds, the controller came back on the radio. "Cessna Four Charlie Lima cleared to the Santa Isabella Municipal Airport. Off Runway Two-Seven, radar vectors Mantika, Victor two-eight-eight, Harding Bay, direct. Climb and maintain three thousand. Expect six thousand within five minutes of departure. Departure frequency one-two-five-point-four. Squawk four-seven-seven-six."

I wrote it all down on a notepad and repeated it back verbatim.

"Cessna Four Charlie Lima, read-back correct. Contact ground when ready to taxi. Safe flight."

I double-tapped a thank-you on the push-to-talk mic button mounted on the yoke, then radioed ground control and received permission to taxi. In the run-up area, I advanced the throttle to one thousand seven hundred rpms, made sure all systems were in the green, reduced the throttle, then continued taxiing to Runway Two-Seven.

"Tower, Cessna Four Charlie Lima is ready at Two-Seven."

"Cessna Four Charlie Lima, winds variable at three. Cleared for takeoff, Two-Seven."

I read back the instructions to the tower, rolled out onto the runway, and took off. Within seconds, the earth below me faded from view and I was cocooned in a solid mantle of white.

The first few seconds of instrument flying, having to trust

your gauges instead of your eyes and inner ears to distinguish up from down, is never comfortable, even for an experienced aviator. It's like forcing yourself to draw that first breath from the bottle of oxygen strapped to your back when you go scuba diving. There's something unnatural about it. Then your training kicks in, and the feeling quickly passes. Less than a minute went by before the gloomy shroud enveloping the *Duck* thinned and we climbed into sunshine. From horizon to horizon below us, the planet was blanketed in a batting of stratus broken only by the peaks of the coastal mountains to my right. The view never ceased to remind me why we fly. Fifty-five uneventful minutes later, I touched down in Santa Isabella and taxied to the ramp outside the BillionAir Jet Center.

Many fixed-base operators like BillionAir make their money selling overpriced fuel to well-heeled jet customers. Catering to those customers means offering comfortable lounges, gourmet coffee, warm homemade cookies, and other perks for being rich. Some even offer private rooms where you can take a hot shower and a nap between flights. And all at no extra charge (also the markup on gas more than covers the freebies). But here's the thing: Most FBOs treat guys who fly single-engine beaters like me no differently than they do those who drive $45 million Dassault Falcons. A pilot is a pilot as far as they're concerned. They must figure that a guy who shows up in a junk heap Cessna Skyhawk like the *Duck* might come taxiing in next time behind the controls of a Dassault Falcon. There's nothing wrong with that.

The line boy had a pep to his stride and the fresh-scrubbed looked of a high school scholar-athlete, like one of those cheerful go-getters one might've found at their friendly, full-service filling station during the Eisenhower administration. He vectored me with crisp hand signals to a parking spot next to a Gulfstream G550. The *Duck* looked like somebody's neglected foster child by comparison. I unlatched my door. Pinned to his blue BillionAir polo shirt was an engraved gold name tag that said, "Chad."

"Welcome to Santa Isabella, sir. Will you be needing any fuel today?"

"How many gallons to waive your ramp fee for the afternoon?"

"Ten-gallon minimum."

"Make it eleven. Five and a half in each tank."

"Yes, sir. Anything else I can do for you today?"

"Do you guys happen to have a crew car?"

"We do, yessir. Check at the front desk, but I believe it's available."

"Thanks, Chad." I tipped him five bucks. You would've thought by his smile he'd won the lottery.

The crew car. Another pilot perk. Most FBOs maintain at least one. Usually, it's a junker they let you borrow to drive into town to get yourself a burger while you're waiting for your plane to be refueled or the weather to clear. BillionAir's crew car was no junker.

Stationed behind the reception desk inside were two lush-haired twenty-somethings, one a blonde, the other brunette, each wearing a white blouse unbuttoned seductively but not too seductively, a fitted navy blazer, and tight matching skirt. If they both weren't working fashion model gigs on the side, they should've been.

The brunette's name tag said, "Kimberleigh." She handed me a set of car keys with a slightly mischievous gleam in her light-brown eyes.

"Just please make sure you bring it back full."

"Will do."

The crew car was a showroom-fresh Jeep Cherokee SUV,

black, showing less than three thousand miles on the odometer. I added another three driving to Chocks's last known address.

The house was three blocks west of the 101 freeway, close enough that you could hear the Jake brakes of 18-wheelers rolling by. Two stories. Colonial Spanish–style with wrought iron balconies and a sloping red tile roof. Easily four or five thousand square feet. Not too shabby for a former fighter pilot. The twin front doors looked like they were better suited to a cathedral. The doorbell chimed like Westminster Abbey. Then the door on the right opened, producing a bloated, leering man with a shaved head who reminded me of every bully I've ever known. You've seen the type. Plenty of gold chains around his neck to let you know how much money he has. Sleeveless T-shirts to show you his gym-rat arms, hoping you don't notice his Budweiser gut. I could hear a small dog yapping inside.

"Whatever it is you're selling," he said with a sneer, "we're not buying. Get lost."

"My name is Cordell Logan. I served with Pete Hostetler. I'm looking for his wife. Is she in?"

The guy went to shut the door. I blocked it with my hand. "I've come a long way and I'd really like to talk with her. Just for a few minutes. It would mean a lot. I'd really appreciate it. Thanks."

His eyes were daggers. "I said get lost."

He had fifty pounds on me, but they were pasta Alfredo pounds, too-many-taco-Tuesday pounds. Why all the hostility, I had no idea. It would've been easy teaching him a lesson in fundamental civility, free of charge. It's what I would've done without thinking twice before I found Buddhism. The Buddha frowns on violence. One is not noble who harms living beings. One is noble who doesn't harm.

"Get your hand off the door," the guy was screaming, "or I'm gonna rip it off your arm and stuff it down your throat!"

I counted silently to three, hoping the burning sensation that rose in my throat would pass. It didn't.

"Here's the thing, chief," I said. "There's a vacancy sign on your fat ass and my right foot's looking to rent. Now, either you tell Mrs. Hostetler I'd like a few moments of her time, or my size twelve Merrell is moving in. Your call."

His beanbag face went wan, and his jaws opened in disbelief, like he wasn't used to anybody standing up to him. I'd seen the same expression on the faces of many other dickwads who weren't used to being taught basic manners, either, right before I took them to school.

"Who in the living fuc—" he started to say when a throaty female voice from somewhere inside the house cut him off.

"Who is it, Marvin?"

"Some dickhead. Says he knew Pete. Probably trying to sell you something. Just like the rest of 'em."

"Tell him to hang on."

The interior of the house was dark. The curtains and shades were all drawn. Standing outside in the sun, I couldn't see much of anything beyond Marvin, who stood there flexing his biceps. Then the door opened wider, and a woman emerged from the gloom wearing a red silk kimono. Every American serviceman who ever deployed to East Asia brought the same kimono back home to his wife or girlfriend. Sometimes both.

The kimono hung on Miranda Hostetler like a shroud. She was thin but not in a healthy way. Blonde but not born that way. Good bone structure. You could tell she'd once been a lithe, athletic beauty. A pom-pom girl or a cheerleader, but you could also tell that was a long time ago.

"How did you know my husband?" she asked, rubbing her dark, tired eyes.

"Well, as I was telling Marvin here, Pete and I flew together. He was my wingman during Desert Storm."

She seemed to brighten with the additional information. Her eyes weren't dark at all. They were amber, the color of honey. And when she smiled, I could see that she wasn't as old as I'd first thought.

"You're Cordell Logan. Peter talked about you all the time."

"In a good way, I hope."

"Always. Come in, please."

Marvin stepped aside, still eyeing me like I was planning to steal the silverware.

"Nothing personal," Miranda said, "but you don't look anything like the way Peter described you. I envisioned somebody about ten feet tall, with a big *S* on their chest."

"Funny. That's exactly how I remember Pete."

The barking belonged to a heavyset beagle named Ack-Ack who kept running laps around me and wagging his tail. The living room was bigger than my apartment and furnished in the style of a classic Spanish manor house. Cowhide furniture. Wrought iron lamps and tables. A wrought iron light fixture the size of a wagon wheel hung from the soaring cathedral ceiling. Over the fireplace, smiling alluringly behind a handheld lace fan, was an oil painting of a Spanish maiden, the kind you'd find in an art museum.

"Don't mind the dog, or my brother," Miranda said, pushing Marvin aside. "They think I'm vulnerable. They both have this compulsion to protect me. We've had a lot of weirdos come around since Peter died." She lowered herself into a throne-sized, red velvet armchair and gestured toward the matching one beside it. I sat. Ack-Ack immediately jumped up in my lap and tried to lick my face.

"Ack-Ack, down!" Miranda commanded.

The dog ignored her.

"He'll settle down, eventually," she said. "Marvin, too. He gets a little grumpy if he hasn't had breakfast."

Marvin hadn't stopped glaring at me. "You sure you're OK with this guy, Miranda?"

"Go. Eat."

Marvin shot me parting look that said, *I've got my eye on you*, and lumbered, stoop-shouldered, into the kitchen, his arms swinging like Bigfoot's.

Chocks's widow and I sat for what seemed like a long time, neither of us quite sure what to say, Ack-Ack lunging and trying every few seconds to lick me on the lips, which wasn't going to happen, before I offered my condolences. I told her how sorry I was for not having reconnected with her husband after we both resigned our commissions. She smiled sadly and stared at the floor.

"Pete was an outstanding fighter pilot," I said, "and one of the best men I ever knew."

Seconds passed before Miranda Hostetler looked back up at me. The smile was still there, but there was nothing warm about it.

"But my husband, Mr. Logan, was a habitual liar," she said. "He got what he deserved."

THREE

By the time an embittered wife gets to the I'm-glad-he's-dead chapter of an unhappy marriage, it's usually several years in, not less than two, as was the case with Miranda Hostetler. It was Chocks's third marriage. Hers as well. She knew they were in trouble early on.

"Pete led a secret life almost from the beginning," she said, gathering her kimono around her in the chair. "I really had no clue where he went off to every morning, or what he was doing from one day to the next, working late or not coming home at all. All those last-minute 'business trips' he was always going on. He forgot to turn off his phone one morning. That's when I saw the text messages from *her*."

"'Her'?"

"The other woman."

The Pete Hostetler I remembered was an honor-bound man not inclined to cheat at anything. His word was his bond, an officer who always said what he meant and meant what he said. He wasn't married back then. He didn't even have a steady squeeze, from what I recalled. But the truth was, we hadn't seen or talked to each other for more than a decade. People change over time, not always for the better.

"That must've been pretty difficult for you," was the best I could do in the moment.

Miranda massaged her temples. "I can't say I was surprised. Of course, there'd been others. You want a drink?"

"No, thanks."

"Well, then you won't mind if I have one. It's five o'clock somewhere, right?"

Across the room stood an antique buffet backed by a beveled mirror and topped with green marble, upon which sat various bottles of booze. Miranda got up and walked over.

"I'm trying to find out who killed Chocks," I said.

"Chocks?"

"His call sign. We called him Chocks."

"Chocks. How cute."

She filled a crystal tumbler with bourbon and downed half the glass in one gulp.

"Any idea how it happened?" I asked. "Or why?"

"How what happened?"

"How he died?"

"He fell out of the sky and landed on a trailer."

"I meant, do the authorities know why? Do they have any suspects?"

Miranda drained her glass and promptly refilled it. "They're not telling me anything. And frankly, I really don't care. I know that must sound horrible to you, but you don't know what it was like, living with . . . *Chocks*, was it? All the deceit, the lies."

I said I understood, even if I didn't. How does someone in the span of less than two years go from saying "until death do us part" to "good riddance"?

"He told me once he'd heard you were living somewhere

down near LA," Miranda said, returning to her chair and crossing her legs, showing me more thigh than was appropriate.

"Rancho Bonita," I said.

"Lucky you." She smiled and sat back. "Such a beautiful city. Mountains, the ocean. Perfect weather. Not like here. Get away from that sea breeze a couple miles, feels like the Sahara Desert half the time."

I didn't need her reminding me that I was fortunate to live where I did.

"He always meant to look you up," Miranda said. "I suppose he never did, though, huh?"

"Pete was stationed at Pope Air Force Base last time we talked, out in North Carolina. But that was a long time ago."

"Yeah, well, I guess he was always too busy chasing all those little bitches on the side to bother keeping in touch with his old buddies."

I didn't say anything.

Miranda held her glass of bourbon up to the light. "Who knows?" she said. "Could be it was one of those whores who killed him. Them and a hundred other people. Pete was a first-rate asshole. All he ever cared about was himself."

I could have told her about having to punch out south of Baghdad at two thousand feet after an SA-16 sheared off the right wing of my A-10, how I never saw the missile before it made contact and exploded. How Chocks earned the Air Force Cross that day after making one strafing run after another on the Republican Guard troops closing in on me, keeping them at bay, running out of fuel long past bingo, until the Pave Lows showed and airlifted me out. But I knew none of it would matter to Miranda Hostetler. I had expected to fly to Santa Isabella and comfort the grieving widow of an old friend. What I found instead was a woman scorned, happy he was dead.

"Was Pete still doing any flying?"

"Not that I'm aware of," Miranda said. "He told me when we were dating that he'd had enough of that in the air force, and that's why he went to work for Delta. But he eventually got sick of that, too, so he went to work for Electrogenics. Are you sure I can't get you anything? Coffee? Juice? Some eggs, maybe?"

"I'm good, thanks."

"Yeah, I bet you are."

She smiled inappropriately. Uncomfortable seconds passed. I thanked her for her time and wished her well. I was getting up to go when the doorbell chimed.

"Can you get that, Marvin?" Miranda shouted.

"I'm cooking," her brother responded from the kitchen.

Miranda muttered something obscene under her breath and went to the door but didn't open it.

"Who is it?"

"It's Cy."

Her demeanor changed in an instant. "Well, this is a surprise," she said to the man on her front step in khakis and a black jacket, wearing a white clerical collar.

"Hope I'm not disturbing anything," he said, peering past her at me. "My wife insisted that I stop by on my way to the sanctuary to see if there was anything you needed before tomorrow."

"How kind of her, Pastor. I'm surviving, for now. Come in, please. You can meet one of my husband's old air force buddies."

The pastor was in his mid-fifties, paunchy, with a florid, cherubic face. Thinning strands of sandy hair were plastered across his balding pink pate like guitar strings.

"Pastor Cyrus Simpson," Miranda said. "I've been worshipping at his church for as long as I've lived in Santa Isabella. Usually alone. Peter was never religious. Cyrus, this Cordell Logan."

We shook hands.

"Pastor."

"Mr. Logan. A pleasure." There was a soft-spoken, almost effeminate tone in his voice.

"Cy is officiating tomorrow at Peter's memorial service," Miranda said. "We had to wait several days until the coroner released his body. I hope you'll be able to attend."

"Wouldn't miss it for anything."

"And what is it you do for a living, Mr. Logan?" the pastor asked affably.

"As little as possible."

He tilted his head back and laughed like he meant it.

"Actually," I said, "I'm a flight instructor for the most part."

"A flight instructor? Wow. How exciting. I've always wanted to learn to fly."

"Well, come on down to Rancho Bonita and take a free introductory lesson. We'll do a little sightseeing up and down the coast. You can get a feel for the plane."

"Don't tempt me. Free? Really?"

"Peter and Mr. Logan were classmates at the Air Force Academy together," Miranda said. "Peter would always tell me how they played football together, and how they used to blow up tanks after they graduated."

"Never ours, though, usually," I said.

Pastor Simpson laughed that laugh again. "My goodness," he said, "I would certainly hope not."

He told me about his church, and how proud he was of his congregation. I listened politely and smiled in the right places. I thanked Miranda again for taking the time to see me and told her I would see them both the next day at Chocks's graveside service. The pastor gave me the name of the cemetery and told me what time it was scheduled. He asked me for a business card.

I dug one out of my wallet. It looked like it had been through the washing machine, which gives you an idea how often people ask for my card.

"'Above the Clouds Aviation,'" he said, reading it. "'Flight training, whale watching, and aerial charters.' Must keep you pretty busy."

"Not as much as you'd think."

He smiled. "I may just take you up on that free ride."

"Anytime, Pastor."

We shook hands again. Miranda walked me to the door.

"I know I come off as a shrew," she said, "but just so you know, Peter thought the world of you. I know he'd be honored you came."

"The honor's mine."

Honor, I've discovered, takes a back seat to trust when the bullets start flying, along with God, country, and the American Way. What that matters in those moments, when people who salute a different flag are trying to kill you, is knowing that you can count on the person beside you to willingly do whatever it takes to get you home, even at the risk of their own life, and that they can count on you to do the same for them. Chocks had proven himself as willing as they come. I owed him nothing less than attending his funeral service.

That and bringing down whoever killed him.

Like Rancho Bonita, Santa Isabella, California, is a clean college town with little crime and a vibrant central business district, the kind of community where the residents bake blueberry muffins for the homeless and buy overpriced produce at farmer's markets to support local agriculture. A place where everyone is nice to everyone else, and the rest of the world's ills seem far away, indeed. So it came as something of a surprise that Tom Kasparov, the Santa Isabella County Sheriff's homicide detective handling the investigation into Chocks's death, was, as Mrs. Schmulowitz might say, something of a schmuck right from the get-go.

"Kasparov—any relation to Garry Kasparov, the chess master?" I asked him. "I remember when he played that IBM computer."

"No," Kasparov said, like he had a dozen better things to do than waste his time talking to me. "What'd you say your name was again?"

"Logan."

"Look, Mr. Logan, I don't mean to be rude, but I have no shortage of other cases I'm juggling right now. You told the deputy at the front desk you knew Pete Hostetler. If you have information that would be relevant to the case, I'm all ears. Otherwise, I really do need to get back upstairs."

In fact, Detective Tom Kasparov, no relation to the Russian chess master, was virtually all ears. A short, pasty young man who rocked a crew cut, the requisite bristle-brush cop moustache, and what looked like two oyster shells protruding from either side of his head. We were standing in the lobby of Santa Isabella County Sheriff's headquarters, with its glassed-in front counter and polished terra-cotta tile floors. Kasparov had come down from his second-floor office in his perfectly creased gray suit pants; a short-sleeved white dress shirt, open at the collar; lizard-skin cowboy boots with walking heels that looked new; and diamond rings on either pinkie finger. A .44 Magnum Desert Eagle pistol dangled from a black basketweave shoulder holster under his left armpit. As the old saying goes, "The smaller the cop, the bigger the gun."

"His widow tells me he wasn't exactly the most devoted husband in the world," I said.

"We've explored that angle," Kasparov said. "There's nothing there. Anything else?"

"What about aircraft ground tracks?"

"What about them?"

"You can look up most planes or helicopters by tail numbers, and see which ones were flying over Santa Isabella that night."

"Holy cow. Really?"

"Really," I said.

"You mean publicly available records that *anybody* can access online on a dozen free websites?" Kasparov smirked, his condescending, sarcastic tone hard to miss. "We may not be Scotland Yard around here, Mr. Logan, but we're not Andy of Mayberry, either."

"I'm just trying to help, Detective."

"Your help is not needed. Anything else?"

I asked him how familiar he was with the terrorist Abu Nidal.

Kasparov glanced impatiently at his watch. "Never heard of 'em," he said.

I explained how Chocks and I had been tasked during Desert Storm with taking out Nidal's most prolific bombmaker, Hakim Elbaz. Flying at what would've been treetop level had there been any trees, we tracked inbound along the Euphrates until we located his mud hut outside Ramadi, then shredded it and him with iron bombs and Gatling guns. Intel analysts told us later that Nidal had placed a one-million-dollar bounty on each of our heads.

"You're telling me, some terrorist flew all the way over here from Iraq thirty years after the fact for, what, a little payback?"

"Well," I said, "you know what they say. Revenge is a dish best served cold."

"Thanks for coming in," Kasparov said like he wasn't thankful at all, then wheeled around and walked back upstairs to his office.

Electrogenics, Inc., where Chocks worked before he was killed, was headquartered in an industrial park less than a mile south of downtown Santa Isabella, along Hesperia Street, just north of the airport. The place looked like Walmart—a cavernous warehouse, but without signs or public access. There was one more thing that appeared decidedly un-Walmart like:

The level of security was extreme for a company specializing in something as innocent as the manufacture of children's toys. I've set foot on top-secret military installations that looked less impenetrable.

Ten-foot chain-link fencing topped by concertina wire ringed the plant. Multiple surveillance cameras on swivel mounts covered every avenue of approach. Two uniformed guards prowled the employee parking lot in one of those tiny Fiat clown cars with a fluorescent yellow sign on the hatchback that said, "Courtesy Officer." A decal of the company's logo was affixed to either side of the car—a happy cartoon hippo and lion flanking a doe-eyed giraffe. Two other courtesy officers, both bearded and buffed, manned the lone gatehouse affording the only access to the plant. Red Beard and Black Beard. They reminded me of SEAL Team Six operators I'd worked with overseas. Both were garbed in sky-blue ball caps and jumpsuits that also bore the company's logo. Neither appeared armed.

I rolled down the window of my borrowed crew car. While Red Beard came around from behind and peered into the Jeep's back seats, Black Beard leaned in and said like he'd said a thousand times, "Welcome to Electrogenics, where children make all the difference. Can I help you?"

"I'm here to see your company president."

"Do you have an appointment?"

"Negative."

"OK, then, you're gonna have to turn your vehicle around and—"

"Tell him it's about Pete Hostetler."

"*Who?*"

"Your company's recently deceased chief operating officer."

Black Beard blinked, unsure how to respond, before his more senior partner, Red Beard, stepped in.

"What's the purpose of your visit today, sir?"

"I'm a licensed private investigator."

"You got any ID on you?"

I showed him my driver's license. He looked at it like he was studying a foreign language.

"This doesn't say anything about being a private investigator."

"My application's under review in Sacramento. They're gonna approve it any day now."

"Regardless," Red Beard said, "you're gonna have to turn your vehicle around."

I asked him if he was ex-military.

"What's that got to do with anything?" he asked.

"It's just that, you've got the look, you know?"

"Army. Eighty-second Airborne," Red Beard said, puffing out his chest a little. "You?"

"Air force."

Black Beard smirked. "You mean *chair* force."

I chuckled as if I'd never heard the insult before. "Look," I said, "you guys served; I served. We all know how it works.

You're making a command decision here. Your commanding officer finds out later that I had some vital information to pass along, and that you told me to beat it without bothering to check with him first? Somebody's gonna get their pee-pee whacked."

Red Beard looked at me. Then he and Black Beard looked at each other. Then Black Beard walked back to the guard shack, picked up a red phone, and made a call.

———

Electrogenics's reception area resembled a small Toys"R"Us. Display shelves were crammed with brightly colored stuffed animals. On the opposite wall from where I'd been sitting for more than half an hour, waiting for the company's CEO to meet with me, a large flat-screen monitor replayed TV commercials on an endless loop advertising Electrogenics's stuffed animals, all singing nursery rhymes in cutesy voices with their mouths flapping robotically. It was like being in a fever dream you couldn't wake up from. How Chocks could've endured working every day in such a place was beyond me. I wondered the same about the receptionist, a dowdy older woman with a shock of Martha Washington hair and a gaggle of silver bracelets on both wrists that jangled like Santa's sleigh bells whenever she answered the phone. She seemed oblivious to the repetitive music and video loop. I walked over to her desk.

"Any idea how much longer it'll be?"

She stared up at me over her half-glasses with a look that could curdle milk. "Mr. Millisohn is a very busy man, as I'm sure you can imagine."

Just then a door clicked open to my right and a tall, gaunt man of about my age with mischievous eyes and crazy Einstein hair breezed into the lobby. He was wearing flip-flops, pink cargo shorts, and a Grateful Dead T-shirt.

"You must be Mr. Logan. Ed Millisohn. Sorry to keep you waiting," he said like he meant it. "We just got a big order in this morning from Australia, of all places. They've gone bonkers down there for our baby koalas and kangaroos. It's our newest product line."

We shook hands. "Hard not to love a marsupial," I said.

"Indeed. So, I understand you have some info for me on Pete Hostetler."

"Actually, Mr. Millisohn—"

"Call me Ed, please."

"Actually, *Ed*, I was hoping *you* might have some information for *me*."

"Excuse me?"

"Pete was a buddy. I'm looking into his murder. Any information about who might've wanted him dead would be much appreciated."

The pleasantness melted from Millisohn's face. "In other words, you lied. You gained entry here under false pretense."

"I'm not trying to defraud anybody here, Ed. Pete and I served together. Maybe you'd understand better if you'd been in the military yourself."

"Who says I wasn't?"

I glanced at the multicolored peace sign tattooed on his toothpick forearm. Ed Millisohn glowered.

"You want information, Mr. Logan? No problem. I'll tell you what I told the sheriff's department. I don't know a damn thing about who killed your buddy. He hasn't worked here in a long time. He didn't have a drinking problem. He had a full-on drunk-all-the-time problem. He also had an embezzling problem. I gave him abundant opportunities to clean himself up, to give back what he'd stolen from my company and me. He didn't, so I fired him. My only regret is that I didn't do it sooner. Now, get off my property."

I left before he called security.

A beeping sound caught my attention as I got to my car. An 18-wheeler was slowly backing into the loading docks at the rear of the factory. Air brakes hissed, the truck's engine shut down, and the driver climbed down from the cab garbed in a zookeeper jumpsuit identical to those worn by the guards.

A forklift emerged from inside the plant carrying a wooden crate the size of a refrigerator. Three other workers in jumpsuits emerged from the building and carefully guided the forklift and its cargo inside the truck's trailer. A submachine gun with a collapsible stock was slung over one of the worker's shoulders. It looked like an H&K MP5. Standard-issue weapon for SWAT teams and special forces. *Why would a guard at a toy factory need that kind of heavy weaponry?*

From across the parking lot, I could see a security clown car speeding in my direction. I snapped a few pictures on my phone of the guy with the gun, threw the Jeep into gear, and took off.

FOUR

After flying back that afternoon to Rancho Bonita, I found Larry perched on a ladder in his hangar, tacking up red, white, and blue bunting for a fundraiser to kick-start Mrs. Schmulowitz's city council run. She was directing his efforts and dressed appropriately for the occasion: high-topped red sneakers, white leggings, an American flag blouse, and a blue ball cap that said, "Don't be shy, give Mrs. Schmulowitz a try."

"A little higher, Larry."

"Here, Mrs. Schmulowitz?"

"Higher."

"I go any higher, my hernia's gonna get a hernia."

I reminded the candidate that the Rancho Bonita Airport was a secure facility and that her supporters simply wouldn't be able to walk in off the street. Only a few transient pilots and other aviation geeks with gate passes would ever see the decorations. Not to worry, Mrs. Schmulowitz said. She intended to live stream the event after doing some research on "the Googles," and was merely factoring in camera angles.

"An old trick I learned from my weekend rendezvous with

JFK," Mrs. Schmulowitz said. "You hang the bunting up high, in the background, position the camera so your audience is looking up at you, and boom, suddenly you're huge, larger than life. Voters don't like small, bubby. They like big."

"Wait a minute. You had a fling with John F. Kennedy, Mrs. Schmulowitz?"

She flapped her hand like it was no big deal. "Ships passing in the night."

I was inclined to take her at her word. The last time I openly doubted one of her implausible tales—she'd claimed to have beaten legendary sprinter Wilma Rudolph in the fifty-yard dash at a Madison Square Garden track meet in 1961—she dug out an old black-and-white photo snapped at the finish line showing her doing exactly that.

"A fling with Kennedy. You'll have to fill me in on the details sometime," I said.

Mrs. Schmulowitz winked. "Good girls never kiss and tell, bubby."

She was right, as always.

———

Layne peered at the photos on my phone of the crate being loaded into the truck at Electrogenics, and the guard with the submachine gun.

"Looks like an MP7, not a five," she said. "The SEALs transitioned to it seven years ago. Bigger mag capacity, less recoil."

"I'm not saying these were team guys, Layne. I'm saying they *looked* like team guys."

"Email me these pics. I want to take a closer look at them."

"Wilco."

We were lounging together in the rope hammock under the

oak tree in Mrs. Schmulowitz's backyard. Kiddiot was asleep on my lap with his front leg curled underneath him and his tongue hanging out the side of his mouth.

"What do you think it means?" Layne asked.

"I think it means he has tongue-management issues."

"I meant the weapon, Logan."

"It means either Electrogenics is the most security-conscious toymaker this side of North Korea, or they're making stuff in there that has nothing to do with robotic animals for little kids. Which could explain why Chocks was working there in the first place."

I told her what the company's CEO had told me. That Chocks was a drunk who'd been stealing money.

"Do you believe him?"

I shrugged. "Maybe Chocks had a Chivas Regal problem—hell, we all had one back then—but he was no thief. It wasn't in his DNA."

"So, if it's not animatronic animals, what exactly *are* they making in there?"

"That's what I'm hoping you can find out. Reach out to your friends at Langley. They might know."

Layne sat up and looked over at me. "Is that all I am to you, Logan? An intelligence asset?"

"Are you kidding me? Not with those lips."

She jabbed me playfully in the chest. "There's something important I need to show you."

"Let's see it."

"Not here. Inside."

I savored the sway of her hips and the way she paused to turn back toward me at the door of our garage apartment with that smile, right before she slowly, seductively peeled off her top and disappeared inside. I picked Kiddiot up, moved him off me, and followed her in. The cat never stirred. I certainly did.

The next morning, I retrieved the one serviceable sports coat and necktie I owned. Somehow, I remembered how to tie a Windsor knot. I spit shined my dress shoes to the extent any twenty-year-old pair of patent leather, air force–issued oxfords can be rehabilitated, and flew the *Duck* back up Santa Isabella to attend Chocks's memorial service.

———

Pastor Cyrus Simpson preached love, forgiveness, and eternal life using a wireless, battery-operated microphone to the twenty or so individuals who'd gathered in a horseshoe of plastic folding chairs to remember my former teammate and wingman. I sat in the back.

Chocks's closed casket was a bargain-basement pine box. There was no missing-man flyover. No color guard or gun salute. No folded flag handed to a grieving widow with thanks from a grateful nation. There was only the traffic noise from the 101 freeway a quarter mile away and the cawing of crows in the cemetery's dogwood trees, in whose dwindling shade we all sought refuge as the sun rose higher in a cloudless sky. Miranda Hostetler sat dry-eyed with her brother, Marvin, fanning herself with what looked like a checkbook. She was wearing spike heels, an inappropriately low-cut little black dress, and an air of complete indifference.

"Amen," the pastor finally intoned, nearly an hour after he'd begun his sermon.

"Amen," the rest of us mumbled, grateful he was finally, mercifully finished—everyone but Miranda, who stared straight ahead without expression.

Even in the shade, it was well over one hundred degrees. The bereaved were sweating through their funereal clothes and looking anxious to leave. Pastor Simpson was perspiring, too, profusely, but seemed in no hurry to call it a day.

"As we all are, brother Peter was a flawed child of God," Simpson said, smiling beneficently and blotting his beaded forehead with a handkerchief for the umpteenth time, "but he also had many, many fine qualities. If there's anyone who'd like to share a few words celebrating Peter's life, you may do so at this time."

Everybody was staring at their shoes except Miranda, who stared straight ahead, sphinxlike.

I stood and cleared my throat.

"Pete Hostetler and I played football together in college. We flew jets together in the military. The pastor's correct. Pete had many fine qualities, not the least of which were courage and loyalty. He didn't deserve to go the way he did. If anyone has *any* information, *any*thing at all, that might help bring whoever killed him to justice, I'd very much like to talk with you after this service is over—assuming it ever is."

Simpson smiled thinly. No one else responded.

"Anything at all," I repeated. The mourners were all silent.

Only then did I glance back and notice Detective Tom Kasparov watching the service from the circular lane behind us, near where I'd parked the Jeep that Kimberleigh, my new best friend at the Santa Isabella Airport, had been kind enough to let me borrow for two straight days. The detective was leaning against a black unmarked Crown Vic with his arms folded and Wayfarers on. Standing beside him, mirroring his posture and sunglasses, was an exceedingly tall, stout man in a dark suit with a gold sheriff's badge clipped to his belt—Kasparov's partner. I knew why they were both there, and it wasn't to help mourn the passing of my fellow fighter pilot. It was to assess the body language and mannerisms of the mourners. Homicide cops attend the funeral services of murder victims because sometimes the murderers do, too.

I returned to my chair as Miranda's brother, Marvin, quickly jumped to his feet. "The man cleans up pretty good" was not an expression that came readily to my mind. Sweaty and unkempt, in a wrinkled, ill-fitting linen suit, he looked like something that had washed up on the beach after floating offshore for a long time.

"I'll be honest with you people," he said. "I hated Pete Hostetler. Like, I mean, *really* hated him. The way he treated my sister, the disrespect he showed her, the abuse she had to take from him day in and day out . . ." Marvin looked down and shook his big sweaty head. "I thought about taking him out myself. More than once, believe me. But I'll tell you one thing. Nobody deserves to go the way he did, naked, crashing into that trailer. Nobody. I hope they catch whoever did it. And that's all I got to say."

Marvin sat back down. His sister gave him an approving pat on the knee. No one else stood up or said a word.

"Thank you all for coming," Pastor Simpson said. "May you all go in peace."

Thus ended Chocks Hostetler's memorial service.

I started to make my way over to Miranda, to tell her that if she ever needed anything, I'd be there for her, when my path was blocked by a fat, bearded man in jeans, scuffed cowboy boots, a green plaid shirt with pearl snaps, and a turquoise bolo tie. His hands hung at his sides, big as shovel blades.

"Looking pretty good for an old fart, Logan."

"Thanks. You, too."

I know I'd seen him somewhere before. The question was where. He could see in my face I had trouble placing his.

"Must be the beard," he said, grinning broadly.

That's when it hit me: his teeth. They looked like a DIY project gone terribly wrong. Chipped. Crooked. A hot mess. You don't forget chompers like that. "Dickie Burrows," I said. "What's up, brother?"

"Not much. Just living the dream." His hand engulfed mine. "Heard you lost your wings a few years back and joined some super-secret-squirrel, spec-ops deal."

"I can neither confirm nor deny," I said.

"Yeah, I know, you could tell me, but then you'd have to kill me, right?" Dickie grinned again.

I tried not to focus on his teeth, or to roll my eyes at his use of the world's most overused line. We used to joke in the locker room that Dickie's IQ was lower than plant life. He did, however, happen to be among the meanest offensive tackles ever to suit up for the academy. On that basis alone, he'd somehow managed to graduate. Too big to squeeze into a cockpit, too short-fused to be trusted inside the underground launch capsule of a Minuteman III nuclear missile battery, the last I heard, he'd been assigned to some admin desk job at Ellsworth Air Force Base in South Dakota. There, he'd satisfied the four years of indentured servitude he owed the government for his college education, then promptly resigned his commission and vanished into the civilian sector.

"I didn't know you and Pete Hostetler were close," I said.

"Two peas in a pod," Miranda said, walking over. "Dickie flies in every couple of months on his way to Vegas from that big cattle spread of his up north. They'd always go out on the town and tie one on—I mean, *really* tie it on. Then Peter would come home and beat the living hell out of me. Isn't that right, Dickie?"

Dickie's eyes stormed. "Pete never laid a hand on you, Miranda, and you know it."

"You're absolutely right, Dickie," she said. "He never hit me with his hand, only with whatever was handy." She pulled her hair back to reveal a ragged scar zigzagging her scalp line. "This one he did with the shot glass he threw at me when I told him he needed to stop drinking." She hiked up the hem of her skirt to reveal three circular patches of scarred skin, each the size of a dime, on her left thigh. "These he did with one of his cigars the night I told him I was sick of all his little affairs."

"You got no right to bad-mouth him like that," Dickie said. "He's not even here to defend himself. Besides, you never loved him, and you know it. All you was ever in it for was the money."

"Pete told you that, did he?"

"Yes, ma'am, he sure did. Many times."

Miranda laughed, low and angry. "You poor, stupid sonofabitch," she said, "your good friend Pete Hostetler was flat broke when I met him, and he was just as broke when I left him last year. Every dollar he made, he blew on booze or on all his little bar skanks. Who do you think covered the mortgage? Who do you think paid the bills?"

She thanked me for attending Pete's service and asked me to swing by the house on my way out of town. She said she had something she wanted to give me, something Chocks would've wanted me to have. Then she walked away, but not before telling Dickie to go perform a sex act on himself that was anatomically impossible.

"That bitch is out of her mind and straight-up mean," he said, watching Miranda stride arm in arm with her brother toward a silver Mercedes coupe parked behind my borrowed Jeep. "Wouldn't surprise me one bit if she killed him herself or hired somebody to do it."

"You got any proof of that, Dickie?"

"If I did, I would've gone to the police already with it. I'm telling you, man, she's bad news. Pete knew it, too."

"She said you flew into town."

"Used to. Lost my medical. Had a Meridian before that. Good airplane in the climb. Lotta useful load. Now I drive."

He nodded toward a pristine white Ford F-250 with Oregon plates and dual rear tires. The truck was as big as an armored personnel carrier. I asked him how he'd heard about Chocks's funeral. The question caught him off guard.

"How I *heard* about it?"

"Well," I said, "it's just that, after watching that little interaction between you and Miranda, I'm guessing you weren't exactly invited."

Dickie stammered, avoiding my eyes. "I dunno, I, uh, I must've heard about it on the news or something. I don't remember too good these days, Logan. All those full-contact drills, all those scrimmages, you know? Pete was a halfway decent tight end. A better blocker than a receiver. You weren't a bad receiver yourself. I do remember that."

He asked me if I wanted to grab a drink with him in town. I told him I quit drinking years ago. Alcohol always brought out the beast in me, a persona I did my best to keep in check. Dickie nodded like he understood with his big paws shoved into the front pockets of his jeans, but the dull void behind his eyes suggested he didn't understand at all.

"We should get together sometime, Logan, catch up on old times. Maybe I'll fly down to Rancho Bonita. You can show me the town. Do it up right."

We both knew it would never happen.

"Good seeing you again, Dickie," I said.

"You, too, man. Watch your six out there."

"Always."

The day was growing warmer by the minute. My inclination was to retreat to the air-conditioned comfort of my borrowed

SUV, but I had questions for Detective Kasparov, and I wanted to catch him before he left. When I turned, he and the tall guy with him were already approaching me. Kasparov introduced the guy as his partner, Detective Lloyd Gregory.

"I hear you were a Hog driver," Gregory said with an accent that sounded distinctly Big Apple. "I was army myself. Ranger qualified. We used to call you guys up all the time for close-air support. A-10s are badass, what with that Gatling gun. Saved my ass more than once."

I asked him if he was from Brooklyn or the Bronx.

"Staten Island," Gregory said. "Put in my twenty with the NYPD and headed West. You can't get a decent Italian deli to save your life. That is a scientific fact. But you take the good with the bad. Am I right?"

"The yin and the yang," I said.

We high-fived.

Kasparov looked disapprovingly at his partner. "We received a complaint from Electrogenics," he said, turning back and scowling at me. "You were trespassing on company property."

"Trespassing requires criminal intent, Detective. I'm only trying to find out who killed my buddy."

"That's *our* job, Mr. Logan, not yours," Kasparov said. "Fair warning: I get another complaint like that from Electrogenics or anybody else in this county that you're sticking your nose where it doesn't belong, you're going to jail."

"Why are security personnel at a toy manufacturer carrying automatic weapons?"

"I don't know what you're talking about," Kasparov said, trading a quick, disconcerted glance with his partner.

"Heckler & Koch MP7s," I said. "Your own SWAT team probably uses them."

Gregory grinned. "What are you, a gun nut?"

"Look," I said, "I can help you guys. We can help each other. Trade information. Hunt down whoever did this."

Kasparov scoffed. "Sworn members of law enforcement don't *trade* information with civilians, Logan, especially in active criminal investigations."

"Not that it matters," I said, "but I used to be assigned to a counterterrorism unit reporting directly to the White House with Tier One Ultra status. I'd tell you all about it, but I can't because you guys no doubt lack the necessary security clearances. What I *can* tell you is that Electrogenics is a front. They're building something in there other than little toy animals. My gut tells me that whatever that something is, it got my buddy killed."

"Tier One Ultra, huh?" Lloyd Gregory's grin reminded me of every sinister B-movie bad guy I've ever seen. "Sounds like a bunch of made-up Hollywood bullshit to me."

The conversation was going nowhere. I urged them both to have a lovely day and turned to walk away. That's when Kasparov said, "I served, too, OK? Marine Corps. Eight years."

"Infantry?"

"They sent me to language school, then embassy duty." He sounded embarrassed about it. "Even though I shouldn't, Logan, I'm gonna throw you a bone. One veteran to another. Just so you can go back to Rancho Bonita, stop spinning your wheels, and let us do our job."

"I'm listening."

"You think your buddy Hostetler was solid? I'm here to tell you, he wasn't."

"Meaning what exactly?"

"Meaning," Kasparov said, "that Pete Hostetler was balls-deep in the Pascua drug cartel."

"And that," Gregory said, "is scientific fact." The B-movie bad guy grin never left Lloyd Gregory's face.

FIVE

It's one thing for a detective to allege your deceased former wingman had worked for a Mexican drug lord. It's quite another when the same detective refuses to give you any details backing up his allegation. The Chocks Hostetler I remembered was as hard-core a right-wing zealot as any you'd find at the academy when we were going to school there, which is saying something. I could recall him arguing more than once in our third-year ethics class how the only viable way to end narcotics abuse was to line all the pushers against a wall and put them permanently out of business. The notion that he would've ever associated in any capacity with *any* drug kingpin like Gervasio Pascua made zero sense. It was antithetical to the man I had known. Then again, so was his widow's assertion that he'd drunkenly and repeatedly assaulted her.

I stopped by Miranda's house after the funeral service, as she'd requested. A for-sale sign from some realtor had been freshly planted on the lawn. Miranda was standing on the front steps next to a dog crate. Inside the crate was their beagle, Ack-Ack.

"The place I'm moving to doesn't allow dogs or cats," she said.

"That's unfortunate," I said.

"I know Peter would want you to have him."

"Who?"

"Ack-Ack."

"You wanted me to come by so you could give me your *dog*?"

"Not my dog. Peter's dog."

"I appreciate the offer, Miranda, but I already have a cat."

"Great. I'm sure they'll be good friends."

I wanted to tell her to forget it, no way, that the last thing I needed was another thing in my life to be responsible for. But then Ack-Ack laid down in the crate with his head on his front paws and gazed at me with his sad, brown, persuasively irresistible eyes, as if he realized his fate hung in the balance. How could I have possibly said no?

Miranda muttered a perfunctory "thank you," ducked back in the house, and returned with a big bag of kibble, along with a rolling suitcase filled with chew toys. Then she gave me a hug.

"Peter was a drunk and first-class jerk, but he thought the world of you. Take care of yourself, Logan."

She went back inside without saying goodbye to the dog. She didn't even look at him. I'm not saying such indifference makes you a murder suspect, but it did leave me wondering.

Layne was sitting at the folding table. She glanced over from her laptop as I walked in lugging Ack-Ack in his crate.

"Who's this?"

"Chocks's dog. He barked the entire flight back. *And* in the truck the entire drive home."

Kiddiot looked on, sitting calmly with his skinny, pipe-cleaner tail wrapped around his front legs. When I set the crate down and opened the door, the dog came bursting out like a racehorse exploding out of the starting gate. Barking and wagging, ears flopping, he immediately made a beeline for Kiddiot, who rewarded his enthusiasm with a lightning-quick swipe of claws across his snout that produced a terrified yelp but no blood. Ack-Ack quickly retreated to a neutral corner, whimpering, and was suddenly a model of canine decorum.

Layne knelt to comfort him. "We definitely do not need a dog, Logan."

I explained how Miranda had all but forced him on me. Then Ack-Ack rolled over on his back, like he was competing for the World's Cutest Dog award. He gazed soulfully at Layne, upside down, ears flopped back, with all four paws in the air.

"OK," Layne said, getting down on all fours to pet his belly, "I was wrong. We definitely need *this* dog. Such *a* sweet boy. What kind of woman could ever possibly give you up?"

"The kind Chocks was married to." I grabbed a bowl from the cupboard and filled it with water from the sink. Ack-Ack wagged his tail gratefully as I set the bowl down, then stepped into the bowl with his front paws and drank enthusiastically, sloshing water all over the kitchen floor with his entire back end swaying.

"I'm in love already," Layne said.

The same could not be said for Kiddiot, who tossed us both a look of disgust and sauntered out his cat door.

As she'd promised, Layne had conducted a deep dive online into Electrogenics while I'd been attending Chocks's funeral service up in Santa Isabella. She hadn't dug up much beyond the company's proof of long-standing membership in the American Toy Association, along with a handful of stories featuring Electrogenics's wild-haired CEO, Ed Millisohn, publicizing his products in obscure industry trade publications. All the articles only reinforced the image of what Millisohn's company outwardly appeared to be: a legally licensed producer of children's cuddly playthings. The company even maintained a triple-A rating with the Better Business Bureau. Layne's former intelligence analyst colleagues at the CIA, she noted, said the agency had no connection with the company.

"The agency would never admit to a connection even if one existed," I said.

"True." She poured us a couple of glasses of orange juice while I cleaned up Ack-Ack's spilled water. He kept trying to bite the sponge, growling playfully.

"The cops think Chocks had ties to the Pascua cartel," I said.

"You believe them?"

"Not for one second."

"Interesting," Layne said.

"How so?"

She walked the seven steps from the kitchen counter to our home office, such as it was—a folding table upon which our laptops and phone chargers and a printer were stationed amid an impossible tangle of power cords—and handed me a three-page printout.

"Pulled this from the California Secretary of State's website, business entities section."

I read the pages over. "You said you didn't find much."

Layne smiled. "I lied."

State records showed that Electrogenics had reported borrowing $16.3 million eight months earlier from something called the Grande Summit Financial Group. Layne's research showed that the group was headquartered in the Cayman Islands. Grande Summit rang no bells, though the Caymans certainly did. The islands served as a tax-dodge haven for tens of thousands of companies. When I was with Alpha, we'd gone after plenty of well-heeled jihadists and other terrorists whose assets were held in secret Cayman accounts.

"What do we know about Grande Summit?"

"Funny you should ask," Layne said.

She handed me another printout—the executive summary of a confidential Drug Enforcement Administration intelligence briefing. It showed that Grande Summit was suspected of laundering tens of millions of dollars in profits from none other than the Pascua drug cartel. It also showed that Grande Summit maintained branch offices in West Palm Beach, Florida; Scarsdale, New York; University Park, Texas; Indian Hills, Ohio; and Santa Isabella—a half mile from Electrogenics's manufacturing plant. The report identified the local Grande Summit branch manager as one Gerald Whitlock, forty-two, who'd recently been paroled after serving a one-year sentence for tax evasion at the minimum security federal lockup in Dublin, California.

"One more report you may be interested in," Layne said, smiling because we both were aware she was good at her work.

This one showed the results of what was described as a comprehensive database search of all DEA intelligence files dating back at least twenty years. The records showed that Peter Gordon "Chocks" Hostetler was never a narcotics suspect, an investigative source, a witness, or a victim.

There was not a single mention of him. Not one.

As the Buddha once observed so profoundly: From a negative can come a positive. It was in that context I phoned Paul Horvath from the Federal Aviation Administration's Flight Standards District Office in Van Nuys. We'd met under the most negative of circumstances years earlier, after some joker sabotaged the *Duck* and I crashed on takeoff near San Diego. Fortunately, neither I nor my passenger, a San Diego cop, was injured. Horvath, a bearded, button-down, senior accident investigator, had been tasked with finding the cause of the crash. We'd hardly become buddies over the course of his analysis, but we did establish a mutual respect of sorts. The FAA routinely presumes that the pilot is at fault whenever an aircraft is seriously damaged or destroyed. Not in my case, however. In my case, Horvath had shown himself to be thorough and objective in concluding that the *Duck* had gone down through no fault of my own.

"I hope you're not calling to tell me you've wrecked another perfectly good airplane," he said.

"Not yet," I said, "though the day is young."

"Then why are you calling me?"

I watched Kiddiot slowly sneaking up on Ack-Ack, who was asleep at my feet. His paws were twitching. "Actually, I need a personal favor."

"The FAA is not in the habit of granting personal favors, Mr. Logan."

"I wouldn't ask if it wasn't important."

Horvath sighed. "I'm listening."

I told him I needed records of all FAA radar tracks, tail numbers, and owner registrations for all aircraft that were operating in or around Santa Isabella's airspace the night Chocks Hostetler fell out of the sky.

"We served together," I said. "He was my wingman."

No sympathy. No "sorry for your loss." Horvath was as aloof as the agency he worked for.

"Current registrations and aircraft ownership records are public," Horvath said. "You can find them online, like everyone else."

"Not if they've been blocked at the owner's request. Some records are private."

It was at that moment Kiddiot pounced. Ack-Ack yelped and ran into the bathroom.

"Was that a dog?" Horvath asked over the phone.

"More like a cat toy," I said.

"What you're asking me to do, Mr. Logan, is highly irregular."

"I'm aware of that. I'm also aware that you don't owe me anything, Paul, but your help could make a difference. The man was a national hero. Whoever killed him needs to be hunted down and made to pay for what they did."

A long pause followed.

"I can't make any promises," Horvath said.

I said I more than understood.

That night, I discovered that Ack-Ack was no beagle. He was a purebred bed hog. So was Kiddiot. By the time the sun rose, Layne and I were clinging to our respective edges of the bed while the two pets were stretched out together in the middle, snoring.

We got up, fed the animals, had a quick breakfast, and drove to Santa Isabella in my old pickup truck to find out what more we could about Grande Summit Financial Group. We would've flown, but Layne didn't like traveling in small planes. They made her anxious, she said. The perfect woman who was afraid of flying. The yin and the yang. You take the good with the bad. No relationship is perfect.

Mrs. Schmulowitz was out watering her geraniums as we were leaving. I introduced her to Ack-Ack and asked her if she wouldn't mind keeping an eye on him for a few hours while we were away. I might as well have asked her if she wouldn't mind making every day of the year Hanukkah. I wasn't sure which one fell more instantly in love with the other—the old lady or the dog. She set her watering can aside, plopped down on the grass, and they engaged in a tail-wagging hug fest.

"I'm taking him out with me on the campaign trail this morning," she said. "Big canasta tournament over at the senior center. He's got vote-getter written all over him."

She said he reminded her of her last dog, Pantene.

"Oh, how I miss that little pooch," Mrs. Schmulowitz said, fighting off Ack-Ack, who insisted on repeatedly trying to kiss her on the lips. "A happier creature you've never seen in your life. He loved baths like nobody's business."

"Pantene. What an unusual name," Layne said. "What breed of dog was he, Mrs. Schmulowitz?"

"A shampoodle."

"Of course he was," I said.

We drove up the coast highway. The ocean was the color of new blue jeans. There was no wind. The water was so calm and flat you could see the ruffle of a breeze offshore. Layne looked over from the passenger seat.

"By the way, I forgot to tell you. Dee called."

"Who's Dee?"

"The realtor."

"You mean your personal trainer."

"She wants us to look at that condo tomorrow."

"Swell," I said.

"I get that you're not enthused about moving, Logan. But what about Ack-Ack? He could have his own yard."

"Ack-Ack already has his own yard."

Layne looked out the window and shook her head.

"You saw how Mrs. Schmulowitz responded to him, and how he responded to her," I said. "They love each other."

"Mrs. Schmulowitz can come over to visit as often as she wants."

I reminded her that our fledgling private investigative agency wasn't exactly setting the financial world on fire, and neither was my flight school. I was losing sleep, I said, at the prospect of taking on additional living expenses without additional income beyond Layne's monthly government pension.

"We can afford this, Logan," she said. "The other thing is, I have money in the bank."

"Oh, yeah? How much?"

"Enough."

I set my jaw and focused on the road ahead, two hands on the wheel.

"Look," she said, "I know you have a loyalty to Mrs. Schmulowitz. I'm just trying to make your life a little better, that's all." She reached out and stroked the side of my face. "Can you understand that?"

I told her that I could. Compromise is the cornerstone of any workable relationship, which explained why none of my relationships with women had ever worked out in the long-term. After a certain age, most people get stuck in their ways like a truck in a ditch. Even the mere suggestion of being told what to do can send mud flying. The thing about it was, though, I wanted this relationship to work as much as I'd ever wanted anything. I wanted us to be together from here on out. I wanted to make Layne happy.

"If it's what you really want," I said, disregarding the bile that rose sour and hot up the back of my throat, "we'll go take a look at the condo tomorrow."

She leaned over and hugged me around the neck. Not like

she'd won. Nothing like that. It was like she genuinely understood what I was feeling and appreciated me for being me.

A rare commodity, indeed.

The offices of Grande Summit Financial Group were located on Hesperia Street in a plain, flat-roofed, two-story commercial building flanked by a Jiffy Lube and the Slice of Heaven pizza parlor. All the building's windows were darkly tinted. You couldn't see inside. Layne and I drove past and parked at a metered space down the street where we could observe anyone coming or going through the truck's mirrors.

"Check this out," she said. "A little spook magic."

I watched her open some super-secret-squirrel app on her phone that she wouldn't let me see directly because, as she put it only half-jokingly, my security clearance had expired long ago. Then she tapped in a series of commands that replaced her actual phone number and caller ID with a 202 Washington, DC, number and "US Justice Department." Illegal? Probably. Necessary? Debatable. I wasn't about to turn her in, however. Layne put the phone on speaker.

"Good morning, Grande Summit Financial Group. How may I direct your call?" The receptionist sounded young and intimidated. She'd obviously seen "Justice Department" pop up on her phone.

"I'm looking for Mr. Gerald Whitlock," Layne said in her best federal agent voice.

"I'm, umm, not sure if Mr. Whitlock has come in this morning. May I ask what this is regarding?"

"His parole revocation."

Seconds passed as the receptionist debated what to do before she said, "One moment, please."

We traded a smile and listened on hold for maybe twenty seconds to an annoying flute version of Simon and Garfunkel's "Feelin' Groovy." Then a male voice came on the line. He sounded as edgy as his receptionist.

"This is Gerald Whitlock. How can I help you?"

"Meet us behind Slice of Heaven," Layne said in her best badass, fed voice. "Ten minutes."

"I'm sorry. *Who* is this?"

"This, Gerald, is your future. Back in prison or not. It's your call." She hung up.

"Well played," I said.

"It's what I do," she said, "or used to."

The pizza joint was a two-minute walk from Gerald Whitlock's office. He drove over. I understood why as soon as he squeezed himself out of his silver two-seat BMW sportster. The man was pushing three hundred and fifty pounds. His dark-gray business suit hung on him like a circus tent. The salt-and-pepper goatee he wore did nothing to camouflage the fact that his chin had chins. Just getting out of his car seemed to exhaust him.

Layne and I emerged from behind the dumpster. It smelled like moldy tomato sauce.

"Show me some tin," Whitlock said.

It was the one time in my life when I could've said, "Badges? We don't need no stinkin' badges." Somehow, I restrained myself.

"Look, Gerald," Layne said, disregarding his demand to see credentials which we obviously didn't have, "this can go one of two ways. Either you give us what we want and you go on your merry way, or you'll be really, really sorry."

I looked over at her. "*You'll be really, really sorry*? What the hell kind of threat is that? You might as well tell him, 'Either cooperate with us, or we're gonna steal your lunch money.'"

Layne ignored me, focused on Whitlock. "Tell us what you know about Peter Hostetler," she said.

"Who?"

"Peter Hostetler. Chief operating officer at Electrogenics."

"Never heard of him."

"The guy who landed on that trailer last week," I said.

"Seriously, I don't know what you're talking about, man."

"We need to know what Hostetler's relationship was with your clients down in Mexico," Layne said.

Whitlock held up both palms. His hands were shaking. "OK, look, whatever this is about, I assure you, I have no clients in Mexico, OK? I don't even know anybody in Mexico."

I took a step toward him. He took two terrified steps back, his eyes as wide as silver dollars.

Layne grabbed my arm and pretended to hold me back. "Not yet. Let's give him one more chance."

"Either this bloated piece of excrement comes clean on Electrogenics and Gervasio Pascua," I said, "or he's gonna be enjoying his next meal out of a sippy cup."

"Please," Whitlock begged, "I don't know what you're talking about."

"You want to go back to prison, Gerald?" Layne asked him.

"God, no."

"Good," she said. "Then you better figure out real quick what it is we *are* talking about."

He ran a chubby trembling hand across his chubby face. "OK, OK. Maybe I do know something. But I'm gonna need some time to think, make some plans. My family. My kids. I don't want them to get hurt. Can you understand that?"

"You've got until noon tomorrow," I said. "And I promise you. We *will* find you."

We watched him hustle back to his car.

"You know, for a big guy like that, he moves surprisingly well," Layne said.

"Ever been fishing?" I asked her.

"No."

"You bait the hook with a small fish," I said as we headed back to my truck, "then you throw the line out and cross your fingers. Same deal here."

We didn't have to wait long for a bite.

SIX

Santa Isabella is a tidy little community laid out on a straightforward street grid aligned north and south, with only a few traffic lights. In other words, it's easy to tail someone through town, especially if they're too stupid or freaked out to realize they're being followed. Gerald Whitlock was both. He drove straight to Electrogenics and into the employee lot like his sports car was on fire.

Layne and I pulled in and stopped across Hesperia Street at the ARCO gas station, about a hundred meters away. She fired up a telescopic device built into her iPhone that you won't find for sale at the Apple Store.

"He's making a phone call," she said, squinting through the phone.

"Could be he's ordering a pizza. The man looks like he doesn't miss too many meals."

She ignored me. Electrogenics's frizzy-haired CEO, Ed Millisohn, emerged from the building's main entrance seconds later. He glanced around nervously, didn't see us, then made a beeline for Whitlock's car; he got in quickly and pulled the door shut.

"Any chance that top-secret phone of yours has distance-monitoring capability, so we can listen in on whatever they're saying?"

"You've been watching too many spy movies, Logan."

"I don't watch spy movies. They never get the details right."

"Tell me about it."

"Well," I said, "I suppose there's one way to find out what they're discussing." I cranked the ignition and jammed the truck into gear. "Buckle up."

Layne looked over at me like I was crazier than her favorite David Sedaris book. "What are you doing, Logan?"

I didn't answer as we roared through a yellow light at the intersection and headed for Electrogenics at twice the posted thirty-mile-per-hour speed limit. Layne had braced one hand on the dashboard and was crossing herself with the other.

"You're gonna get us killed."

I didn't answer her.

With Gerald Whitlock's BMW in my sights, we slalomed through the parking lot. Neither man saw us coming. I jammed on the brakes, fishtailed to a stop, and was out of the truck before they knew what was happening. That's what I assumed, anyway, that I'd gotten the jump on them, until I pulled open the front passenger door and was met by the business end of the .40-caliber Sig in Millisohn's right hand. The muzzle looked like it belonged on a howitzer. It was a good thing I was unarmed. I would've been shot dead before I could've drawn my own weapon. Which never happens in spy movies.

"Take it easy," I said, slowly raising my arms.

Layne joined me with her hands in the air. "All we want is some information," she said.

"These are the two feds I was just telling you about," Whitlock said. "From the Justice Department."

"*Justice Department?*" Millisohn's lips spread in an incredulous smile as he sat in Whitlock's car, looking Layne up and down. "I don't know who the babe is, but this wiseass here talked his way into my office two days ago wanting to know about his alcoholic dead buddy. I told him to take a hike. He obviously doesn't comprehend the meaning of the word no."

"One among my many character flaws," I said. "What exactly is it that you people manufacture here, Ed? Because I think we both know it's not just 'for the kids.'"

Before Millisohn could answer, a siren keened from across the parking lot as a "courtesy" guard in one of the company's clown-car patrol Fiats came speeding toward us with its rooftop gumball light flashing. Tires screeched, the driver's door flew open, and out stepped a slab of a man in an Electrogenics baseball cap and jumpsuit. In his left hand was a collapsible aluminum police baton which he extended with a menacing flick of his wrist.

"Everything OK, boss? You want I should escort these individuals off the premises?"

"That won't be necessary," Layne said. "We were just leaving. Weren't we, Logan?"

"Actually," I said, "no, we're not. Not until we get a handle on what it is you're making here at Electrogenics, Ed—what you're *really* making."

Ed Millisohn smiled enigmatically. His eyes and pistol were still trained on my face. "Call the sheriff," he ordered the guard. "Tell them that the president of the Santa Isabella Sheriff's Citizen Advisory Council is being threatened on company property by a deranged nutcase."

"Yes, sir." The guard had been thumping his baton in his palm, waiting for any excuse to tune me up. Now he got out his phone like he was almost disappointed.

Layne was giving me a look that said, *Let's get the hell out of here before we both end up in jail.* I forced the issue no further. I'd already achieved my fundamental objective: by immediately running to Millisohn, the CEO of Electrogenics, Gerald Whitlock had unwittingly confirmed the connection between the company and Mexican narcotics money.

"If I find out you had anything to do with what happened to Pete Hostetler," I told him, "you'll wish your parents never met."

I thought about blowing him a kiss as we drove away, but I didn't want to leave the wrong impression. Layne was looking over at me from the passenger seat with her mouth open.

"What the hell was all *that* about back there?"

"Go on offense. Dominate. Be dynamic in the field. They didn't teach you that at the Farm?"

"What they taught me, Logan, is that there's no room in a dynamic environment for impulsivity. What they taught me was that rash behavior, like that which I just witnessed, can get you killed in the field."

"Who dares wins," I said.

"Not always," Layne said.

I looked over at her. "Did we not just catch a bigger fish? Whitlock led us back to Millisohn. We rattled Millisohn's cage. He could lead us straight to whoever killed Chocks—assuming Millisohn didn't do it himself or pay somebody to do it for him. What part of fishing don't you understand?"

Layne glared at me. "Thank you *so* much for mansplaining it to me like that, Logan. With my little lady brain, I could've never understood all that in a million years."

"I'm sorry. Seriously. I didn't mean to be demeaning, and I didn't mean to frighten you."

"Yeah, well, you were, and you did." She stared out the window without speaking, biting her lower lip, and shaking her head. "I'm not sure this is working out, Logan," she said after a while.

I knew she wasn't talking about our investigation of Chocks Hostetler's murder.

Hesperia Street transitioned to the southbound lanes of the 101 freeway. Traffic was light. Neither of us said another word the entire drive back to Rancho Bonita.

———

We were three blocks from home when things got even more chilly between us, which was ironic given the day had turned into a scorcher—one of those cloudless California afternoons when the wind feels like a blowtorch and the threat of wildfire is the first thought on everyone's mind. My truck's air-conditioning had given up the ghost long ago. Both windows were open. As I exited the freeway and stopped at the intersection of Garrido Avenue and Eden, a vintage Cadillac convertible, cherry red, all tail fins and polished chrome, eased to a stop in the turn lane to my left. The driver and his passenger were screaming profanely at each other.

Both looked to be in their thirties, both all-American flawless in appearance, in that way every model on every TV commercial used to look before the gurus on Madison Avenue realized that most people don't look that way in real life. Both were blessed with perfect tans, highly desirable hair, and the best teeth money could buy. Both were wearing aviator sunglasses of the style no actual aviator ever wears. I made him for some up-and-coming actor. Her, too. Hollywood types love getting away to Rancho Bonita, where they're half a tank of gas from Los Angeles, yet far enough away that they won't get caught cheating on their partners. I couldn't tell what they were arguing about, only that the fight was escalating quickly.

"You think you're all that? Well, you're not. You're nothing. You're less than nothing," he yelled at her. "I should've dumped you back in Albuquerque."

"You can go to hell, Troy!" she shot back.

Two D-list actors running lines from some B-movie script. That's what I thought at first. But then she struggled desperately to climb out of the Caddie, and Troy yanked her back by her chestnut mane, and I knew her screams were no act.

"Let her go, Troy."

He looked past the woman, still clutching a fistful of her hair, and growled at me with a teeth-bearing grimace that did not reach his eyes.

"Kiss off, Grampa."

Grampa? Who the hell was he calling *Grampa*? I was only old enough to have been his father, and I still felt like I was twenty-five—at least when I was lying down and not moving.

The turn arrow slid from red to green. The Caddie burned rubber through the intersection, Troy steering with one hand and manhandling his still-screaming passenger with the other. I slammed my foot down on the accelerator, veered into the turn lane, and gave chase, cutting off a kid in a blue VW who laid on his tinny horn in complaint.

"This isn't your fight, Logan," Layne pleaded.

"Did you hear what he just called me?"

"So what?"

"I'm not old enough to be a grandfather."

"Some idiot insults your fragile male ego, and now you're going to beat him up. What planet am I living on?"

"He needs to learn some manners."

"You're not Miss Manners, Logan!"

I ignored her as the speedometer climbed over fifty. In seconds, I was riding his back bumper.

"I'm calling the police," Layne said. "This is their job, not yours."

"This guy'll be long gone before the cops show up."

As far as car chases go, it wasn't much of one. Troy saw me in his rearview, pulled over in front of the Church of Skatan skateboard shop, and jumped out.

"You want a piece of this, old man? Is that what you want? Fine. Let's go!"

I stepped out of the truck.

"Please don't do this, Logan," Layne begged.

I ignored her.

Veins bulged in the guy's neck. His eyes were wide and glowed like magma. Focused as he was on me, he didn't notice the woman vaulting out of his convertible and fleeing. By the time he realized what had happened, she was too far gone to catch. It made him even madder.

"I'm gonna enjoy kicking your sorry ass," he said, lacing his fingers together and cracking his knuckles.

I sighed. It wasn't the first time I'd found myself facing down a jerk in defense of some woman I didn't even know. Was it the result of having grown up in one foster home after another, watching my foster moms getting knocked around by the drunks they were unfortunately married to, and being too small to protect them? Or was it a coincidence?

This particular jerk would've ended up in the emergency room like so many before him had Layne not burst out of my truck and taken him on herself. Before I knew it, she strode past me and had the guy in a straight arm bar, slamming him face-first into the curb with her knee in his back.

"Repeat after me," she said. "Only cowards lay hands in anger on a woman."

He was groaning. "You broke my wrist, you bitch."

She bent his arm back even farther. He groaned louder.

"Say it," Layne said.

"Only a coward lays hands in anger on a woman."

"Very good. Only this time, say it with feeling."

He repeated the line with feeling. Layne made him promise to get some counseling before she let him go. He promised. I believed him about as much as I did in the Easter Bunny. We watched him get back in his Caddie. He flipped us off as he drove away.

"Nice form," I told Layne. "Thanks for the assist."

She gave me a sideways glance that screamed disapproval. The skin around her eyes was drawn tight with strain. "Maybe you haven't heard, Logan, but there are these things now. They're called laws. You just can't go around taking them into your own hands, no matter how righteous you think you are."

"He was hurting that girl."

"He called you *Grampa*. Admit it. That's what set you off, not whatever bizarro hero-complex it is you seem to be suffering from."

"Somebody had to do something, Layne."

"Where does it say you have to ride to the rescue all the time?" Several seconds passed before she turned her head and fixed me with as flinty a look as I'd ever seen. "To repeat," she said. "I don't know if this is working out."

She was right about one thing: There *are* laws. But they came in two flavors as far I was concerned: the formal kind found in statute books and the informal but no less immutable kind that aren't. I'd spent the better part of eight years upholding the latter while serving as the air force's lone representative among a band of interservice meat-eaters whose violent means always justified the ends without regard to international boundaries. We rid the world of more murdering thugs and genocidal crazies than I'm willing to admit publicly, even if each of them more than deserved a taste of their own medicine. The risk, however, in abiding by those kinds of conventions long enough is that enforcing them becomes muscle memory, even when both your current love interest and the Buddha's teachings are telling you to stand down.

I apologized to her. She registered no response. We got back in the truck, and she maintained radio silence for the remainder of the ride home. Her body language made it abundantly clear that Layne Sterling and I were history.

We arrived to find Mrs. Schmulowitz holding a campaign fundraiser in her tiny backyard. Her red, white, and blue bib overalls matched her tennis shoes. Her campaign manager, otherwise known as my airplane mechanic, Larry Kropf, was playing waiter and making the rounds in a T-shirt designed to look like a tuxedo, offering attendees Ritz crackers laden with Velveeta cheese on a silver tray. Those in attendance included members of Mrs. Schmulowitz's mahjong club and other blue-hairs from the hot yoga class she taught twice weekly at the Rancho Bonita Senior Center. Also present were Kiddiot and Ack-Ack, who followed Larry around in tandem, waiting for crackers to fall off the tray. The place was hopping.

"You're both just in time," Mrs. Schmulowitz said, working her way through the crowd to give Layne a peck on the cheek and me a hug. "I'm about to deliver a major policy address on the local homeless situation."

"I'd love to hear it, Mrs. Schmulowitz," Layne said, "but I have a splitting migraine. If you'll excuse me."

The chilly sidelong glance Layne gave me as she walked

inside and slammed the door of our garage abode was not lost on our landlady.

"You know what they say, bubby: Behind every angry woman is a man who has absolutely no idea what he did wrong."

"That's the problem, Mrs. Schmulowitz. I know exactly what I did wrong."

"Mazel tov." She patted me on the cheek. "Then consider yourself ahead of the game."

———

Layne and I didn't do much talking that night beyond me trying to explain why I'd reacted the way I had to that dickwad in the Cadillac, and why I'd felt the need to go racing into the parking lot of Electrogenics up in Santa Isabella like a cheetah chasing its prey across the savanna.

"You need to not be so impulsive next time, Logan. You're gonna get yourself killed."

"There won't be a next time, Layne. I promise."

She said she accepted my apology, but her unyielding silence afterward suggested otherwise.

We were both asleep about three hours later, turned away from each other at opposing edges of the bed, with the cat and dog cuddled in between us, when my phone chimed. I picked it up off the floor. There was a new text message. It read:

> You've been asking many questions
> re PH.
>
> 31° 47' 43" N 116° 36' .09" W
>
> 20:00 Z mañana.

I rolled over on my back as quietly as I could, trying not to disturb Layne or the pets, and typed the latitude and longitude into a converter app on my phone. The coordinates were those of the Ensenada International Airport, about eighty-five miles south of the United States-Mexico border, down the Baja Peninsula. The reference to "20:00 Z *mañana*" translated to eight P.M. Greenwich mean time—or "Zulu" as it's known in aviation circles—a seven-hour difference from Pacific Daylight Savings Time. The sender wanted me to rendezvous with them at the airport at one P.M. the next day.

You've been asking many questions re PH.

Indeed, I had. My wingman, Pete Hostetler, had died a gruesome and undeserved death. One way or the other, I intended to keep asking questions until I got the answers I was looking for.

Given the suspicion that Chocks was associated with the Pascua narcotics cartel and that Gervasio Pascua was known to control much of the Baja, something told me I wouldn't be meeting with the tooth fairy.

SEVEN

Lawfully flying a private airplane into Mexico makes an IRS tax audit look effortless by comparison. I was up early, gathering all the necessary paperwork and emailing the proper aeronautical authorities the details of my planned flight while Layne cooked me scrambled eggs and pretend, plant-based sausage. The silent treatment was still largely in effect, but her fear for my safety in flying down to Mexico to meet with Gervasio Pascua overshadowed the fact that she was still upset with me over my behavior the day before.

"I don't get it," she said, standing over the stove, stirring the eggs as I sat at the table.

"Neither do I. And neither do they." I nodded to the dog and cat who were sitting hip to hip at Layne's feet, looking up at her and waiting expectantly for food to fall on the floor. "Why can't we all have real sausage?"

"Because real sausage will kill you, Logan. Maybe not as fast as meeting face-to-face with the most cold-blooded cartel boss in the Western Hemisphere, but kill you, nonetheless. At least let me come with you. You need some backup."

I reminded her how she hated flying in small planes, and how the flight to Ensenada in the *Ruptured Duck* would take close to three hours, depending on the wind. I also reminded her how a ruthless drug dealer with unlimited resources would have little need to invite me south of the border to kill me when he could just as easily do it north of the border.

"Either Pascua's going to tell me that (a) Chocks had nothing to do with their operations, or (b) he's going to tell me to stop asking so many questions unless I want to get thrown out of some aircraft in the middle of the night, too."

Layne stepped around and over the pets and brought me my breakfast. The eggs and pretend sausage were mixed with sautéed onions and seasoned with basil. I didn't even know we had basil.

"Smells and looks terrific," I said. "Thank you."

"You're forgetting (c)," Layne said. "Pascua rightfully concludes you're the type of guy who'll never quit until you find the truth, and you're never seen again."

She crossed to the sink and started rinsing dishes while I slipped a chunk of pretend sausage each to Kiddiot and Ack-Ack. The cat sniffed it like I was trying to poison him. The dog wolfed his down like he couldn't remember his last meal, even though his last meal had been served an hour earlier. His wagging tail thumped my leg.

"You're forgetting, Layne. I've hunted drug guys. Granted, most if not all have the conscience of a rattlesnake, but they usually don't go around killing foreign nationals without good reason. They would have zero reason to kill me."

"Keep telling yourself that, Logan," she said, scrubbing a pan. "You're forgetting. I've hunted them, too."

She wished me luck and pecked me on the cheek before I left. At least that was something.

The *Duck* and I played cat and mouse with the clouds, level at seven thousand feet on an IFR flight plan. One minute we would be enjoying unlimited visibility, flying above a solid batten of white. The next minute the clouds would rise ahead of us like the Andes, and I'd be on instruments, barely able to see past the end of the *Duck*'s nose. Air traffic control routed us along the coast and directly over LAX, where I watched departing jetliners climbing up through the deck below me, rising like ghosts out of the gloom. The air was bumpy—"light-to-moderate chop," we pilots like to call it. It wasn't until the *Duck* and I were south of Dana Point with San Juan Capistrano off the left wingtip that the clouds thinned to clear but hazy skies. San Diego soon beckoned ahead with its glass-and-chrome skyline and the majestic blue swoosh of the Coronado Bay Bridge. We overflew *nuevo* mansions in La Jolla, sailboats plying Mission Bay, and gray navy frigates and supply ships berthed in Chula Vista, south of the city.

"Skyhawk Four Charlie Lima, contact Tijuana Approach now on one-one-niner-point-five. Good day."

"One-one-niner-point-five," I radioed back. "Four Charlie Lima, thanks for the help."

But for an imaginary line on my iPad's moving map and the barely discernible Mexican accent of the new air traffic controller I was handed off to, I would've never known that I was exiting the United States and entering the airspace of a foreign country. Private pilots used to venture south of the border all the time to fish for tuna and dorado and to lounge on the beaches in ridiculously affordable hotels, gorging themselves on cheap lobster and beer. Those days were long over. A crackdown on drug trafficking and rocky relations between Washington and

Mexico City had put a major dent in general aviation traffic heading south of the border. Where the Baja once boasted two hundred airfields there were now less than two dozen, most controlled by corrupt military commanders with their hands out. *Mordida*, the Mexicans called it. Often as not you either greased their palms with bribe money or you could kiss your airplane goodbye. Sometimes you went to jail.

Far to my left, barely blue in the late morning haze, was the Sea of Cortez, made famous by John Steinbeck. To my immediate right, stretching to eternity, was the vast Pacific. Beneath me but for the occasional struggling farm or vineyard was a rocky, foreboding desertscape. You pay particular attention to the gauges and the sounds your engine makes when flying over such terrain and keep a sharp lookout for where to put down in an emergency if you must. Fortunately, the *Duck*'s one-hundred-and-sixty-horsepower Lycoming thrummed along with nary a hiccup. The female controller at Tijuana Approach had handed me off to the Ensenada International Airport tower. I started my descent over an azure harbor clogged with small fishing boats and a luxury cruise ship belching smoke from its stacks and entered the pattern on the downwind leg to Runway Two-Niner. Five minutes later, I was parked in front of a sunbaked, prefab, single-story building at the base of the tower—Mexican Customs Enforcement.

Two young soldiers emerged in camouflage fatigues, the bills of their crush caps pulled down badass-style over their brows. Slung across each of their chests was an FX-05 assault rifle, a weapon that looked like the love child of an M4 carbine and an AK-47. I unlatched my door, stepped out, and gave them my most charming tourista smile.

"Hola. Buenos días."

"Your documents, please," the taller of the two said,

sounding less like a Mexican serviceman and more like a Gestapo agent in every World War II movie ever made.

By "documents" he meant an original copy of the *Duck*'s insurance policy, original logbooks, the *Duck*'s radio license, weight-and-balance calculations, and, for all I knew, proof that I wasn't a creature from some faraway galaxy. Then he added, with the trace of a smile, "And the required entry fees."

"How does twenty dollars apiece sound, amigo?"

The heavier one said, "About a thousand dollars short . . . amigo."

Talk about inflation. The last time I'd flown into Mexico, it was to pick up the son of a wealthy, older Rancho Bonita couple whose son had been badly injured dirt biking outside Maneadero. The friendly Mexican sergeant on duty that day at the Bahía Soledad Airstrip hit me up for ten bucks. These two dudes seemed nowhere near that benevolent.

"I'm here to meet somebody," I said, stalling for time while I scrounged around the *Duck*'s back seat for the necessary paperwork.

"*¿Quién?*" the taller one asked.

"Gervasio Pascua."

After they were finished laughing, the heavier one said, "The entry fee just went up to two thousand dollars, my friend."

I was pleading poverty when a line of three black Chevy Suburbans drove onto the tarmac and straight toward us. The two soldiers' cocky demeanors changed instantly to outright fear.

A pair of slick-haired, muscled-up goons emerged from the lead Suburban wearing jeans, pastel polo shirts, and wraparound sunglasses made for shooting. Each had an Israeli-made Uzi submachine gun slung over his shoulder. Another two goons, similarly armed, got out of the rear SUV. The soldiers blanched and hurried back to the customs building. Only then did the rear passenger door of the middle SUV open and a gangly man with dark receding hair step out.

"Mr. Logan?" His attire was business casual. A crisp, open-collar white dress shirt, gabardine slacks, and an Ivy League navy blazer with brass buttons. His smile reminded me of piano keys. "Welcome to Ensenada."

"Mr. Pascua?"

"Armando Berganza," he said, correcting me. "I'm Mr. Pascua's personal assistant. You may call me Armando, please."

He raised his eyebrows like he expected me to recognize his name. I didn't.

"If you're worried about your airplane," he said, "don't be. It will be safe during your visit here. Now, if you would be kind enough to turn around, please, with your hands behind your back."

"What for?"

Armando Berganza smiled again, soothingly. "Your own safety, señor."

All four goons were waiting and watching me. Under the circumstances, what choice did I have? I turned around. Berganza zip-tied my wrists, frisked me, then nodded to one of the gunmen who threw a burlap sack over my head.

I couldn't see much through the bag, but I could smell plenty as I bumped over bad roads in the Suburban's back seat. The stench of fish and the salty perfume of the nearby sea mixed with Armando's aftershave which smelled like oranges and insect repellent. I could hear the melodic strains of a violin and guitars as we passed by a mariachi band. They were playing and singing "Cielito Lindo"—Lovely Sweet One. The SUV made a hard left turn that caused me to lean into Armando Berganza, who was sitting close beside me. Another left turn followed by two turns to the right, then we stopped and the doors opened. Instantly, the stifling heat of the day filtered in.

Berganza maneuvered me by the crook of my arm, steering me out of the SUV—"Watch your step"—then inside an air-conditioned building where he lowered me gently but forcefully onto an unpadded wooden chair with the bag still over my head. I heard a switchblade click open. Someone cut the plastic tie binding my hands. A door opened and closed behind me.

Silence.

I pulled off the bag to find myself in a windowless room stacked floor to ceiling with cases of bottled Mexican beer. Above me was a skylight the size of a twin bed. On the barnwood table in front of me was a set of silverware, a glass of ice water, and an earthenware plate upon which lay the most impressive chile verde burrito I'd ever seen. The thing was the size of a brick and smelled the way I imagined heaven might. I concluded that if anyone were planning to kill me, it wouldn't be by filling a steaming homemade tortilla with slow-cooked chile verde, rice, and black beans, all smothered in green sauce. I ate every delectable bite.

A couple of minutes later, the door opened. I could hear cantina music and people laughing. One of the goons I'd observed earlier walked in. His nose was crooked from too many fistfights, and his eyes were too small for his face. He wore his moustache Fu Manchu–style. You don't see that kind of facial hair too often these days. He glanced around the room like he was running a security check, then turned over his shoulder and nodded an all clear.

The short, wiry man who followed him in bore the casual look of a Silicon Valley executive, not the drug lord I presumed him to be. Tight-fitting white V-neck T-shirt, eight-hundred-dollar Gucci sneakers, black jeans. Late forties but trying hard not to look it. He had a Fitbit smartwatch, ruby studs in either earlobe, and the narrow eyes of a carnivore. I could see fine scars under his chin from what looked to be a recent neck lift.

"A pleasure to meet you, Mr. Logan. My name is Gervasio Pascua." He extended his hand to shake mine. His skin was as cold as quartz. "My apologies for making you wait. Business called. How was the burrito? To your liking, I hope. My people tell me you're something of an aficionado in that regard."

"Excellent burrito. I can feel my arteries clogging already."

"So glad you enjoyed it." Pascua smiled like he meant it. "You flew a great distance to see me on short notice. A good meal was the least I could do."

Fu Manchu took up a position just inside the door. I could see other goons standing guard outside the room, lining a long, dark hallway. Pascua sat down in a chair on the other side of the table.

"So," he said, "I understand you've been making inquiries regarding Peter Hostetler. I was quite saddened to learn of his passing. I'm told the two of you served together in the military."

"You knew Pete?"

Pascua nodded. "He flew for me. Briefly."

"That's funny. His wife told me he hadn't flown since he left the airlines."

"What man shares with his woman everything he does when he's out of her sight?"

"Pete transported narcotics for you. Is that what you're telling me?"

Gervasio Pascua smiled again and calmly crossed his legs, brushing an imaginary piece of lint from the right thigh of his jeans. No, he said, that wasn't what he was telling me.

"I own homes in Tampico, in Guadalajara, on Cozumel," he said. "My wife enjoys spending time in all of them. My personal pilot, a man who had flown us for many years, retired and bought a coffee plantation in Chiapas."

"So you hired Pete?"

Pascua leaned forward in his chair, folding his hands on the table. "Your friend was looking for a job. My people came across his résumé online somewhere. We arranged to meet. I liked him immediately. An open and honest man. Trustworthy. And an excellent pilot. He was paid well for his services. Those services, however, had nothing to do with my business ventures. He worked for me for, I would say, a month, no more than that, before my accountant advised me that joining a chartered jet service was much less expensive than owning your own jet."

"So you fired him."

Pascua shrugged. "I employ many people, Mr. Logan. They come and they go."

"How many of them end up falling out of the sky?"

The mustachioed goon standing guard at the door walked over, leaned down, and whispered something in Pascua's ear. Pascua nodded, never taking his eyes off me.

"If you're asking me, did I have anything to do with what happened to your friend, Mr. Logan, the answer is no."

"Can you prove that?"

"You're asking me to prove a negative, Mr. Logan. Proving a negative is impossible."

"Why did you ask me to come down here?"

"Why?" Pascua leaned forward in his chair with his elbows on his knees. "To express to you, sincerely, how much I admired your friend Peter as a pilot and as a man, even though he didn't work for me long, and to assure you I had nothing to do with his death. Also, I wanted to gauge what sort of man *you* are, to see if you might be interested in coming to come work for me."

"I wouldn't, but I appreciate the offer. Who told you I was looking into Pete's murder?"

"I'm not at liberty to say."

"What is your connection to Electrogenics?"

"I'm afraid I don't know what that is."

"I'm afraid I find that hard to believe, Mr. Pascua."

"Are you calling me a liar?"

"I'm just calling it like I see it."

Again Fu Manchu leaned down and whispered in Pascua's ear. Again Pascua nodded, eyeing me.

"Well," he said with a sigh, "I'm afraid we have a bit of a problem."

"And what would that be?"

Pascua tilted his head in Fu's direction. "My associate, Mr. Zuniga, tells me he has a bad feeling about you, a very bad feeling. He believes you'll continue asking questions and making trouble for me, drawing attention to my business activities, no matter how adamantly I insist I had nothing to do with the death of your friend. I trust Mr. Zuniga's instincts explicitly. He believes we have no choice but to kill you."

"Bummer. And just when I thought things were going so well between us."

"Don't get me wrong, Mr. Logan. Personally, I find you oddly charming—in a blunt-spoken, excessively self-assured sort of way. But if Mr. Zuniga believes that it's in my best interest you must die, well, so be it."

"If it's not too much to ask, can I ask how Mr. Zuniga plans to kill me?"

"He intends to slice you into small pieces, then go chumming for dorado."

"Unless?"

Pascua sighed and examined his fingernails. "You've played

your hand, Mr. Logan. Unfortunately for you, there is no *unless*."

"There's always *unless*." I ran my fork around the plate my burrito had been served on, licking off the last bit of sauce. "OK, how about this: I take you at your word that you had nothing to do with my friend's murder, your people give me a ride back to my plane, and we never met."

"I'm not sure you understand," Pascua said. "You see, once an idea takes seed in Mr. Zuniga's prehistoric head, well, I've found that it's all but impossible to remove the idea. For you and I to come to such an arrangement, I'm afraid you'd have to kill him before he killed you."

I heard a click and looked over. Sunlight filtered down from the skylight overhead and glinted off the shiny steel blade of the stiletto in Zuniga's right hand. He was grinning. His front teeth were solid gold.

"Doesn't seem like a fair fight," I said.

"True enough," Pascua said. "No one ever said life is fair, did they?"

"You misunderstand me, Mr. Pascua," I said. "What I meant was, it's not fair to him."

I flung the plate like a Frisbee, aiming for Zuniga's head. He ducked and the plate hit the wall behind him. Pieces of earthenware clattered to the floor. He came lumbering toward me, thrusting and slashing with his stiletto. I narrowly danced clear of the blade—my Muhammad Ali to his Joe Frazier—but the room was small and he kept coming.

I grabbed my chair and threw it at him. He blocked it with his ham hock of an arm and kept coming, anticipating my moves before I made them, grinning at me with those teeth. Each time he tried to stick me, I sidestepped him and counterpunched, but I was nearly twice his age, and he had a solid fifty pounds on me. It was like hitting a cement block for all the good my fists did as he kept cutting off the angle, maneuvering me steadily into a corner. Being stabbed to death was not a question of if, but when. I was determined, however, to make him work for it.

Adapt and overcome. Whatever it takes. That's when I thought of the fork.

Backing up, I grabbed it off the table as he slashed at me savagely, swung around to his left, and drove the tangs deep into the flesh below his ribs. Even that didn't stop him. Groaning, he pulled the fork out, tossed it aside, and kept coming.

Then I heard a gunshot.

Zuniga stopped in his tracks, his eyes wide with surprise, dropped to his knees, and flopped over on the floor, as dead as dead gets, with a bullet hole spilling blood at the base of his neck.

Behind him, Gervasio Pascua lounged casually in his chair with a bemused look on his face, like he'd just watched a good movie. A whiff of gun smoke rose from the barrel of the small-frame, chrome-plated pistol in his hand. Berganza and two bodyguards came rushing in with their own pistols aimed at me.

"No, no, no." Pascua raised an index finger. "Leave him alone." He stood, stepped over the body, and extended his hand to me, careful to avoid getting any blood on his shoes.

"You are a worthy adversary, Mr. Logan. Are you sure you won't come work for me?"

"Dead sure." I shook his hand. All things considered, it was the courteous thing to do.

I couldn't understand why he had shot his own man, especially in the middle of a gladiator fight his guy was winning—until Pascua conveyed his suspicions that Zuniga had been working as an informant for the Drug Enforcement Administration. Pascua gazed down at the corpse and shrugged. "He was beginning to annoy me anyway. I never much liked that moustache, either. Always with the hypermasculinity."

He insisted on driving me to the airport himself, without bodyguards. He swore on the lives of his children and his late sainted mother that he had nothing to do with my former wingman's demise. The last thing he said before I exited his Suburban was, "We all have our troubles, Mr. Logan. Your friend was no exception. But he was a good man and a fine pilot. My family always felt safe when he was in the cockpit. I hope you find whoever killed him and make them pay."

Gervasio Pascua sounded sincere.

I wanted to believe him. I almost did.

The sun looked like a giant glowing basketball sliding into the Pacific by the time I got the *Duck* refueled and lifted off from Ensenada—that hour of the day between late afternoon and early evening when winds fade, the air turns glassy, and a pilot has time to think. I barely thought about the goon I had watched die that afternoon. Was he really a DEA informant? Did he leave behind a loving family? Was he kind to kittens? None of that mattered. The guy tried to kill me. He got killed first. I wasn't going to lose any sleep over it.

No, what I thought about was Chocks.

Gervasio Pascua was right about one thing. We all have our troubles. From everything I'd learned, Chocks had encountered plenty after our paths diverged. But helping transport illegal narcotics in the employ of a Mexican drug cartel appeared not to be one of them, despite what detectives from the Santa Isabella

County Sheriff's Department claimed. I took some comfort in that. I took none in knowing I was still far from tracking down whoever had killed my buddy—a man I owed my life to.

All private aircraft flying in from Baja are required to land and clear inspection at either of two ports of entry near San Diego—Brown Field, south of the city, or at Calexico, some one hundred miles to the east. The US Customs and Border Protection agents at Brown Field have a reputation for being overachievers who'll strip down your airplane, looking for contraband, at the slightest provocation. I opted to fly to less-busy Calexico. It was dark by the time I landed there.

I taxied into the terminal, toggled off the *Duck*'s avionics master switch, pulled the air-fuel control to idle cutoff, and shut down the engine. The propeller sputtered to a stop. I'd no sooner unbuckled my shoulder strap and opened my door when a squad of men in military camo, helmets, and ballistic armor came swarming out of a gray Pilatus that had taxied in right behind me. Next thing I knew, I was face down on the tarmac with a lot of guns pointed at me and my wrists zip-tied behind my back.

"Welcome to America," one of them said.

EIGHT

The US Customs Enforcement agent in charge at the Calexico airport was a soft-spoken, gum-chewing cinder block who looked as if he might've spent a couple of hours every day working out. "S. Mori" was the name stitched on the chestplate of his desert camo tactical vest. He tossed me a bottle of ice-cold evian water and grabbed a chair across the table from me in the alcove that passed for the agency's interrogation room. I took a long sip and read the label on the bottle.

"Imported from France. Isn't there some kind of law against this?"

The bags under his eyes were as big as walnut shells. "We have drone video of you meeting in Ensenada with Gervasio Pascua."

"Hopefully, you caught my good side," I said.

Mori sat back in his chair with his arms folded across his girthy chest, working his chewing gum. "You think this is some sort of game, Logan? Is that what you think?"

"Au contraire." I gulped more French water. It tasted a lot like American water. "You guys serve a vital national security function; I respect that, even if you do serve your guests water from France."

Mori stopped short of a smile. "Pascua never comes out from under his rock for face-to-face get-togethers with anyone, Logan, let alone an American. You must be pretty special."

"Tell that to my cat."

"What was the purpose of your meeting with Pascua?"

"I'm a private investigator."

Mori leaned forward in his chair and flipped through a computer printout. "Says here you're a civilian flight instructor."

I could've filled him in on my pending application with the state of California or my years at Alpha, but I knew none of that would have mattered. Agent Mori didn't give a hoot about my work history. He was only interested in Gervasio Pascua or, more specifically, in *arresting* Gervasio Pascua.

"A buddy I flew with in the air force, my wingman, was killed up in Santa Isabella last week," I said. "Somebody threw him out of an airplane or a helicopter."

"I read about that guy," Mori said. "Landed on a doublewide. Helluva way to go."

"There's a rumor he worked for Pascua. I decided to go find out."

"So the biggest drug kingpin in North American agrees to meet with you, in person? Just like that?"

I shrugged.

A second camo-garbed customs agent was leaning in the doorway with his arms folded, listening in. A crescent-shaped scar curved diagonally from his upper lip across the left side of his jawbone. Brown curly hair. Wire-frame glasses. His nameplate read "Kordrich."

"This friend of yours who fell out of the aircraft," he said, "what was his name?"

"Peter Hostetler. Call sign Chocks."

"He flew drugs for Pascua?" Mori asked.

I shook my head. "Personal pilot. He flew Pascua and his family around."

"How do you know that?"

"Pascua told me."

"And you believe him?"

"He gave me no reason not to."

"Sounds like you two developed quite the camaraderie," Mori said.

"First, it's French water, now it's French words. What is it with you guys?"

The two feds traded a look that said, *Who does this jack hole think he is?* Then Mori said to me, "We'd like you to go back, meet with Pascua again."

"And do what?" I asked. "Convince him to let me fly him across the border so you don't have to jump through all the legal hoops snatching him out of Mexico?"

"There'd be reward money in it," Kordrich said. "High six figures. Maybe even seven."

"No thanks," I said.

"You'd be wise to at least think about it, Mr. Logan," Mori said.

"Look, guys, I'd like to help you out. Really, I would. But the yacht's all paid off and so is my ski chalet in Aspen. I'm not interested in your money."

"Then I suppose service to country won't persuade you, either," Kordrich said.

I almost smiled. "My former team and I used to round up folks like Gervasio Pascua for the good old US of A at least twice a month. Sometimes more. Some we'd snatch and fly to some black site in Poland or Romania where they'd stand trial in some kangaroo tribunal that never made the news. But mostly they never made it that far. Most we just liquidated on the spot, right where we hunted them down. Quicker that way. Cleaner. Saved the American taxpayer a ton of money. And you can't get more patriotic than saving money, right?"

"Your *team*?" Mori looked at me like I was delusional. "What're you, on crack?"

I pushed my chair back and got to my feet. "I'm guessing by now your drug-sniffing K-9 and the guy out there with the Geiger counter looking for nuclear material have gone through every inch of my plane and found nothing, nada, yes?"

Kordrich looked out the window at the flight line where the *Duck* was parked, then turned back and gave Mori a nod. I might've been concerned about them finding out about my involvement in the death of a possible DEA informant that afternoon in Baja, but I knew how the game was played, having played it a few times myself. What happens in the back rooms of cantinas south of the border stayed there. Just like what happens in the mud huts of Kandahar, deep in the jungles of the Philippines, and in dozens of other dark corners of the globe where I'd traveled in service to my country to exterminate those who would do it harm.

"You boys stay frosty," I said and walked out to my airplane. They didn't stop me.

Southern California glowed like a patchwork of white and gold through a gauzy mantle of clouds a mile below the *Duck*'s wings. Flying through the dark, bathed in the dim red of the instruments, the sky was a familiar and comforting cocoon where everything made perfect sense—everything but the murder of my friend Chocks. That the narcotics trade could've been responsible for his violent death made no sense.

What I knew of Chocks's personal history, and what I witnessed of his valor in combat, convinced me that the sheriff's detectives investigating his death had no idea what they were talking about. Gervasio Pascua only affirmed that. The drug lord's impressions of my former wingman mirrored my own. He would not have risked meeting with me unless he was telling the truth, that he had nothing to do with Chocks's death.

Did it bother me that my former wingman had flown, however briefly, for a man who peddled addiction and misery? It did not. As a commercially rated pilot, I'd flown plenty of sketchy individuals plenty of places without regard to whether they'd earned their fortunes legally or otherwise. When you live month to month on a government pension check, trying to keep the lights on and the bill collectors at bay, you don't ask too many questions of your customers.

"Cessna Four Charlie Lima, contact Point Mugu Approach now on one-twenty-four-point-seven. Take care."

The female controller's voice in my headset yanked me from my deliberations. "Point Mugu one-twenty-four-seven," I said. "Thanks for the help."

Midnight had come and gone by the time I touched down in Rancho Bonita. I was exhausted. The day had been a long one, and my landing was hardly textbook, but it didn't make the earth wince, so there was that. I tied down the *Duck* and drove home.

The dog and cat were both snoring, sandwiched together in Kiddiot's bed, buddies for life. Ack-Ack barely raised his head as I walked in and offered me a bleary yawn before returning to canine dreamland. Kiddiot stirred nary a muscle. I'd never known him to genuinely like anyone or anything, apart from Mrs. Schmulowitz and her brisket. And now here he was, besties with a beagle. The Buddha would've been proud of them both.

I slipped off my shoes, stripped down to my skivvies, and maneuvered as quietly as I could into bed. Layne was on her side with her back to me. I snuggled in. Her concave to my convex. No bones on bones. No limbs losing circulation. Some people fit together ergonomically. That was Layne and me. The jury was still out, however, on how well we paired emotionally.

"How'd it go down there?" she asked softly without turning around.

"Not too bad. I ate an amazing burrito. *Muy authentico.*"

"That's not what I meant, Logan."

"I know what you meant, babe."

I left out the part about sticking a fork in a man in the back room of a Mexican cantina. I told her nothing about being forced onto my stomach by federal agents on the tarmac at the Calexico airport. I only told her how Pascua had denied having anything to do with what happened to Chocks.

"He was adamant. There was no drug-running. Nothing like that. Chocks flew him and his family around to their various vacation villas. Worked for him about a month."

Layne rolled over toward me. Even in the dark, I could see the doubt in her eyes. "And you believe him?"

"Look, Layne, it's not that I don't appreciate your professional skepticism, but you didn't know Chocks. He would've been the *last* guy on this rock to get wrapped up in that kind of crap."

"So, if Pascua didn't kill him, who did?"

"I'm working on it." My eyelids felt like lead. All I wanted to do was go to sleep, but that would've been wrong, not before demonstrating that I was capable of being the kind of supportive, considerate partner she deserved.

"How was *your* day?" I asked her.

"Thanks for asking. Not that you really care."

"That's not fair. I care a lot."

"Sure you do."

Layne was spoiling for a fight. I was too tired to give her one. "You can believe me or not," I said. "I just want to know how your day went, that's all."

Reluctantly, she told me how she'd driven my ancient landlady all over town, persuading business owners to display Mrs. Schmulowitz's city council campaign poster in their windows. The poster featured a picture of Kiddiot looking into the camera wearing his usual expression—displeasure. "Why is this cat grumpy?" the caption read. "Because he didn't vote for Mrs. Schmulowitz."

"I also managed to get a copy of this," Layne said. She reached over to the nightstand and handed me a half-dozen sheets of paper stapled together. I turned on the light on my phone. It was a copy of Chocks's final autopsy report from the Santa Isabella County Coroner's Office.

"Nice going. They usually don't make these available during an ongoing investigation."

She didn't volunteer how she'd gotten the report, and I didn't push it. Methods are never as important as results. Layne pulled the covers up over her shoulder and rolled back away from me. I gave her a thank-you kiss on the back of her neck. There was no reaction.

Carefully sidestepping the still-snoozing pets, I climbed out of bed, sat down at the card table, and turned on a gooseneck desk lamp. I bypassed the gory forensic analysis of Chocks's injuries and focused instead on the report's toxicological results.

"They found traces of ketamine in his bloodstream. They use that stuff to tranquilize horses."

"It's also a big date-rape drug," Layne said. "Slip it into some girl's drink at a bar, makes it hard for her to move or speak."

"Maybe that explains how they managed to get a guy who played tight end in college into an aircraft—I'm assuming against his will—then pushed him out. But why horse tranquilizer? Seems pretty obscure."

"No idea," Layne said. "Good night, Logan."

"Good night."

I turned off the lamp and read by the light of my phone. Chocks, according to the coroner, had picked up a few tattoos since we'd last seen each other. One was the number 84—the same number Chocks wore during his playing days at the academy. The other was twin lightning bolts, which I took to represent the formal name of the A-10 Thunderbolt IIs we used to fly. The coroner speculated in his narrative summary that the tattoos were associated with white supremacy. I would've laughed aloud, but I didn't want to disturb the pets. The Chocks I knew was no racist.

Layne sighed from bed. "I can't sleep."

"I'm sorry. I didn't mean to wake you up."

"Forget it. I was up anyway, waiting for you to come home. I'm just glad you're OK."

"I'm good."

She pulled on her robe, came over, and sat down at the table. "What was Deep Fury?"

I looked over at her. "Where'd you hear about that?"

"Online, digging around this afternoon on Chocks. It said he got the Air Force Cross, but I couldn't find the actual citation."

"Nobody remembers that stuff anymore, Layne, much less cares."

"You do. I'm just curious, that's all."

I kept it short. How our squadron had been tasked during Desert Storm with hunting enemy armor in a kill box above Phase Line Lucifer, northwest of Ramadi—Republican Guard country. Some creative whiz kid at Central Command had dubbed the operation "Deep Fury."

Chocks and I rolled in as the sun was coming up. The Iraqi tanks were easy to spot. Most had pulled off the road and shut down for the night, but their engines still glowed red against the sand on our sensors. We began nailing them with IR-guided Maverick missiles. When we ran out of those, we used our cannons. We dove steeply and engaged at close range to get good hits. The jet shook every time I squeezed the trigger. I remembered my oxygen mask filling with the burning smell of thirty-millimeter rounds. Every time I scored a kill and came off the target, I jotted a *K* with a grease pencil on the inside of my canopy before swinging back around on another gun run. In less than five minutes, I'd destroyed nine tanks, most of them T-72s. That's when I got hit.

"I rolled in and felt a shudder. Chocks told me later it was an SA-9. Anyway, next thing I knew, the jet's inverted and everything's on fire, including my boots."

I told her how I ejected, hit the ground hard, scrambled out of my parachute, and took cover in a dry river channel with my pistol, hoping my emergency locator transmitter still functioned. I could see a column of enemy troop carriers—what looked like an entire mechanized infantry company—coming to get me.

"Then, out of nowhere, here comes Chocks, blazing away. One pass after another, blowing up bad guys. He took a thirty-seven-millimeter round in his leg on one pass, but he stayed on station even though he was bleeding and running out of fuel. Kept 'em pinned down until the helos came to get me out. Both engines flamed out on his way into Khalid. Had to dead-stick his landing. They quit counting the shell holes in his ship when they got to two hundred. Command staff put him in for a big blue, but those usually go to the grunts."

"Big blue?"

"The Medal of Honor."

Layne stared down at the table for a long moment. "I'm sorry if I made it sound like he was anything less than a hero, Logan."

No apologies were necessary, I said. "Believe me, I'm still scratching my head, too, Layne, wondering how a hero like that could end up dying the way he did."

She reached out and held my hand. Her skin was soft and warm. We sat there together for what felt like a couple of minutes with neither of us saying a word. Then Layne said, "Oh, I almost forgot." She got up, gathered her robe around her, and walked over to the kitchen counter. "Those photos you shot of the loading dock at Electrogenics? I forwarded them to a friend at the agency who works IMINT."

Imagery intelligence—the most thankless job in the espionage community, where faceless analysts once hunched over light tables with jeweler's loupes, trying to make sense of high-altitude reconnaissance photos. These days, they relied on computer-imaging software to assess shots mostly taken from satellites in low orbit.

"This is the one you're gonna want to see," Layne said, returning with two printouts and turning on the desk lamp.

The first printout was a duplicate of the photo I'd taken of the forklift maneuvering that large wooden crate into the tractor-trailer at the loading docks behind Electrogenics. The second printout was a blowup of the same photo, focused on a bar-coded shipping label that was tucked into a protective, transparent plastic sleeve taped to the side of the crate. Even with state-of-the-art magnification, the distance from which I shot the picture rendered the label's small print illegible. But I could easily read the big print:

Contents: Boo Boo Cuddle Bears

Deliver to: APRAD/OSD

AVOCLA

CPDA

NA

808733553944(G)

"Not the most sophisticated coding," Layne said, "but good enough to keep the masses guessing."

"Defense Sciences Office, Defense Advanced Research Projects Agency," I said.

Layne smiled. "Give that man a cookie."

DARPA was the Defense Department's research and development arm tasked with conceiving top-secret technologies designed to benefit America's warfighters—everything from nuclear space planes to robotic exoskeletons for infantrymen. Without a necessary compartmentalized clearance, getting information out of DARPA was next to impossible. I didn't know anyone who worked there. Neither did Layne. I asked her what she thought "A-D-P-C" printed on the shipping label stood for.

"I played with that one for a while," she said, rubbing the back of her neck. "Near as I can figure, it's either a scrambled abbreviation for the National Alcohol and Drug Policy Commission or something called 'antenna displaced phase centering.'"

"Antenna displaced phase centering. Sounds like it's got something to do with radar."

"Don't ask me," Layne said. "I was a philosophy major."

"What about these numbers—eight zero eight, etcetera?"

She shrugged. "Your guess is as good as mine."

Now it was my turn to do some neck-rubbing. I studied the magnified photo. Had I been a betting man, I would've wagered that there wasn't one single Boo Boo Cuddle Bear in that crate going to DARPA's Defense Sciences Office in Virginia. Truth be told, I didn't know what was in there.

But I was fairly certain I knew someone who might.

NINE

The next morning, a Saturday, broke warm and dry. Winds were gusting out of the high desert at near-gale force. Along California's central coast, that means red-flag warnings and wildfires. One moron with a Weedwacker or a carelessly tossed cigarette butt, and three hundred houses go up in flames. Layne stayed home with the cat, loading essentials in her car just in case we had to evacuate. Ack-Ack rode with me to the airport, where I found Mrs. Schmulowitz and Larry in his hangar, blowing up red, white, and blue balloons for her big campaign rally that night.

The beagle moaned with happiness, his tail wagging, popping balloons with his claws without intending to, and straining at his leash to greet her. She saved him the trouble and sat down on the floor. Their lovefest was a thing of beauty.

"Larry thinks I'm too old to be running for political office," Mrs. Schmulowitz said.

"I didn't say that," Larry said. "All I said was, people tend to slow down when they get to be your age, not run around all over town with their hair on fire, trying to change the world."

"I happen to like being this age. There are certain advantages."

"Yeah? Name one," Larry said.

"Hostage situations," Mrs. Schmulowitz said. "Guess who gets released first? Somebody who looks like the Little Old Lady from Pasadena or somebody like you, Larry, who looks like that big furry animal—what's his name, Cookie?—from that crazy outer space movie."

"I think you meant 'Wookiee,' Mrs. Schmulowitz," I said.

"Wookiee, schmookie. The point is, I get the senior discount at IHOP. Larry does not."

"I had my fill of pancakes in the navy," Larry said, blowing up another balloon. "That's all there was left for breakfast after you'd been at sea for three months. Couldn't eat another one if you forced my mouth open."

"Weren't you a radar tech on some aircraft carrier?" I asked him. "On the old *Constellation*, if memory serves?"

"The *Kitty Hawk*." Larry knotted the balloon. He was out of breath. "Since when did you become interested in my illustrious military service, Logan?"

"I need somebody to school me on antenna displaced phase centering."

"Come again?"

"Antenna. Displaced. Phase. Centering. I need you to help me understand it better."

"What the hell for?"

"It's a long story."

"Not as long as it would take me to explain it to you. I'm trying to manage a hotly contested political race here, Logan."

"Looks to me like all you're doing is blowing up balloons."

Larry pushed his glasses back up his nose and gave me a condescending look. "For your information, Logan, balloons have played an essential role throughout American political history. What national convention would be complete without the big balloon drop at the end?"

"I don't need chapter and verse, Larry. The CliffsNotes version will do me fine."

"That would be impossible. We're talking highly technical concepts, Logan. They sent me to school for months to learn that stuff."

"Don't be a pain in the tuchus, Larry," Mrs. Schmulowitz said, keeping Ack-Ack at bay as he tried to lick her on the lips. "Enough with the balloons. We got enough balloons already. Go on. Be a mensch and just tell him."

"Fine." Larry exhaled like he was doing me a big favor. "I'll try to make it as simple as I can. You use antenna displaced phase center-capable circuitry and phase-coherent klystron transmitters in airborne, moving-target-indication radars to better separate the wheat from the chaff."

"You call that simple?" Mrs. Schmulowitz smirked. "Sounded like a bunch of gobbledygook to me."

"Ditto," I said.

Larry closed his eyes and dropped his head, like he couldn't believe anyone could be so dense. "OK, look, basically what we're talking about is computer hardware that lets you find the *real* enemy and kill him before he can find and kill you. ADPC enhances moving-target-indication capabilities. The enemy employs electronic countermeasures to confuse your defenses, to make it look on your radar scope like you're getting attacked by a thousand missiles or a thousand planes, not one or two."

"Which ups the chances of their *real* missiles and aircraft breaking through your defenses?"

"Now you're starting to get it, Logan," Larry said. "Both the Chinese and Russkies have upped their game over the last, say, twenty years. We've been playing catch-up. With the technology we got and the technology they got, they could come after us right now, and there wouldn't be much we could do to pick out their real airplanes and missiles from the fake targets. I mean, it's a big-ass problem."

"Maybe so," I said, "but there's one thing we've got that they don't."

"Yeah? What's that?"

"Boo Boo Cuddle Bears."

Three things can't remain hidden, the Buddha said: the sun, the moon, and the truth. I was convinced Chocks's widow was hiding the latter. She'd told me that her late husband hadn't flown since leaving Delta Airlines. That obviously didn't fly with what Gervasio Pascua had said, that Chocks had served, however briefly, as Pascua's personal pilot. I needed to talk to her again, face-to-face—more forcefully this time, if necessary.

Looking at it from the ground, the sky seemed deceptively placid, as blue as a rich man's swimming pool. As soon as I took off, I discovered otherwise. The air was like a churning, gale-driven sea. With a thirty-knot headwind, the *Duck* bounced and shuddered through the invisible breakers like a freighter steering bow-on into a typhoon. The top of my skull slammed into the roof of the cockpit so often and so violently that I thought for sure the turbulence would cause me to dent both. By the time we finally returned safely to earth in Santa Isabella, my shoulders ached from wrestling the yoke, and my arms felt like jelly.

The good news was that a crew car was available at BillionAir. The bad news was that the brand-new Jeep I'd gotten comfortable driving had been borrowed by the crew of a Dassault Falcon that had flown in earlier from Tucson. The good news, my friend Kimberleigh, the comely customer service rep at BillionAir, informed me, was that the FBO maintained a backup crew car. They referred to it affectionately as "Little Red Riding Hood."

"Feel free to use her whenever you like," she said. "Don't worry about checking in and out. Just bring her back full, with the keys under the floor mat and the doors unlocked."

"You sure you don't want me to lock it?"

Kimberleigh suppressed a knowing giggle. "Trust me. Nobody's gonna want to steal Little Red Riding Hood. It's not exactly eye candy."

She wasn't kidding. Waiting for me in the parking lot was a four-door, primer-red Plymouth Reliant, circa 1981, rocking three-hundred-thousand-plus odometer miles. The driver's seat was little more than exposed springs covered by a folded beach towel. The windshield wipers wouldn't turn on and the radio wouldn't turn off. I would have hesitated parking the car in front of a museum for fear that somebody might tow it inside, but hey, free transportation is free transportation. I drove to Chocks's house listening to a soccer game with Spanish play-by-play.

―――

Miranda Hostetler answered the door in lime-green yoga pants and a matching sports bra. Her breath reeked of bourbon.

"Forget it, Logan. The beagle's yours. No take backs," she said, swaying a little unsteadily on her feet.

"I'm good with the dog, Miranda. That's not why I'm here."

Her eyes were half hooded from the booze. "You're not?"

"No. I'm—"

"Good," she said, cutting me off and heading back inside. "Then you can help me pack up Peter's stuff."

I followed her up the stairs, which she navigated unsteadily, to her bedroom. Suitcases and moving boxes were strewn about. She grabbed a pink-striped, short-sleeve shirt hanging in the closet and pressed it against my chest.

"He was a huge clotheshorse. Calvin Klein this, Ralph Lauren that. Fits you perfect. Want it? It's yours."

"I'm not much into pastels, Miranda."

"You sure? Cuz it's going in the dump otherwise. All of it. What do I need all his crap for? I'm moving. Starting over fresh." She started yanking men's pants and shirts off hangers and tossing them over her shoulder onto the floor.

"You told me Pete quit flying after he left Delta."

"You sure you don't want these pants? They're Armani."

"You lied to me, Miranda."

"I have no idea what you're talking about."

"Gervasio Pascua."

She turned and looked at me, swaying unsteadily, her arms full of Chocks's clothes.

"Sorry," she said, "*no habla Español.*"

"Gervasio Pascua. The Mexican drug dealer. I'm told Pete flew for him, briefly."

"Yeah, well, I wouldn't know anything about that. Peter never talked to me about his work. After a while, he never talked to me about anything." Miranda dumped the clothes in a box, sidestepped me, and headed back downstairs, into the kitchen. I followed her.

"I need a beer," she said. "Want one?"

"I don't drink."

"Well, aren't we special? Mister superior being." She grabbed a Miller Lite out of the refrigerator.

"Did Peter ever tell you what he did at Electrogenics, the nature of his work?"

Miranda kicked the door of the fridge shut with her bare foot. "You don't seem to understand. We didn't have that kind of relationship. We never did. He just said some of it was hush-hush and I didn't ask." She twisted open the bottle and eyed me with something between curiosity and contempt. "You married?"

"No."

"Ever been?"

I nodded.

"But not now?"

"No. Not now."

"What happened?"

"She passed away, unfortunately."

"That's too bad. What was her name?"

"Savannah."

"Like the town in Florida, you mean?"

"Close enough."

Miranda gulped a swig of beer. "So, then, OK, you've been married. You know that some questions, you just don't ask."

Have you gained weight? How long has it been since you shaved your legs? When is our anniversary? Those were the kinds of questions I would've never dared ask my late wife. *How did work go today?* was not one of them.

"Why would somebody want to kill your husband, Miranda?"

"Who knows? Peter was into all kinds of nutty things."

"You said he never talked to you about anything."

"OK, if that's what I said."

"So, he never told you he was flying for a drug dealer?"

"Why are you asking me all these questions?" She downed

her beer, opened a cabinet next to the refrigerator, and got out a bottle of vodka. "He was scared of it. I know that much."

"Scared of what?"

"Flying."

"Your husband was an experienced combat and airline pilot, Miranda. Guys like that are, generally speaking, not afraid of flying."

"Yeah, well, this one was." She drank straight from the bottle, then propped her elbows on the counter, showing more cleavage than I really needed to see. "Marvin offered to take him flying plenty of times. Peter would just shake his head. He'd say, 'I'm never going back up there. Not after everything I've been through.'"

At first, I wasn't sure I heard her right.

"You mean Marvin, your brother?"

She shot me a half-inebriated look. "No, Marvin the mailman."

"Your brother's a pilot?"

"Yeah. So what? What if he is?"

"A private pilot?"

"He used to work for one of those regional airlines. I can't remember the name right now. Flew puddle jumpers. Had his own helicopter for a while, too. That was before he decided to open a jewelry store."

"You don't find all that coincidental?"

"Find what coincidental?"

"Your husband either fell out or was pushed out of an airplane or a helicopter, Miranda. You just told me your brother knows how to fly both."

She narrowed her bloodshot eyes. "You think my *brother* murdered my husband?"

"I dunno. You tell me."

Her face grew redder by the second. "Get out of my house."

"Maybe you should ask Marvin directly."

"I said, get out of my house!"

"I *will* find who killed Pete, Miranda. I promise you that. You can help me or not."

Down came the vodka bottle, crashing against the edge of the counter and into a thousand shards of glass.

"Get out!"

Little Red Riding Hood was parked across the street in the shade of a flowering magnolia. The tree's branches danced the hula on a toasty, gusting wind. I had just stepped off the sidewalk in front of Miranda's house and was about to cross the street when a silver Mercedes coupe came roaring up and screeched to a stop. I had to jump back to avoid getting hit. The driver clambered out and stormed toward me like an unguided missile—Miranda's brother, Marvin.

"Your ears must've been burning," I said. "We were just talking about you."

"Nobody hurts my sister. Nobody!"

He was yelling about having just seen Ring footage of me assaulting her in her own home. I wanted to ask him what the hell rings had to do with anything, but I never got the chance. He launched a ragged, off-balance swing in the general direction of my head. I dodged the punch easily.

"Chill out, Marvin. Whatever you think you saw, you didn't. She broke a vodka bottle. I didn't lay a hand on her."

"You're a goddamn liar!"

That's when he reached under his shirt and pulled out a six-inch .357. I kicked the revolver out of his grasp before he could bring it to bear. This enraged him even more, and he came at me with his teeth bared and hands raised like grizzly claws. A short, crisp uppercut to the solar plexus, and he dropped like a marionette with its strings suddenly cut.

By now, drivers had stopped in both directions to watch the fight. An older bearded guy leaned his head out the window of a white Range Rover. "You need me to call the police or anything?"

"No, we're fine. Thanks," I said, picking up the revolver and stuffing it into the back of my belt. "Just a little misunderstanding, that's all."

The man motored on. I yanked Marvin to his feet by the back of his shirt and guided him to the side of the road before he got run over. He was moaning and clutching his belly where I'd hit him.

"Gimme back my gun."

"You're the *last* guy who needs his gun back, Marvin."

"I got a concealed carry permit, goddammit!"

"Congratulations. You're still not getting the gun back."

"You sucker punched me," he said.

A man tries to knock your face into next week, then pulls a revolver on you, leaving you no choice but to defend yourself, and suddenly *you're* the one accused of taking a cheap shot? Ridiculous.

"Your sister tells me you're a pilot."

"My sister drinks too much. And you better damn well stay away from her if you know what's good for you."

"You didn't happen to kill your brother-in-law, did you, Marvin?"

Rocking and groaning and still looked up at me with a sliver of a smile. "Why would I ever go and do something like that?"

"You just told me nobody hurts your sister. Pete used to hurt her all the time, to hear her side of it."

Marvin slowly unbent himself and stood. "I didn't kill

nobody," he said, less than convincingly. "Now, you gonna give me my gun back or what?"

We both knew the answer to that one. He stared at me. I stared at him.

"I catch you around here again, bothering my sister," he said, "it'll be the last thing you ever do."

"Whatever you say, Marvin."

The old me might've put him on his butt again, if only to serve notice that I didn't appreciate gratuitous threats. Being an aspiring Buddhist, however, is all about finding the good in your fellow man, even if you've yet to rule them out as a suspect in the murder of your former wingman.

Marvin got back in his Benz, pulled into his sister's driveway, got out, and flipped me off as I drove away.

Something told me it wouldn't be the last time we'd be seeing each other.

TEN

Detective Tom Kasparov's cubicle on the sun-splashed second floor of the Santa Isabella County Sheriff's Department was a testament to obsessive-compulsive behavior. Everything on his pristine desktop was positioned at right angles. Nothing out of place. His partner's desk, meanwhile, looked like it qualified for federal disaster relief funds, heaped as it was with police reports, old newspapers, and junk food wrappers. Leftover sandwiches could've been buried under the mess that was Detective Lloyd Gregory's workstation and no one would've been the wiser but for the stench.

"Smells like tuna fish," I said. "Either that or Jimmy Hoffa."

Kasparov didn't smile. Neither did Gregory. The latter was leaning back in his faux leather swivel chair, clipping his fingernails. "So," he said, "you're telling us that Gervasio Pascua, a stone-cold killer who's on the FBI's Ten Most Wanted List, who murdered hundreds of innocent people, didn't do your boy, Hostetler—that Hostetler's brother-in-law killed him?"

"What I'm telling you is that it's worth looking into," I said. "But, hey, you two are the pros from Dover. I'm not telling you how to go about doing your jobs."

"That's exactly what you're telling us, Logan," Kasparov said, "and I'm getting pretty sick of it." His cell phone vibrated on his desk. He picked it up, peered at the number, swiveled away from me, and took the call. "Yeah, now's not a good time," he said, cupping the phone with his voice lowered. "Yeah, he's here now . . . No, yeah . . . I'll deal with it." Kasparov hung up, tossed the phone back on his desk, and turned to face me. His jaw was tight. "You were saying?"

"I checked FAA records online," I said. "Marvin's a licensed pilot. He holds commercial and helicopter ratings."

Kasparov rubbed his throat. His blue button-down dress shirt was open at the neck, revealing a collection of gold chains worthy of Mr. T. "That's your big theory, Logan? That Hostetler's brother-in-law somehow got him into an airplane or a helicopter, stripped him down, then dropped him, *Thirty Seconds Over Tokyo*–style, on the Sun Country RV and Trailer Park?"

"That's what I'm telling you."

"Where's the motive?"

"Marvin's very protective of his sister. He's convinced himself she was married to a wife-beater. That and the fact that I asked him point-blank if he had anything to do with Pete's death. He didn't exactly deny it."

Lloyd Gregory finished trimming the last of his nails and licked his fingertips. "For your information, Marvin Garnhardt is a respected member of the local business community, Logan, and a friend of this department. He donates big bucks to the local Boys & Girls Clubs. He sponsors our Coffee with a Cop community get-together every month. He's never gotten so much as a jaywalking ticket, so far as I'm aware of."

"He claims to have a concealed carry permit."

"He transports a lot of expensive jewelry on a regular basis to his store from the big wholesalers down in Los Angeles,"

Gregory said. "He has a lawful right to protect himself as much as anybody."

"He unlawfully pulled a .357 Magnum on me not more than an hour ago."

"Maybe you were harassing his sister," Kasparov said. "Maybe you had it coming."

I was no math major but subtracting the benefit of the doubt from the smug, knowing expression on Kasparov's face, I calculated that it was none other than Marvin Garnhardt who'd been on the phone moments earlier to tell him all about our encounter outside Marvin's sister's house.

"That jewelry store must be pretty nice," I said.

"Biggest one in town," Kasparov said.

I nodded toward the detective's many gold necklaces. "So is that where you got all that bling you're wearing? From your friend, the respected local merchant who sponsors your little Coffee with a Cop get-togethers?"

Kasparov's head wheeled slowly in my direction like a gun turret on a battleship. "Mr. Garnhardt," he said, "would like his revolver back."

"Mr. Garnhardt has a hair-trigger and no business running around with a loaded gun. I threw it away."

"Where?"

"In the river."

Kasparov glowered. "That's called theft of private property, Logan. We could arrest you right now."

"You could," I said, "but you won't. Not unless you want it coming out in open court that you and your friend Marvin enjoy a cozy arrangement where you get the law enforcement discount on pricey jewelry in exchange for a concealed weapons permit, along with the leeway to skate on major crimes like felony battery and brandishing a firearm."

Kasparov rocked back in his chair, his fingers interlaced across his prodigious stomach, trying a little too hard to look like he still had the upper hand. "You want some friendly advice?"

"Always."

"Get out of town, Logan, while the getting's still good. And don't come back."

I got the clear impression he wasn't being friendly at all.

Marvin Garnhardt's revolver was still under Little Red Riding Hood's driver's seat where I had stashed it for safekeeping before paying a visit to the Santa Isabella County Sheriff's Department. OK, so maybe I hadn't been truthful in telling Kasparov that I'd thrown the gun away. A lie is a lie, as the Buddha said, but as I believe, a loaded, fully functioning, .357-caliber Smith & Wesson should never be discarded without careful consideration.

I was still sitting parked outside the sheriff's department in my rusting borrowed crew car, wondering whether the two detectives assigned to Chocks's case were even trying to find his killer, when Layne called.

"Just checking in to see how things are going up there," she said.

"Well, let's see. So far today, I nearly got run over, came close to getting shot, and, just now, I was ordered by the local gendarmerie to get out of Dodge, or else. Other than that, things are going swimmingly. How about you?"

"I have some news," Layne said.

My heart leapt into my throat. The tone in her voice was alarming. For a second, I thought she was going to tell me that a wind-driven fire had erupted in the hills and was bearing down on Rancho Bonita, as wildfires are inclined to do, and that she was evacuating. Or that maybe something had happened to Mrs. Schmulowitz, or to the pets. But, to my relief, it was nothing like that.

"I got a response this morning from a gal I knew at DST," Layne said. "I was one of her bridesmaids. We went through training together. I emailed her yesterday to see if they had anything on file regarding Electrogenics. You'll never guess what she came back with."

I could've humored her and guessed, but we would've been there all day. I'd traded actionable intelligence a few times with DST, the CIA's Directorate of Science and Technology, when I was with Alpha. The directorate employed a vast array of brilliant but quirky experts, from computer savants to clairvoyants. Their collective mission was to think creatively. The results were often bizarre. It was DST that once wired a house cat with transmitting gear mounted in its collar and attempted to train the kitty to become a mobile eavesdropping receiver. Predictably, the cat wasn't interested in the job.

"Do me a favor, Layne. Just tell me what she sent you."

"You don't want to guess?"

"Why should I have to guess?"

Seconds of stony silence were followed by, "I'll email it to you."

Before I could explain that I was simply tired and that I didn't mean anything by it, she hung up.

Things obviously were still not going well between us. Most of that, I realized, was on me. Like many men of my generation, I needed to do a better job of communicating with my partner, of being more sensitive to her sensitivities. But you know what they say about new tricks and old dogs.

Just then, Detective Kasparov came running out of the sheriff's department with the tails of his sports coat flapping in his wake. He piled into his unmarked Crown Vic, seeming not to notice me sitting three rows away in a tired, bucket-of-bolts Plymouth, then backed up and peeled out of the parking lot like he was chasing the devil himself. For about three seconds, I thought about tailing him, wondering if where he was off to in such a hurry had something to do with Chocks, but then my phone beeped with an incoming email from Layne. The one-page memo she attached to it only confirmed that playing along with her guessing game would've indeed been a pointless waste of time. I would've never guessed right. Not in a million years.

The subject line read, "Electrogenics, LLC," but most of the page had been blacked out. Blocks of black ink obscured entire paragraphs. Virtually every remaining sentence had been marked through with [REDACTED], leaving only disjointed words and cryptic phrases like "domestic collection" and "EEI," and "advisory tasking." Then there was this:

[REDACTED] asset [REDACTED] I&W
[REDACTED] [REDACTED] [REDACTED]
possibly 29155 [REDACTED].

Had I finished my government service with the air force and not gone to work for the Dark Side, such cryptic language would've meant nothing to me. But those words and abbreviations, and that number, could've just as easily been printed on my brain in neon. EEI—or essential elements of information—related to foreign military activities that CIA section chiefs deemed threatening enough to pass along to their superiors. Time-sensitive indication and warning (I&W) intelligence-gathering activities encompassed threats of enemy actions indicating a possible major attack on the American homeland in the offing. Then there was 29155. I knew that wasn't a zip code. Unit 29155, alternately called the 64th Special Service Center—or, in NATO parlance, "Double Carbine"—was the Russian military's ultrasecret electronics warfare directorate. I reread the email, then read it again, filling in blanks and connecting dots. A likely scenario emerged in my mind:

A domestic intelligence asset whose name was redacted from the file had tipped off the Central Intelligence Agency to a possible covert link between Electrogenics and a Russian military intelligence operation. Langley had deemed the link so significant, it had assigned it priority attention among the agency's internal investigators.

I pulled up and studied the photos I'd recorded days earlier on my phone, of heavily armed Electrogenics security guards loading that crate of radar components into a semitruck bound for DARPA's facilities in Virginia. *What we're talking about, Larry had told me, is hardware that lets you find the real enemy and kill him before he can find and kill you.* Was Chocks Hostetler the intelligence asset referred to in the memo Layne's source had passed along? Is that why my former wingman was killed, because he had uncovered the illicit transfer to Moscow of some powerful, classified piece of technology developed by his employer, Electrogenics?

I called Layne back to find out what other insights, if any, her former colleague might've provided, but she didn't answer her phone. I left a message.

"Hey, it's me. Thanks for the email. Good stuff. Way to go. It definitely pays to have a girlfriend who used to work for Christians In Action. Listen, if you haven't already, I'm wondering if you could please get back to your contacts at your former employer and brief them, if they don't already know, about what happened to Chocks. They might be willing to team up with us and help track down whoever did him. It's worth a shot. Thanks, Layne."

I hung up. Electrogenics was five minutes away. I drove.

My plan was to wait until CEO Ed Millisohn emerged from the building and got in his car, then to follow him and force him to the side of the road where I could get some answers without being harassed by his security guards. I parked across busy Hesperia Street with a view of the company's main entrance, sat back, and waited.

An hour dragged into two. Under an unrelenting afternoon sun, with a twenty-knot wind out of the east swirling hot as a blowtorch, Little Red Riding Hood began to bake. I would've cranked up the air-conditioning, but there was no air-conditioning. Sweat poured off me as if I were sitting in a sauna. I began seeing spots. I needed to get out of the sun and get something cold to drink or risk passing out from dehydration—if heatstroke didn't kill me first.

On the opposite corner was a twenty-four-hour convenience store, but one unlike any I'd ever seen before, built with a decidedly Indo-Islamic vibe, right down to the mini minarets. Inside, it looked like every 7-Eleven I'd ever been in. I took my time walking around, pretending to shop, and trying to cool off.

The clerk behind the checkout counter was probably in his mid-twenties but looked twice that old. He had bug eyes, stringy dark hair, and the posture of a cashew nut.

"Find everything OK?" he asked.

"All set." Still dripping sweat, I got out my wallet to pay for my thirty-ounce Big Gulp of root beer.

"Processed sugar, man," the clerk said, nodding approvingly of my purchase as he rang me up. "Way better than crack, right? They shouldn't call it diabetes. They should call it *enjoy*-a-betes."

"Thanks for the medical advice, Dr. Phil." I handed him

a five-spot. He reached into the cash drawer to make change when I glanced over my shoulder and spotted Ed Millisohn with his crazy Einstein hair walking out of Electrogenics across the road. With him was a petite blonde. They were kissing. I left my Big Gulp sitting on the counter and bolted out of the door.

"You don't want your change, man?"

"Keep it."

I ducked behind a telephone pole, got out my phone, and snapped several photos of Millisohn and the blonde going at it hot and heavy in the parking lot before they parted company and walked to their respective vehicles. Millisohn eased into a blue Tesla. The woman climbed into a black Chevy Silverado pickup truck with oversized off-road tires. I jumped back into Little Red Riding Hood, jammed the key into the ignition, and cranked it. The engine offered up what sounded like a death rattle, then nothing.

"C'mon, Red, don't do this to me now." I twisted the key again.

Nothing.

Patience, the Buddha said, is the greatest prayer. I closed my eyes, counted to ten, and tried it again. This time, the engine caught and came to life, but by then, Ed Millisohn's car was gone. The blonde in the black truck, meanwhile, was just pulling out of the company parking lot.

As she made a right turn onto northbound Hesperia, I caught the green light, hooked a left at the intersection, and fell in behind her, making sure to keep at least two other vehicles between us. Through the rear window of the truck's cab, I could see her talking animatedly on her phone. She was laughing and seemed not to notice that she was being followed.

Affixed to the pickup's tailgate was a bumper sticker. *My other ride is a Learjet.* The truck also sported a vanity license plate, one of those black-and-gold retro tags the California DMV began issuing a few years back. This one read, "N29VG." To a non-pilot, it wouldn't have meant much. To someone who's flown most of his adult life, the combination of letters and numbers preceded by an *N* signified only one thing: the tail number of a US-registered aircraft. I couldn't help wondering if it was the aircraft from which Chocks Hostetler plummeted to his death.

The truck changed from the left lane to the right. I called Layne again, hoping she could lean on her sources to run a quick registration check on the license plate, but she still wasn't answering her phone. Then the blonde turned right without signaling into a gas station. I purposely drove on, made a U-turn two blocks away, and pulled in behind her just as she was stepping out of the truck. She stuffed an empty soda can and a baseball-sized wad of papers into a trash can at the end of the fuel island. Then she slid a credit card into the payment terminal, yanked the hose out, jammed the nozzle into the truck's fuel intake, and began pumping gas.

She looked young enough to have been Ed Millisohn's granddaughter. Mirrored, oversized Ray-Bans. A nose ring. Multiple studs in both ears. A slender hottie in a chartreuse crop top, suede ankle boots, and a leather miniskirt.

"You must be a jet jockey," I said, pretending to pump gas.

"Excuse me?"

I nodded toward her truck. "Your bumper sticker, and your license plate," I said, delivering what I hoped was my most charming smile. "That's gotta be your tail number, right?"

"It's my boss's truck," she said.

"Roger that. Well, anyway, I will say you do look like a real pilot with those shades on. I happen to be one myself, actually. A pilot, I mean."

"Whatever, dude."

She clearly thought I was trying to hit on her. I wasn't.

"So, who's your boss, if you don't mind me asking?"

"None of your business."

"I'm sorry. I didn't mean anything by it. I was just curious, that's all."

"Yeah, well, obviously, you haven't heard," she said, pulling out the nozzle and sliding it back in the pump.

"Heard what?"

"Curiosity killed the cat."

She snatched her receipt from the machine, climbed back into the truck, and, with a haughty flip of her hair, peeled out from the gas station, tires squealing.

I walked over and fished out the wad of paper she'd crammed into the garbage can.

I uncrumpled the papers which included the bottom half of a residential electrical bill with the address torn off, a partial grocery list scrawled in a masculine hand (cheese, chips, bean dip, beer), and the top half of a receipt for the purchase of three cases of proprietor's reserve pinot noir, dated that morning, from a winery, Onas Seco Vineyards, to the tune of $4,322. Talk about expensive vino. The price, however, wasn't nearly as eyebrow-raising as the customer who bought the wine. His name was printed on the bottom of the receipt:

My murdered wingman, Peter Hostetler.

ELEVEN

Layne's side of the closet was as empty as the sky. All of her clothes and shoes had been cleaned out. Taped to the refrigerator was a note written in her fluid, feminine hand:

> *We need some time apart so that both of us can decide what exactly we want out of this relationship. If, in fact, we want anything.* —L

The dog and cat were sitting hip to hip on the floor, staring up at me like it was all my fault.

"There are always two sides to every coin," I said.

Kiddiot put his ears back and coughed like he was getting ready to hack up a hair ball.

"If you wanna know where your gorgeous sweetie went off to," Mrs. Schmulowitz said, peering in through my screen door, "she got a condo with an ocean view over near City College. Not that I'm being a yenta or anything."

"You're not being a yenta, Mrs. Schmulowitz. Thanks for letting me know."

"She told me to tell you that you could come over and check it out anytime you wanted. No big whoop. Here you go." Layne had written down her new address on a piece of paper. I opened the screen door. Mrs. Schmulowitz handed it to me. "That young lady's quite the catch, if you want my two cents, bubby. I wouldn't blame you if you moved out to be with her."

"I have no immediate plans to move, Mrs. Schmulowitz."

She seemed both relieved and a little sad. "Well, all I can say is that I hope it works out one way or the other. But just remember, there are two ways to argue with a woman. Both are equally wrong. By the way, I'm making pork chops tomorrow night and you're invited—but only on the condition that it remains our little secret. My third husband memorized the Torah back to front. He'd be rolling over in his grave if he knew what was on the menu, may he rest in peace."

"How do you have time to cook, Mrs. Schmulowitz? Aren't you in the middle of a hotly contested city council race?"

"Actually, I'm taking a few days off from the campaign trail. Gotta let things cool down a little from last night's debate."

"Why? What happened at the debate?"

"Well, let us just say that things got a little out of control. My esteemed opponent kept cutting me off every time I tried to speak. Such a chauvinistic piece of you-know-what, this man. You have no idea. Finally, I said to him, 'Mitch, do you know what the difference is between a career politician like you and a flying pig? The letter *F*.' You should've seen his face. It practically melted. Shall we say tomorrow night at six? Bring the pets."

"We wouldn't miss it for the world," I said.

An online search of the FAA's aircraft registry produced no record of a Learjet with the tail number N29VG, or any other aircraft with that number. So I reached out again to Paul Horvath at the FAA. He thought I was calling to complain about how long my request for radar ground tracks was taking.

"I emailed our records section," Horvath said, sounding more than a little put off by my call. "They'll get to it when they can. That's the best I can do for you, Logan."

I told him I appreciated his efforts, but that I had another favor to ask in the interim. His response was silence, followed by a strained, "What is it now?"

"I found a tail number for a Learjet—November two-niner Victor Golf—that may have been involved in the case I'm looking into, only there's no record of it online. Any chance you could do some digging around for me?"

"I'm a civil servant, Mr. Logan, not your personal assistant," Horvath shot back. "And I am certainly not in the habit of ignoring federal aviation regulations for the benefit of a private pilot who mistakenly believes that just because I happened to have investigated a plane crash he was involved in that now, years later, I somehow owe him limitless special attention."

"You're right, Paul. You're a busy man. Forget I even asked."

Another long silence. Another long sigh. Reluctantly, Horvath said he'd see what, if anything, he could find on N29VG.

My next call was to Onas Seco Vineyards in Santa Isabella. More than a week after his death, Chocks Hostetler had somehow stocked up on premium wines there, according to the discarded receipt I'd pulled out of the trash at that gas station.

"G'day. Thanks for calling Onas Seco Vineyards. This is Oliver. How can I help you?" He sounded Australian.

"This is Peter Hostetler," I said. "I was there this morning. I bought three cases of wine—two pinots and a zin. I need to speak with whoever sold them to me. Would that be you, Oliver?"

"No, sir. I don't work mornings. You probably dealt with Freddie. He'll be back tomorrow morning. Is there something I can help you with?"

"There's nobody else who was working this morning I can talk to?"

"Just Freddie. We're a small operation, mate. Why, what's up?"

How do you explain to someone over the phone that you're investigating a murder without scaring them into silence? How do you explain that you need to show Freddie a photo of your late friend to confirm that it was someone else who bought wine using a dead man's credit card? How do you get Freddie to describe who that someone else was? The short answer is, you can only do it in person, not over the phone.

"Did you say Freddie will be back tomorrow?"

"Nine o'clock sharp."

"I'll stop by then."

"Cheers."

Ack-Ack was sitting by the door, looking back at me like he had an urgent need to go outside. He was too big to fit through the cat door. I let him out and watched him lift his leg on Mrs. Schmulowitz's rosebushes.

"Saves me on my water bill," she said, standing at her kitchen window, wearing yellow gloves and washing dishes. "Who's a good boy?"

I waited for the dog to finish his business, let him back in, then drove over to Layne's new digs.

———

No question, it would've represented a substantial improvement from garage living. The condominium was sunlit and airy. French doors led to a trampoline-sized terrace with unobstructed views of the Pacific. There was an extra bedroom, a wood-burning fireplace, and real oak floors.

"Nice crib," I said.

"A two-minute walk to the beach," Layne said. "And the best part?" She opened a louvered door and showed me the stacked washer and dryer. "No more having to go to the laundromat."

"You could've told me you were moving out, Layne."

"I *did* tell you."

"By leaving a note on the refrigerator. That's not telling. That's called escaping."

She walked out onto the terrace and shielded her eyes with a visored hand to watch a line of pelicans skim the waves. I joined her.

"I know how much you love Mrs. Schmulowitz," Layne said. "I love her, too. But I'm not some starving artist. I can't live in a converted garage. I'm sorry; I just can't."

"Garage living isn't for everybody," I conceded, "but you do have to admit, it *is* a pretty awesome garage."

I couldn't decide if her smile was one of mild amusement or simmering indignance.

"I'm just trying to make your life a little better, Logan. *Our* lives. Is that so wrong?"

"What if I like my life the way it is?"

Layne shook her head in obvious disappointment. "The lease is month to month. I'll be around," she said, "for a while anyway." Then she kissed me the way she kissed me the first time, slowly and tenderly. I wondered if it would be the last time.

I might've stuck around and tried to broker one of those meet-in-the-middle, your-bed-or-mine-every-other-night kind of arrangements, but Layne Sterling was not the type of woman easily persuaded of anything once her mind was made up. Then my phone rang. Caller ID showed, "A. Berganza."

The jet was a gleaming Cessna Latitude. Easily ten million bucks. I noted the tail number as I climbed the stairs: XA-BYOB. Every aircraft registered in Mexico is assigned a tail number that begins with *XA*. Gervasio Pascua's right-hand man, Armando Berganza, stood in the doorway with a big welcoming smile.

"A pleasure to see you again, Mr. Logan," he said over the whine of the two idling engines. "Thanks for coming on such short notice."

We shook hands.

"Please . . ." Berganza gestured, stepping aside.

With the door pulled shut, the engine noise all but disappeared. "Luxurious" didn't begin to describe the jet's royal blue and gold interior. There were reclining club chairs and couches upholstered in the finest leather. Silk carpeting. Birdseye maple trim. A full galley. A partitioned bedroom suite at the rear of the cabin. And two flight attendants, both of whom looked like they could've competed for Miss Mexico City. And won.

"Cute tail number," I said.

Berganza gave me a confused look.

"BYOB? Bring your own bottle."

He still didn't understand.

I told him to forget it. Through the jet's windows, I glimpsed the *Ruptured Duck* parked forlornly across the ramp in his usual spot outside Larry's hangar. "Tell Mr. Pascua I'll trade him straight across. My Cessna for his."

"Mr. Pascua charters the jet. He doesn't actually own it."

"If I had all of his money," I said, "one of these babies would be the first thing I'd buy. Then maybe some new cat toys."

Berganza smiled civilly. "May I offer you some champagne or mango juice, perhaps? It's fresh-squeezed."

"I'm good, thanks."

He turned to the two women and nodded. They disappeared dutifully into the aft bedroom and closed the door behind them.

"I'm sure you want to know why I called you," Berganza said.

"Please." He gestured to two club chairs facing each other.

We sat.

"I'm heading to San Francisco, then Portland, on company business," Berganza said, "but Mr. Pascua asked that I stop off here in beautiful Rancho Bonita. He wanted me to convey to you, in person, some additional information he thought you might find insightful, even comforting, regarding your . . ." Berganza's words trailed off as he looked out the window and noticed a Rancho Bonita Airport Police SUV slowly approaching along the tarmac.

"Routine patrol," I said. "They make the rounds about every fifteen minutes."

My words seemed of little comfort to Gervasio Pascua's right-hand man. He leaned forward and watched intently until the police car drove out of sight. I was tempted to ask how a jet leased by one of the world's most infamous narcotics traffickers could enter the United States and not immediately be impounded, but that wasn't why I was there.

"You were saying your boss had some information he thought I'd find useful?"

"Indeed, yes. My apologies." Berganza sat back, noticeably relieved by the departing patrol car. "He wanted me to tell you—to reassure you, actually—that your friend Mr. Hostetler died trying to do the right thing."

"*What* right thing?"

"I'm afraid that's all Mr. Pascua has authorized me to disclose."

"That's not very helpful."

"I understand, Mr. Logan, but that's the best I can do for you."

"What do you say we dial up your boss and ask for some additional clarification? I have unlimited texts and data. No roaming charges. Free calls to Mexico *and* Canada."

"Mr. Pascua asked me to pass along what I just told you. He's said all he is willing to say, Mr. Logan. If there's any more he wishes to add, I'm sure he'll reach out." Berganza tapped a button on the arm of his chair, then stood. The two flight attendants/beauty queens reappeared from the aft cabin. "Are you sure I can't offer you anything else before you go?"

The taller of the two gave me her best *Mona Lisa* smile.

I might've been wrong, but it seemed like Berganza was offering me more than fresh mango juice.

Chocks died trying to do the right thing.

My head hurt trying to figure out what it meant as I got back in my truck. What else did Gervasio Pascua know that he wasn't telling? Was Chocks killed to stop him from exposing the covert sale of classified radar components? What if his murder had nothing to do with national security and everything to do with his thuggish, overly protective brother-in-law? What if the Santa Isabella County Sheriff's Department was somehow complicit in him falling out of the sky? My own radar told me there was something sketchy about Detectives Gregory and Kasparov.

I could've used a burrito and a couple of Advils, but that would have to wait.

Predictability can get you killed. Be random. Vary your routines. It's one of the first lessons you learn as an operator, and why I was using a different route driving home that day. Instead of approaching from the east, I circled the neighborhood and came in from the west. Had I not done that, I might not have spotted the surveillance team waiting for me down the street from Mrs. Schmulowitz's house.

The two men were slouched low in the front seat of a gray Dodge Challenger, both keeping an eye on what they presumed was the most logical avenue of approach: the alley behind the house. The mistake they made was to park facing the wrong direction. They never saw my pickup truck cruise past the other end of the block. All I saw of them as I did were the backs of their heads—a Black guy and a white guy. Their choice in unmarked rides suggested they were possibly US Marshals or FBI. But then it hit me: Maybe they weren't feds. Maybe they were apparitions from my not-too-distant past, survivors or associates of high-value targets I'd once helped to neutralize. Revenge in my former line of work remained an occupational hazard.

I reached under my seat for the .357 I'd liberated from Chocks's brother-in-law, Marvin. It felt good in my hand. Familiar. Comforting. As the Buddha said, always be prepared—or was it the Boy Scouts? Doesn't matter. Good advice is good advice.

I tucked the gun into my belt, parked around the corner, and walked through the alley. Mrs. Schmulowitz's six-foot back fence and gate were solid redwood, secured by an industrial-strength dead bolt which I insisted she have installed because, let's face it, the world can be a nasty place, even in genteel Rancho Bonita. I made sure the gate was still locked—it was—which told me that nobody in all likelihood was waiting behind the fence to ambush me. I slipped my key into the lock and entered.

The backyard was empty. Not a dog or cat in sight. I turned

to relock the gate, giving myself more credit than I deserved for being so stealthy, when the muzzle of a gun barrel pressed firmly into the back of my neck.

"Move," a deep voice said behind me, "and it'll be the last thing you ever do."

TWELVE

"To be honest, fellas, it was hardly the most creative death threat I'd ever gotten. 'Move, and they'll be sanding what's left of you off the walls for a week.' Or, 'Move, and your next stop is the *Twilight Zone*.' Now, *those* were creative."

A smile formed on one side of the team leader's big square face like a crack spreading across the edge of a frozen lake. I was sitting on my couch. He was standing over me with a Browning nine-millimeter in his right hand. The two guys I'd observed in the Dodge minutes earlier were now turning my apartment inside out, searching for what, I did not know.

"Looks like we got us a real comedian here, boys," the team leader remarked. "I didn't see anything in his DD-214 about being a quipster."

"Me, neither," said the Black guy, dumping boxes of cereal and flinging cans of cat food out of my kitchen cabinets like he was having way too much fun.

"A complete loser, maybe," said the white guy, who was going through my medicine cabinet, "but definitely not a comedian."

"Perhaps if you gentlemen told me what you're looking for," I said, " I could save you the time and trouble."

Square Face backhanded me across the mouth. "You'll speak when you're spoken to, understood?"

"Whatever you say," I said. "It's your funeral."

His reference to my DD-214, the Defense Department's official record of my years in the military, told me he was familiar with that world. But there was nothing military about these guys. All three looked like it had been a while since any of them had seen the inside of a barbershop, and they had spent too much time at all-you-can-eat buffets. "Scruffy" and "chunky" were two words that came to mind while watching them toss my apartment—earrings, greasy beards, untucked T-shirts but not in the rock star way special operators seek to blend in. No, these jokers reminded me of agency backbenchers I'd occasionally have to contend with—lard-ass frat boys on TDY from Langley or DIA headquarters, hoping to up their chances of promotion by spending a few weeks downrange, but rarely venturing beyond the wire.

I'm no neat freak, but these guys were quickly and thoroughly trashing my humble home. Hard to be Zen when strangers are rifling through your underwear drawer and dumping cornflakes on the kitchen floor. Then there was Kiddiot and the dog hiding under the bed. I could see their little noses peeking out.

"You're scaring my animals," I said.

"I thought I told you to shut up."

Square Face swung at my face again. I caught his fist in midair and twisted it the way you unscrew a pickle jar. The sound the bones in his wrist made as they splintered reminded me of a cracker snapping in half. Down he fell, screaming in pain.

The other two drew their pistols and turned toward me,

yelling for me to get on my face, which prompted Ack-Ack to come lunging out, barking and snarling, from under the bed, which distracted them for a half second, prompting me to spring off the sofa and drop-kick the white guy square in his happy sack, then spin and jam my elbow hard into the Black guy's throat. With all three of them writhing on the floor, the act of gathering up their weapons, along with the revolver Square Face had relieved me of earlier, was as easy as picking daisies.

"Nice work, Ack-Ack."

I would've rewarded him with a dog treat, but he was already busy scarfing up cornflakes off the kitchen floor while the cowardly little lion—otherwise known as my cat—remained under the bed. I slid the magazines from their semiautos into the trash can, ejected the live rounds, then tossed the guns outside, into Mrs. Schmulowitz's rosebushes.

"So, where are you boys from?" I asked with the revolver in my hand, but they were all too busy groaning in pain to answer. "Maybe you didn't understand the question."

I stepped on Square Face's broken right wrist, applying enough pressure that it got his attention.

"Langley," he moaned.

"Well, I'll be darned. Langley. You know, I thought that might be the case. Which leaves me wondering: Why would three knuckle-draggers from CIA headquarters fly all the way out to California to rough up a civilian flight instructor and ransack his apartment?"

No response. Only more groaning.

"Let me repeat the question." I put more weight on his wrist.

"National security interests!" he screamed in agony.

"Too vague. I'm gonna need you to be a little more specific there, hoss," I said, "or I might have to shoot every one of you, just to put y'all out of your misery."

"C'mon, man," he gasped, "you're not *that* stupid—unless you want to spend the rest of your life in prison."

"Let's recap. I come home to find three armed burglars in my apartment. My pets are terrified. I have no choice but to defend them and myself. All three burglars wind up in the morgue. I fail to see how that produces a guilty verdict in any courtroom in America."

"Go to hell, Logan."

"Have it your way." I cocked the hammer.

That's when he told me what I already knew.

———

I cleaned up the kitchen and called Layne to tell her about my three visitors. She sounded out of breath, like she was at the gym working out.

"Did you get any names before you sent them all packing? Maybe I know them."

"I didn't bother with names. I was more interested in what they were looking for. Anyway, after our little set-to, they were all in a big hurry to get to the emergency room, and the dog was starting to barf up cornflakes, so I just let 'em go."

"So, what were they looking for?"

"Nothing."

"*Nothing*? What do you mean, 'nothing'?"

"It was a show of force, Layne. To intimidate me. To get us to stand down."

"That's ridiculous. The CIA is prohibited by law from targeting American citizens domestically. No section chief would've ever issued tasking orders approving an operation like that."

"Look, all I know is what they told me," I said, "which is that you've been asking too many questions of your former colleagues at Langley. Word got back to some of the big kahunas there. They want you to cease and desist."

The mechanical whooshing of the elliptical machine Layne was exercising on quieted as she stopped.

"Gotta be the radar thing," she said after a couple of seconds, breathing hard.

I agreed.

She said she'd reached out to her Science and Technology contacts at Langley to find out what information, if any, they had on file about Chocks.

"They told me they'd never even heard of him," Layne said. "I can definitely go back and push them harder."

"You've already done enough, Layne. I can take it from here."

"Don't tell me what to do, Logan."

"I'm not telling you what to do. It's just that—"

"What," she said, cutting me off, "that I'm a woman? That I can't take care of myself the way a man could? Here we go again with the whole damsel-in-distress thing."

"Layne, we both know the agency would never risk getting caught violating the law by sending out three of their goons on a domestic op unless it was a huge deal. Who knows what these people are capable of next time?"

Layne's voice was laced with resentment. "You're forgetting. I used to work for the agency, remember? Specifically, with that very same flavor of goons. I know what they're capable of, Logan, and if you think for one second that I'm going to be intimated by them or anybody, then you don't know me. And that's a big problem. You don't see me for who I am. You see me for who you *want* me to be. And whatever that image may be, it, I can assure you, is not who I am. I'll let you know if I turn up anything relevant to your purposes."

The line went dead.

I can be accused of many things—of not appreciating the benefits of yoga or the taste of yogurt or the excessive personal grooming habits of the so-called modern male—but I was hardly the flaming chauvinist she made me out to be. Maybe that was our problem, too. Layne didn't see me in an accurate light, either.

I fed the pets and was still straightening up the place when Paul Horvath called. He'd checked FAA files. There were no records, he said, of any aircraft operating in or around Santa Isabella's immediate airspace in the hour before or after Chocks Hostetler's death.

"That's impossible. There *had* to be," I said. "A man crashed through the roof of a mobile home. You don't generate that kind of velocity falling out of a tree."

"It's possible there was an aircraft," Horvath said, "but it might've been flying too low to be picked up on radar. It's also possible its transponder was turned off and not broadcasting."

"Either way," I said, "a satellite would've picked up a ground track, wouldn't it?"

"Look, all I know is what I found on file, Mr. Logan. You asked me to check. I checked. Good night."

"What about the tail number, Paul?"

"What tail number?"

"The tail number I asked you to look up. November two-niner Victor Golf."

"The Federal Aviation Administration has no record of any aircraft in the current civil aviation registry corresponding to that number," Horvath said.

"What about expired airworthiness certificates? Or deregistered aircraft?"

A pause. An annoyed sigh. Then Horvath said, "If I *do* check on those for you, will you *promise* to leave me alone?"

"Probably."

Another pause. Another sigh. He sounded beyond annoyed. I couldn't say I blamed him. "I'm putting you on hold," he said.

"Thank you."

I stood by, trying to sweep the floor while Ack-Ack barked and chewed on the broom's bristles like they were alien invaders. When Horvath returned to the phone, he said the tail number had once been assigned to a Learjet, but that its registration had expired six years earlier. FAA records offered no indication why the certificate was not renewed, though I knew there were only two reasons: either the jet had been destroyed in a crash or sold to a foreign buyer and reregistered abroad.

"What about the last owner of record? Could you check on that for me?"

"No," Horvath said.

I had exhausted whatever special treatment I'd been audacious enough to think he owed me in the first place. He assured me that this would be the last conversation we would ever have.

"I don't know what you're up to, Logan, and I really don't want to know," Horvath said. "But considering your track record, I have a premonition that whatever it is, sooner or later, it's going to get you killed."

I told him that I appreciated his time, then immediately called Buzz, my old battle buddy from Alpha. The first words out of his mouth weren't, "It's been a while, Logan, how've you been?" or "Gee, old pal, it seems like forever since we last talked." No. His first words were:

"Are you aware, Logan, that you're the reason God created the middle finger?"

"You know, Buzz, you're a perfect example that beauty is only skin deep, but ugly goes clean to the bone."

His laugh was as grating as a chain saw.

A true friend is someone who knows everything about your past and still loves you. That was Buzz, though the word "love" was not in his vocabulary—not as it related to other men, anyway. Buzz wasn't merely a dinosaur. He was whatever came before the dinosaurs. His political incorrectness was in keeping with the brash former Delta operator he was at heart, one who'd lost an eye to an RPG on an op outside Benghazi and who'd subsequently joined Alpha shortly before I did. I'd saved his bacon a time or two in the field, but not as many as he had mine. After the White House quietly disbanded our group as a political liability amid rumors that *The New York Times* was planning to publish an exposé on "America's top-secret assassination team," I went the civilian flight instructor route and Buzz went to work riding an analyst's desk at the DIA. These days, he honchoed a small counterterrorist group that answered directly to the joint chiefs and operated under clandestine corporate cover from a large Midwestern city that looked suspiciously liked Cleveland. I always thought that if Buzz had decided to become a newspaperman instead of a warrior, he would've made an excellent gossip columnist. He was well-connected, with sources at every level of the intelligence community.

"Seems like the only time you ever call me anymore, Logan, is when you need me to do something for you. Whatever happened to taking warm showers and watching Lifetime movies together? Remember those swell days?"

"No, Buzz, I don't."

"Yeah, me neither."

We got the preliminaries out of the way. How his wife and kids were doing, and how he was getting sick of having to answer to risk-averse Defense Department bureaucrats afraid to authorize virtually any intelligence-gathering operation for fear of failure. He was considering retiring, he said, which he'd been pondering for as long as I'd known him. The one bright spot in his life was Cleveland, he said, which he considered the perfect covert base of operation because nobody ever mentioned "Cleveland" and "covert" in the same sentence. He'd thought about moving back to DC, he said. Then he discovered pierogies.

"They're like these little dumpling thingies. Very tasty."

"I know what pierogies are, Buzz."

"Why are you calling me, Logan?"

"I'm just wondering if you have contacts at NORAD."

"What for?"

I told him about what had happened to Chocks and how the FAA had been of little use in helping me find whoever killed him. There was a chance, I said, that North American Aerospace Defense Command satellites in synchronous orbit might've uploaded aircraft tracks in the Santa Isabella area that night that FAA radars and its less sophisticated satellite system may have missed.

"Sounds like you and this poor guy Hostetler were pretty tight," Buzz said.

"He was my dash two during Desert Shield and Desert Storm."

"What's a dash two?"

"A wingman. It's fighter pilot lingo, Buzz, not that I'd ever expect a crippled-up ground-pounder like you to know such things."

"You're hurting my feelings, Logan. I thought *I* was your wingman."

"I didn't know you had any feelings, Buzz."

He grunted and said he'd see what he could find out but told me not to hold my breath. He was tight with sources at the alphabet agencies, but NORAD was hardly in his wheelhouse. It would take some time.

"If they got something on what happened to your boy that night," he promised, "I'll get it."

I asked him for one last favor. Buzz had instant computer access to every state motor vehicle record in the country. Would he mind running a registration check on the Chevy Silverado driven by the blonde I'd followed into the gas station in Santa Isabella, the same truck whose license plate matched what I believed was the tail number of a Learjet that Paul Horvath told me didn't show up in current FAA files?

"Give me the number, flyboy," Buzz said.

"November two-niner Victor Golf."

"Say again?"

"*Two*. Niner. Victor. Golf. How did you get to be so hard of hearing, Buzz?"

"Gee, I dunno, Logan. Could it have been those two million rounds of two-two-three ammo I fired during six overseas deployments? Or was it the five-hundred-pound JDAM that idiot air force guy in his F-16 dropped danger-close when I was humping through Helmand Province?"

"Forget I asked."

I could hear the click of computer keys over the phone as Buzz accessed a restricted database intended for use only by law enforcement and intelligence agencies. In less than a minute, I had what I was looking for:

The truck was registered to one Theodore M. Millisohn, age fifty-three, of Santa Isabella, California—no doubt the same Ed Millisohn my former wingman answered to at Electrogenics before Millisohn fired him. Buzz then got me Millisohn's home address. Records showed the Electrogenics CEO lived in a $3 million home in Santa Isabella's ritziest neighborhood with his wife, Corrine, a prominent divorce attorney.

"That's one I owe you, Buzz."

"I'll put it on your tab, asshole, as per usual," he said.

"Let me know if you hear anything from NORAD."

"Copy. But just so you know, Logan, I treasure the time I *don't* spend with you."

There was that chain saw laugh again. The man loved me beyond words, but not as much as I loved him.

I got less than three hours' sleep that night. My brain wouldn't shut down as I struggled, without success, to pull from the deep recesses of my gray matter what it was that had prompted Chocks and me to part company all those many years ago. Competition over some long-forgotten female? A drunken misunderstanding? Jealousy over a promotion or decoration one of us got that the other didn't? The harder I tried to retrieve the memory of whatever it was that explained our falling out, the more the reason eluded me. By the time the sun came up, I had decided it really didn't matter anyway. Chocks had saved my life. I couldn't save his. The only thing left to do was hunt down whoever stole it from him.

THIRTEEN

My thinking went something like this:

Chocks died falling from an aircraft.

He was on bad terms with his former boss, Electrogenics's CEO, Ed Millisohn.

The vanity license plate on Millisohn's truck looked like an aircraft tail number—possibly corresponding to a Learjet, given the "My other ride is a Learjet" bumper sticker affixed to the same truck. Even if the FAA said there were no records of such an airplane registered in the US, that didn't rule out it being registered elsewhere, like, say, Mexico.

It was time to get some straight answers from Millisohn. This time, I would not be deterred by his security guards. This time, I would get the truth.

"You two behave yourself," I told the dog and cat. "I'll be back later."

The irresistible aroma of freshly baked cinnamon rolls filled the air as I approached Mrs. Schmulowitz's back porch. The door was open. Through the screen door, I could see her whipping a bowl of batter and flitting about her kitchen wearing an apron that read, "Messy but Cute."

"Something's come up," I said. "I need to take a rain check on dinner. I should be back later tonight."

"Don't worry about a thing, bubby. I'll feed your kitty and puppy tonight if you want."

"Thanks, Mrs. Schmulowitz. Just do me a favor and save me some of those pork chops you were planning to cook."

"Only if you vote for me," she teased. "Otherwise, forget it."

She handed me a warm cinnamon roll for the road. Buying votes. The old lady was a born politician.

I was preflighting the *Duck*, inspecting the control surfaces because nothing will ruin your day faster than an elevator or aileron falling off your aging airplane in midflight, when Larry came lumbering toward me across the tarmac.

"She's driving me nuts. I can't take it anymore."

"Have you considered marriage counseling?"

"Not my wife, Logan. Your landlady. You heard what happened at the debate last night?"

"She said something about calling her opponent a lying pig."

"She was just getting warmed up. She also said his mother should've thrown him away and kept the stork. She called him a *goniff*. I don't even know what that is. This is a small town, Logan. Mrs. Schmulowitz is ruffling feathers. I'm worried it could hurt my business, me running her campaign."

"So quit."

"And leave her high and dry? I can't do that, Logan. Not without finding a replacement first. Which brings me to—"

A Southwest Airlines 737 started its takeoff roll down

Runway Two-Seven, engines thundering. We turned to watch. It's what airplane geeks do. We can't help ourselves. Larry waited until the jet lifted off and the roar of its engines lessened before continuing.

"Anyway, I was thinking maybe you could, you know, take over for me."

"Run her campaign?"

"She's *your* landlady, Logan. And nobody else is gonna take the job. That woman is a *load*."

I told him I'd give it some thought, even though getting involved in local politics was the furthest thing from my mind.

Flying to Santa Isabella had become so routine that I was now a familiar face at BillionAir. Hardly anyone bothered looking up at me from their desks when I walked in off the flight line. It wasn't lost on me that I was taking advantage of their hospitality, repeatedly borrowing their crew cars, but nobody complained.

Little Red Riding Hood was still parked where I'd left it the last time. The car fired right up. I drove toward the headquarters of Electrogenics where I intended to confront Ed Millisohn, but not before stopping at Onas Seco Vineyards, which was on the way.

The tasting room was spare, industrial-themed. A thin man in his mid-fifties, with bushy sideburns and a caveman's brow, was rinsing wineglasses behind the bar.

"Are you Freddie?"

"That would be me." He looked up from his labors and smiled. "We're pouring some of our best whites today. What can I get you started with?"

"I'm not here for wine, Freddie." I showed him the credit

card receipt with Chocks's name on it from the day before. "This customer came in and bought three cases of pinot noir yesterday. Do you remember what he looked like?"

Freddie's eyes narrowed. "What're you, a cop or something?"

"We can forgo the formalities. You tell me what I want, I was never here. I'm just looking for a little information, that's all."

He wiped his hands on a wine-stained dishrag, slipped on a pair of reading glasses, and took the receipt warily from my hand. "Yeah, I remember," he said, planting both elbows on the bar and peering closely at it. "How could I forget. Blonde. Twenties. A real looker."

"Peter Hostetler. An odd name for a young lady, wouldn't you say, Freddie?"

"She said she was his secretary. I ran the card. It went through no problem."

"You didn't ask her for her name or get her phone number?"

"We don't hit on our customers."

"I'm not talking about that, Freddie. I'm talking about carding her. How do you know she was over twenty-one? Selling spirits to a minor, that's serious stuff. You could lose your liquor license."

Freddie gulped hard. "I dunno, maybe I wasn't thinking about it, OK? We were pretty busy. Maybe I screwed up. Look, she gave me a valid credit card. The card went through. I swear, that's all I know, sir."

The "sir" told me he *did* think I was a cop. The bob in his Adam's apple told me he was too scared to be lying. I thanked him for his time and left.

One more reason to confront Ed Millisohn. He would certainly know who the blonde was. I'd snapped photos of them kissing in his company parking lot. I got back into the car and had just put it in gear when Chocks's widow, Miranda, called. She said she had to see me. Immediately.

"It's super important," she said, slurring her words. Asking her if she'd had a few drinks would have been like asking Elizabeth Taylor if she'd been married a few times. At Miranda's suggestion, we arranged to meet on the north end of Santa Isabella, at a cocktail lounge called Vino Rouge.

The place was elegant in a pretentious kind of way, trying hard to emulate some dark, cozy San Francisco speakeasy and pulsing with the animated conversations of millennial hipsters and stylishly attired wine snobs meeting for an early lunch. Over in the corner, a jazz pianist in a purple silk shirt tickled the ivories with an abundance of goop in his Kenny G hair. I found a booth facing the door. Miranda had not yet arrived.

My waitress was an auburn-haired heartbreaker in a white tuxedo shirt and black pencil skirt.

"How are we doing today?" she asked.

"We're hanging in there."

Her name, she said, was Amber, and she delivered a well-rehearsed dissertation on two special wines Vino Rouge was serving that day. One was a lively pinot offering hints of cherry and coffee with a chocolate finish. The other was a blend of grenache and cabernet, mellowed with a hint of Syrah.

"Just a glass of water for now, thanks," I said.

"You got it." She removed the two pricey wine goblets from my table like I might steal them and left me alone, never to be seen again.

I heard Miranda Hostetler enter before I saw her. She practically stormed in, drunk and loud, apologizing as she bounced off one patron, then another. The crowd seemed to part, and suddenly there she was, standing in front of me in a peach-colored sundress, hair clinging limply to her face in a tangle of sweaty strands that she kept pawing aside with one hand while struggling to keep the strap of her matching tote bag from falling off her sunburned shoulder.

"Well, well. Aren't we punctual?" she said with an inebriated grin as she slid into the booth beside me with all the grace of a bulldozer. Her eyes were glassy. She smelled like a distillery. "You order yet?"

"Water."

"Oh, that's right. I forgot. You're one of those, whatchacallits, teetotalers. Peter never said anything about that." She craned her head left and right, looking for the waitress. "I really could use a drink."

"A little early in the day to be getting blitzed, isn't it, Miranda?"

"You know," she said, turning to peer at me woozily, "you're cute in a caveman kinda way. Anybody ever tell you that?"

"You said you needed to see me, Miranda."

"I did?"

"Yeah, you did."

"Oh, yeah, I did, huh?" She blinked a couple of times. Her eyes regained a glimmer of focus. "I have a secret, but don't tell anybody, Logan, OK?"

"Mum's the word," I said.

She leaned in closer, her breath reeking of barley and hops, and whispered too loudly, "My brother works for the CIA, but he said for me to keep it hush-hush, so that's just between us, OK?"

"Marvin, your brother, the jeweler, works for the CIA."

"Shushhhh." She put a finger to my lips. "He told me they were the ones who murdered him."

"The CIA murdered Pete?"

"Not the CIA, silly. The aliens who work for the CIA—and not the ones from Mexico, either. From outer space."

". . . From outer space."

"Exactly."

I sat back. "OK, I'll bite. Why would the CIA and space aliens want to hurt Pete?"

"To shut his mouth. To silence him. Permanently."

"Why would they want to do that, Miranda?"

She rolled her eyes like I was slow on the uptake. "Don't you get it? All that top-secret stuff they got going on over at Electrogenics? It's all alien stuff, OK?"

"Pete told you all this?"

"I told you. We didn't have that kind of relationship. My brother told me. He said Peter was gonna go to the media and blow the lid off the whole agreement."

"What agreement?"

"Reverse engineering. They're giving us this super advanced stuff—nano stuff, microchip stuff, whatever, the whole nine yards. They're way more advanced than we are. Like, by light-years."

"And what do they get in return, these aliens?"

"Can you keep a secret?"

"Asked and answered," I said.

Miranda leaned in even closer. "The government signed a contract. We get all this cool stuff, and they get to do experiments . . . on *us*." She raised her eyebrows. "Highly sensitive experiments. Of, shall we say, a *sexual* nature."

"Sounds like a pretty good deal to me," I said.

She punched me in the arm and laughed like someone who was twice over the legal blood-alcohol limit. She wanted me to tell the detectives investigating Chocks's death all about the aliens. She said she would've told them herself but was too afraid word might get back to the "mother ship," and that the aliens would murder her, too. Then she passed out with her forehead on the table.

Chocks Hostetler was among the most grounded, clear-eyed

pilots I ever served with. How he could've ended up marrying a woman like Miranda was beyond me. Then again, what right did I have to question anyone else's choice of mates, considering my own dubious track record in that department?

I called Ed Millisohn at Electrogenics. His assistant said he was gone for the day. Would I care to leave a message for him? I would indeed, I said.

"Tell him Cordell Logan called about the blonde in the Silverado. He'll know what I'm talking about. Tell him we can discuss it at his house. I'll be there shortly."

Millisohn lived outside the Santa Isabella city limits on a nouveau-riche, five-acre estate surrounded by vineyards at the base of Bishop Diego Mountain. An ornate pair of wrought iron gates swung open as I pulled in, as if Millisohn were waiting for me to arrive. Bronze sculptures of Greek gods flanked the quarter-mile-long driveway leading to his mansion. The fountain out front was nearly big enough to swim laps in. I parked in the cobblestone motor court, stepped out of Little Red Riding Hood, and was immediately greeted by a pair of Rottweilers that skidded around the corner, barking and snarling, and came rocketing toward me like Sidewinder missiles.

I jumped back in the car and slammed the door shut with barely a second to spare. Ed Millisohn emerged from his McMansion in slippers and a red terrycloth robe with a golf club in his left hand. It looked to be either a nine-iron or a sand wedge. In his right hand was a Glock.

"*Hör auf!*" he shouted at the dogs. Instantly, they stopped barking and sat. "They won't hurt you, Logan—unless I order them to. I told you, if I saw you again, I'd have you arrested."

I stepped out of the car with one eye on his attack dogs.

"Who was the young woman in the truck, Ed?"

"I don't know what you're talking about."

"Black Silverado? Off-road tires? 'My other ride is a Learjet'? Good-looking truck. But not quite as good-looking as the little cutie driving it—the one you were too busy getting busy with in the parking lot to notice me taking pictures from across the street."

Millisohn glanced nervously over his shoulder at the front door.

"Relax, Ed. You give me what I'm looking for, your wife will be none the wiser."

Millisohn swiped at the sweat that had suddenly appeared on his upper lip. "We can talk in your car," he said, setting aside the golf club and stuffing the pistol in the pocket of his robe.

He got in on the passenger side. I slid in behind the wheel. "Lemme see the pictures," he demanded.

"You're not in charge here, Ed. I am. Like I said, you answer my questions openly and honestly, and everything'll be fine."

"You're bluffing. You don't have any pictures."

I showed him and watched the blood drain from his face. "Who is she, Ed?"

"A friend, that's all. Just a friend."

"Your friend bought three cases of red wine with Pete Hostetler's credit card long after he was dead. I have the receipt, Ed."

Millisohn licked his lips. "Yeah, well, I wouldn't know anything about that."

We both knew he was lying.

"Your wife's a divorce lawyer, Ed. A good one, from what I hear. She'll get the house and the cars and probably Hans *und* Franz out there." I nodded toward the dogs. They were still sitting outside the car, waiting to chew on me at the slightest provocation.

"Hostetler was a drunk and a thief," Millisohn said. "He was stealing from my company. Somebody found the card in his desk. I can only assume he forgot to cancel it after I fired his ass. I was just trying to even the score. Balance the ledger. A little payback, that's all. So, yeah, I gave her the card and told her to have a ball."

"What did Pete steal, Ed?"

Millisohn's eyes dodged mine. "Look," he said, "I know why you're here, Logan, so let me make this as perfectly clear to you as I can: I had absolutely nothing to do with what happened to him, OK? Zero. Was I mad at him? You bet I was. I should've turned him over to the sheriff when I found out what he was up to. And I would have, too, if he hadn't been such a big goddamn war hero. But I didn't kill him."

"Stealing *what*, Ed?" I repeated.

"I can't talk about it."

"Fair enough. Then you can kiss this extremely nice hacienda and those two lovable pooches out there goodbye."

He turned toward me. Any amateur could've read the desperation in his eyes. "You don't understand," he said. "It's a matter of national security."

"That's funny. You're the second person who's told me that in two days."

"Please," Millisohn said, "you have to believe me."

"Believe what? Your company builds toys for kids, Ed, animatronic animals. Personally speaking, they weird me out, but that's beside the point. The point is, how are toys for kids a matter of national security?—unless it's all a false front."

"I can't talk about it," he said again.

I asked him about the crate that was shipped to DARPA in Virginia, the one Layne and I watched being forklifted onto the semitruck at Electrogenics's loading docks. The breath seemed to catch in Millisohn's throat.

"How do you know about that?" he demanded.

I let my silence do its bidding. People hate lapses in conversation. They find them unnerving and feel the need to fill them. Ed Millisohn was no exception.

"We do some work on the side for the government," he said. "That's all I'm prepared to say."

"Your company is building phase-centering radar components, Ed. That's what got Pete Hostetler killed, isn't it?"

Millisohn ran a hand nervously across his mouth. His voice grew softer. "Please, Logan. I *really* can't talk about it."

"Which part, Ed? The radar components or Pete's murder?"

He was near tears, looking everywhere but at me.

"Who murdered him, Ed?"

"I don't know."

"Sure you do."

"I just told you. I don't know!"

"What about your jet?"

"I don't have a jet," Millisohn said.

"November two-niner Victor Golf. Ring any bells?"

"Jesus, who *are* you?"

I waited.

Millisohn rubbed his face with both hands. "It was the company's plane. A Lear 55. I sold it when we closed our satellite operation in Phoenix. But that was years ago."

"Who bought it?"

He ran a palm across his mouth. "I don't remember."

"Who killed Peter Hostetler, Ed?"

"What the hell do you want from me?" He hunched over, rocking and cupping his hands over his ears. "How many times do I have to tell you? I had nothing to do with it."

"Hear no evil."

"What the hell's that supposed to mean?"

"It means liars cover their ears when they can't stand hearing themselves lie anymore. It also means you've got about two seconds to come clean, Ed, or things are gonna get awfully ugly in here for you."

He reached into his robe for the Glock. I grabbed his arm before he could and slammed him into the passenger door, which then flew open—hardly a surprise given how rusted Little Red Riding Hood was. Out Millisohn tumbled. *"Fass! Fass!"* he yelled as he got to his feet and sprinted into the house.

I leaned over and pulled the door shut a half second before his Rottweilers could hop in and say *Guten Tag*.

Barking and snarling, the dogs chased my car all the way up the driveway. They gave up and turned back before I reached the county road where uniformed Santa Isabella sheriff's deputies in three black-and-white patrol units had set up a roadblock, waiting to arrest me.

FOURTEEN

Breakfast was undercooked pancakes and powdered scrambled eggs. I'd overnighted before in a few municipal lockups. By comparative standards, the Santa Isabella County Jail was the Ritz-Carlton. No rats. No cockroaches. I even had a private holding cell all to myself.

"Almost like a B&B," I said to the bob-haired, wide-bodied custody officer as she walked me in handcuffs down the corridor and into an interrogation room where Detectives Tom Kasparov and Lloyd Gregory were waiting for me.

"Be sure to leave us a nice review on Tripadvisor," she said.

The room was small and predictably windowless, furnished with the requisite bare metal table and three metal chairs, all bolted to the floor, which was poured cement. The custody officer unlocked my cuffs, pointed to the chair across the table from the two detectives, and left.

"How was breakfast?" Gregory asked like he didn't care either way.

"Four and a half stars," I said, taking a seat. "I would've given it five, but the flapjacks were a tad undercooked."

Kasparov was sipping coffee from a Styrofoam cup with his eel-skin cowboy boots propped up on the table. Gregory was working on a Danish the size of a catcher's mitt.

"What were you doing at Mr. Millisohn's house last night?" Kasparov asked.

"Having a conversation."

"He told us you accused him of murder," Gregory said with his mouth full, pausing to lick frosting from his fingers, "after which you physically assaulted him."

"Only after he tried to pull a gun on me."

Kasparov shook his head. "Do you ever stop to ask yourself, Logan, 'Why is it all these people are always pulling guns on me?'"

I shrugged. "Life is full of mysteries."

"Why don't we start by you telling us your side of the story," Gregory said.

I told them what Millisohn told me. That Electrogenics once owned a jet a man could've easily been shoved out of. I told them about Electrogenics manufacturing highly classified, military-grade radar components. I told them that I was pursuing aviation records that would, I was convinced, establish the identity of any and all aircraft flying above or near Santa Isabella the night Pete Hostetler was murdered. I also told them I intended to keep asking questions until whoever killed my former wingman was identified and brought to justice, either by me or them.

"Use me as an asset," I said. "I'll pass along whatever I find. We can trade information."

"I already told you, Logan," Kasparov said, glancing over at Gregory who was wiping pastry crumbs off his paisley tie. "It doesn't work that way. We don't trade information with civilians, especially ones who show up in our community intending to cause trouble."

"This isn't a two-way street, Logan," Gregory added. "It's a one-way street. The way of law enforcement."

"Nice speech, Joe Friday," I said. "OK, let's play it this way: You guys cut me loose; I'll do my best to stay out of your way. Whatever intel I come across, it's yours, free for the taking. All I want to do is catch whoever killed my friend."

Kasparov studied me with his arms folded. Then he put his feet on the floor. A slim manila folder marked, "Logan, Cordell" was resting on the table between us. He slid it across to me.

"Read it," he said.

Inside was a two-page computer printout of my military records. Included was the year I graduated from the academy, a list of decorations I'd earned, and my various squadron assignments from basic flight training forward. The last entry stated, "Deactivated from flight status, interagency transfer."

"Silver Star. Distinguished Flying Cross." Kasparov sneered. "The air force hands out medals like candy. Unlike the Marine Corps."

"Do not overrate what you have received," I said, "nor envy others. He who envies others does not obtain peace of mind."

"What's that supposed to mean?" Kasparov demanded.

"You'll have to ask the Buddha."

The two cops looked at each other. Then Gregory said, "Why did the air force take you off flight status?"

"I caught a pass over the middle against the University of New Mexico my senior year at the academy and got decleated by their middle linebacker. Three surgeries and twenty years later, the air force decided my knee had degenerated to the point they no longer trusted me bringing back their $18 million airplane in reusable condition."

Kasparov sat back in his chair. "OK," he said, "so, let's say for the sake of argument you were being up-front with us about being assigned to this so-called Ultra unit."

"*Tier One* Ultra," I said, correcting him.

"Fine. Tier One *Ultra*. Let's say we do decide to cut you loose. What are the chances of you reaching out to your old contacts in the intelligence community to find out what's going on at Electrogenics? I mean, what's *really* going on there. Because they're not telling us anything."

"I just told you," I said. "They're manufacturing radar components and shipping them to DARPA."

Kasparov got up and paced the room. "OK, look, here's the deal. I'm gonna be honest with you, Logan. Our investigation's hit a dead end. We're not exactly sure, but we think your friend Hostetler may have stumbled onto something."

"And got killed to keep whatever that is quiet," Gregory said.

"Please do not tell me that 'something' has to do with little green men."

The two detectives looked at each other, then at me, like they had no idea what I was talking about.

"Forget it," I said. "Stumbled on what?"

"We don't know. That's what we're hoping you can help us find out." Kasparov opened the interrogation room door and stood aside. I was obviously free to go. "Keep in touch, Logan," he said.

"Yeah," Gregory added, "and try not to get dead."

The hole Pete Hostetler's body made when it crashed through Walt and Lena Rizzo's roof had been patched over with a new sheet of plywood and galvanized decking screws. Walt had made the repairs himself, he told me proudly, after the couple's insurance carrier decided the damage wasn't covered under their homeowner's policy.

"How is it that these insurance people will cover wind damage and fire damage and every other damage, but not damage from some guy using your roof as a drop zone?" Walt shook his head. "Bunch of money-grubbers is what they are."

"Amen to that, sir," I said.

Lena brought in steaming cups of coffee from the kitchen and a plate of frosted doughnut holes she'd baked herself. Walt insisted on her showing me where she was sitting on the sofa that night, then made his wife show how she got up and walked toward the door that night to let Rambo out.

"Two, three steps, then, *ka-boom!*" he said. "Didn't hear nothing before that. I had my hearing aids out, and Lena's don't work too good to begin with, anyway. Felt like an atom bomb. Sounded like it, too."

"Must've been pretty scary," I said.

"What?"

"He said we must've been scared, Walt!"

"Damn right we were scared."

Lena attempted to interject her own version of events that evening, but her husband was just getting cranked up. He described the gore in detail. How, afterward, the couple tried to scrub the blood clean from everything before finally giving up. How they bought new carpet on sale at Home Depot. How it came with a free pad and free installation. How they replaced the couch with one that was genuine leather—not any of that fake stuff from China—and how they got it for next to nothing on Craigslist from a nice elementary-school teacher who was moving to Phoenix. The story had a much-practiced ring to it, as if Walt had told it many times to anyone who'd listen.

"After the coroner showed up to pick up the body, if that's

what you want to call it, the sheriff's people showed up. They were here about a hundred times, taking pictures, making all these measurements, and—" Walt stopped midsentence. "Who did you say you were again?"

"He was friends with the man, Walt!" Lena said.

"I really appreciate you both taking the time to talk with me," I said. "I wanted to see where Pete died, to pay my respects."

That last part was true. We'd been through a lot together. I *had* wanted to see where Chocks departed this life for whatever, if anything, comes after it. No less significantly, though, I wanted to see for myself the damage he'd caused in crashing through the trailer's roof. I was no forensics expert, but I'd seen more times than I cared to remember what can happen when a human being is blown forcibly through a solid surface like drywall or plywood. Much like a bullet going through glass, the body will produce cratering or splintering opposite the entry point. The pattern of damage often as not will more or less conform to the body's trajectory. The steeper the angle of impact, the greater the damage. Looking up at the plywood-patched hole in the Rizzos' ceiling, I speculated that Chocks had fallen almost straight down.

I asked if they'd mind me looking around on their roof, but not before helping myself to another of Lena's doughnut holes.

"If I were on death row," I said, "I would include these in my last meal."

She beamed proudly. "They're called zeppole. My grandmother's recipe. From the Old Country."

"How d'you think I got this?" Walt rubbed his cannonball tummy. "I'll get my ladder. Just watch your step up there. It ain't exactly built for walking on."

FIFTEEN

There wasn't much to see up on top of Lena and Walt's mobile home—a precariously mounted TV antenna, two galvanized roof vents flanking an opaque plastic skylight, and Walt's plywood patching job, reinforced with roofing nails and gobs of black tar.

How was it possible, I thought to myself, that the life of a hero like Chocks Hostetler could've ended in such an inglorious location, and in such disreputable fashion? I stood on that ladder waiting to feel something more philosophical, but all I felt was guilt. I could've been a better friend to him. I'd have to live with that the rest of my life.

I exhaled and was about to start down the ladder when I glanced to my left and noticed a thin silver necklace chain crumpled under the antenna, with an attached silver medallion about the size of a dime. I reached over and picked it up. Embossed on the medallion was the image of an ancient priest soaring across the sky and holding a crucifix—St. Joseph of Cupertino, patron saint of pilots and air travelers. Chocks's good-luck necklace. I remembered seeing the same medallion dangling around his neck as we suited up in the squadron's ready room before combat missions. He never went to Mass as I recalled, but he always considered himself a good Catholic. The chain must've ripped away as he crashed through the Rizzos' trailer roof.

"A lot of protection it brought you this time, pal," I said to myself, stuffing the necklace and medallion in my pocket.

I've never believed much in divine intervention or in the belief that the dead somehow can communicate with the living from the Great Beyond. But I'd be lying if I said that what happened next as I climbed down off that ladder didn't give me pause.

A plane flew overhead. I looked up. It's what aviators do, turning their eyes automatically to the sky, wishing they were up there, too. The plane, what looked to be a low-wing Piper, was flying northeast to southwest, directly overhead and slowly descending. I watched as it extended its landing gear. Then I heard another plane, a Mooney, tracking the same flight path. I watched as its landing gear came down, too. That's when it occurred to me: one of those eureka moments that don't come along often enough.

I opened ForeFlight, the georeferenced aviation map on my phone. It showed that both airplanes were on approach to landing on Runway Two-Nine at the Santa Isabella Airport. I traced a straight line with my index finger from the airport to the blinking dot on the map that showed my own location, less than a mile from the field. The line I'd traced corresponded precisely to the extended centerline of the runway.

"I'll be damned," I muttered without realizing it.

My theory all along had been that Chocks Hostetler was pushed out of an aircraft overflying the city of Santa Isabella, not one coming in to land. Maybe someone at the airport saw a plane landing that night. Maybe they remembered a tail number. It was worth a shot.

I thanked the Rizzos, got back in Little Red Riding Hood, and headed toward the Santa Isabella Airport.

With the airport's control tower in sight, I stopped at a stop sign across from a vacant lot where a scrawny, hippy-looking college kid in a Jimi Hendrix T-shirt was camped on a beach chair in front of a small tent with a clipboard balanced on his lap. He was peering intently through a tripod-mounted spotting scope aimed in the direction of the approach corridor to Runway Two-Nine. I thought he was watching airplanes.

"Good for you," I said. "Not too many young folks are into flying these days."

"Not me, dude," the kid said with one eye still glued to the scope. "I'm afraid of heights." He pointed to a wooden box mounted high atop a eucalyptus tree on a direct line of sight from the approach end of the runway. "Great horned owl. He's in there right now with his girlfriend. They screw all day and hunt all night."

The kid said he was taking a wildlife biology course at the local community college. He and his classmates were studying the mating habits of birds of prey. For three weeks, they'd maintained round-the-clock surveillance on the tree box.

"Sounds pretty boring," I said.

"Yeah, pretty much, except for the other night, when that dude fell out of the helicopter." The kid said it so matter-of-factly, I wasn't sure at first I heard him correctly.

"Say again?"

"The dude, bro. Who fell out of the helicopter. You didn't hear about it? It was all over the news."

I pulled over and got out of the car. "What's your name, son?"

"Tyler."

"You saw what happened that night, Tyler?"

"Not me, dude. I was home that night, but one of my friends did."

Two of his classmates were on owl duty that night—Mia and Charlotte. Mia was asleep and saw nothing. Charlotte, he said, saw it all.

"You think you might be able to put me in touch with her?"

He pulled away from the spotting scope and eyed me with suspicion.

"The guy who died was a friend of mine. We were in the military together."

Tyler rubbed the side of his face.

"I dunno, dude," he said. "She was pretty freaked. Nobody's really talked to her since that night. She kinda, like, disappeared, you know?"

"I need to find out what Charlotte saw. It's really important, Tyler. Do you think you could reach out to her for me? Seriously, lives are at stake."

Reluctantly, he agreed to call her for me. There was no answer.

"Do you know where she lives?"

"Yeah, I know where she lives."

"You think maybe you can give me her address?"

"I don't know, man. I don't even know who you are."

"I'm just trying to find out what happened to my friend, Tyler."

He thought about it. Then he said, "OK, but you didn't get it from me."

"Deal."

More than two hundred thousand aircraft are registered in the United States. Fewer than 5 percent of those are helicopters. That narrowed the odds appreciably. Determining the helicopter's make and model would narrow them down more. First, though, I had to persuade a frightened coed to talk to me.

SIXTEEN

Charlotte lived on Santa Isabella's east side in an RV campground, a collection of decrepit campers with deceptively adventurous names like the "Deluxe Wanderer" and "Blue Skies." Tyler, her community college classmate, said I'd find her in a white Winnebago with green trim that she shared with her boyfriend, Ethan. It wasn't hard to find. The smoldering strains of Jim Morrison's "Riders on the Storm" oozed out from behind the Winnebago's aluminum walls, along with the stink of ammonia. Somebody was inside, cooking meth.

I rapped on the door. No response. I knocked harder. Instantly, the music went silent. I could hear two people whispering inside. This was followed by a male voice trying hard to sound big and bad.

"Who is it?"

"Not the police," I said.

The door cracked open a few inches with the security chain in place, revealing a shirtless young man who could've easily passed for Jim Morrison, replete with messiah hair and a beaded necklace.

"Yeah?"

"I'm looking for Charlotte."

"Nobody's here by that name." He went to close the door. I blocked it with my shoe.

"Hey, you can't do that!"

"I just want to talk to her, that's all."

"I'm calling the cops."

"Do that," I said. "I'm sure they'll be extremely interested to find what you're whipping up in there."

From behind him came a female voice: "Who is it, Ethan?"

"Some guy. Says he wants to talk to you."

"About what?"

"She wants to know what about?" Ethan said.

"Great horned owls."

The door closed. I could hear the security chain slide free, then the door reopened. Standing there was a tall, thin, barefoot young woman wearing jeans, a green Santa Isabella Community College hoodie, and one of those purse-lipped teenage faces that convey disgust with everybody and everything.

"I'm not coming home," she said. "You can tell my so-called dad to go to hell."

"Your dad didn't contact me, Charlotte. I need your help."

She had big round glasses and unwashed hair the color of mud, and for a moment, her face seemed to soften a little.

"You saw a man fall out of a helicopter," I said.

"No. I didn't." The way she bit her lower lip told me otherwise.

"Your friend Tyler said otherwise, Charlotte."

"Tyler smokes too much weed. Besides, I don't talk to the police. You guys are all part of the problem."

I told her I wasn't a cop and showed her my driver's license. All I was trying to do, I said, was find out who might've wanted Chocks dead. The disgusted expression on her face didn't change.

"I can pay you," I said. "I just need some information."

"How much?" Charlotte asked with her arms folded.

Inside my wallet were two twenties, a five-spot, and a couple of singles. "Forty-seven bucks. You can have it all."

"Forty-seven bucks? Yeah, right." She blew a puff of air through her lips like I'd insulted her and slammed the door in my face.

That old familiar feeling rose in my throat, acidic and blinding. The door was thin metal. The latch was cheap. One well-placed kick, one fistful of hair, and she'd volunteer everything. For what must've been a full minute I stood there, on the bubble, wrestling old demons, before finally ignoring their whispers. The new, semicivilized me. I wondered what Layne would think.

I was halfway to the car when I heard footsteps behind me.

"You see something like that," Charlotte said, "it's hard not to unsee it. In your head, over and over."

"I've been there," I said.

"I'm sorry if I was just . . ." She tucked a strand of stringy hair behind her ear and stared down at her feet. "My boyfriend . . . he doesn't want me to get involved. He thinks I'll get thrown out of a helicopter, too, like that guy."

"How do you know he got thrown out? How do you know it wasn't an accident?"

Charlotte swallowed hard. "By the way he screamed going down."

The RV park's communal area included a coin-operated laundry, a horseshoe pit, volleyball court, a children's swing set, a couple of built-in bring-your-own-charcoal grills, and a half-dozen picnic tables arranged in a circle around a brick firepit. We sat down at the only picnic table where her boyfriend back in the Winnebago couldn't see us.

"Tell me what you saw that night, Charlotte. Anything you can recall. Anything at all."

It took her a while to find the words.

She'd been monitoring the owl box and studying by flashlight for a chemistry midterm. Mia, her classmate, was asleep, curled under a blanket a few feet away. Charlotte remembered the helicopter seeming to come out of nowhere, thundering south to north, flying, by her estimate, less than five hundred feet above the ground.

"I mean, it's really loud, and I'm thinking, 'Is this guy gonna crash or what?' So I look up. Moon's full. Plenty of light that night. Next thing I know, I see this man come falling out, and, I mean, he's screaming. I didn't see him hit cuz those trees over there were in the way, but I heard it." She hung her head. Tears streamed down her cheeks. "The whole thing took, like, five seconds. Mia never even woke up. I just got up and ran. I didn't know what else to do."

I reached across the table and took her hand. "I know this is painful for you, Charlotte."

She gently wiped the bottoms of her eyes with the edges of her index fingers. "I'm OK."

"You said the helicopter looked to be flying from south to north."

She nodded.

"And the moon was pretty full?"

"I could see my shadow."

"Do you remember what color the helicopter was?"

"I dunno. Kinda silver, maybe."

"Did you notice any unusual markings? Numbers? Anything like that?"

"Not that I remember."

"Do you think you could identify what kind of helicopter it was?"

"I dunno. They all sorta look the same to me."

I Googled "Robinson R44 Raven," the best-selling helicopter on the civilian market, and showed her the picture on my phone. Charlotte studied it for a long time.

"Maybe. Like I said . . ."

"They all look the same. I get it." I showed her photos of two other popular helos, the Bell JetRanger and the Eurocopter EC175. Each evoked the same noncommittal shrug and, "Maybe. I dunno." It wasn't until I pulled up a photo of the four-seat McDonnell Douglas 500 with its distinctive, H-shaped tail assembly that she took my phone and looked closely. A smile formed.

"This one." She tapped the screen. "It definitely looked a *lot* like this one."

Most fixed-wing pilots have little regard for their rotor-wing counterparts. I'm no exception. A helicopter is five thousand whirling pieces, all of them trying to kill you. Helicopters don't fly, as the old saying goes, they beat the air into submission. I'd never flown one. Frankly, I never had the desire to. But I'd logged hundreds of hours flying *in* helicopters on missions with Alpha, including countless infiltrations and exfils aboard MH-6 Little Birds, the military's version of the MD 500.

"Are you sure, Charlotte?"

She studied the picture again, taking her time, then nodded. "Just promise me you won't tell the sheriff's department. They can't protect me. I know you can't, either, but . . . I had to tell *somebody*."

"I can't make that promise, Charlotte. It's their job to find who killed my friend. I'm just trying to help them as much as I can."

Charlotte's face flushed red. "Then I'll deny I ever told you anything. I should've never talked to you."

I watched her walk back to the Winnebago. I thought about reaching out to Paul Horvath again at the FAA and asking him to pull ownership data on every silver-colored MD 500 registered in the southwestern United States, but I'd already run that string. Horvath had made it clear he was done providing me favors. Layne, I knew, was also a no-go. She was still upset with me. So I called Buzz again.

"Do you not think I have anything better to do with my day, Logan? If you're calling to yank my chain about your NORAD request, the answer is they haven't gotten back to me yet. Now, leave me alone. I'm trying to do the Lord's work over here."

"My buddy Chocks got thrown out of a helicopter, Buzz, not a fixed-wing aircraft."

"How do you know that?"

I told him what Charlotte had told me without mentioning her name. When I finished, Buzz said, "I got a daughter in college probably about that girl's age. The idea of her seeing something like that? *Hearing* some guy screaming on the way down? Damn."

I'd never known Buzz to be the sentimental type except when it came to his wife and kids. Could be that's why he didn't complain about my hitting him up yet again for information, that and the fact that my latest request for help was probably well within his wheelhouse.

"Boeing bought out McDonnell Douglas back in the nineties," Buzz said. "Maybe Boeing maintains a master list of the ones still flying. I'll see what I can dig up."

"I could use all the help I can get," I said.

"You don't watch out, Logan, they're gonna write that on your tombstone."

He said he'd be in touch.

SEVENTEEN

Small airports are small towns unto themselves. People go drinking together after work. They sleep with each other. They form cliques, make enemies, and have trouble keeping secrets. Presuming my theory held true, that the helicopter Chocks Hostetler was riding in the night he died was on approach to Santa Isabella, all I had to do was track down somebody who might've seen it and could point me in the right direction. The problem was I was based in Rancho Bonita, more than a hundred miles away and knew not a soul at the Santa Isabella Airport except for Kimberleigh, the comely desk clerk at BillionAir.

She was sitting at a patio table tucked off to the side of the FBO, nibbling a sandwich and absorbed in a paperback book.

"Looks like a good read," I said.

She showed me the cover—*Burning the Days* by James Salter.

"Great writer," I said.

Kimberleigh raised her eyebrows. "You know Salter?"

"He wrote *The Hunters*. Best book ever written about fighter pilots at war. Don't let me interrupt your lunch."

"You're not interrupting." She closed the book and gestured

to an empty chair on the opposite side of the table. "You're the first man I ever met who's read Salter. Pretty weird."

"I prefer unusual."

She volunteered that she was taking a literature class online. She hoped to be a schoolteacher someday. "Not that this isn't a good job," Kimberleigh said. "I get to meet a lot of super interesting people. Like you."

"You don't know anything about me."

"True. But you seem like a nice guy." She offered me half her sandwich—peanut butter and strawberry jelly on whole wheat.

"Smooth or crunchy?" I asked.

"Are you serious? Crunchy. Definitely."

"That is the correct answer." I thanked her and took a big bite.

"How's Little Red Riding Hood treating you?" she asked.

"The radio won't turn off, and every time we pass a junkyard, the steering wheel pulls in that direction. No complaints otherwise. Reliable transportation. I appreciate you letting me borrow it as often as I have."

"You've been flying up here a lot," Kimberleigh said.

I figured she was entitled to some answers considering how often I'd been borrowing her company's crew car. I told what had had happened to Chocks.

"But you're not a cop?" she asked.

"I'm a flight instructor. Mostly, anyway. The guy who was killed was friend. He was a good pilot. We served together in the air force."

"I'm sorry for your loss," she said.

I nodded my appreciation.

Kimberleigh stifled a smile.

"What's funny?"

"Nothing. It just reminds me of a little joke. I'm kind of weird that way."

"Let's hear it."

She paused like she knew she was about to make a mistake, then made it anyway. "You know what the difference is between God and a pilot?"

"God doesn't think he's a pilot," I said.

"You heard it before, huh?"

"A few times."

She reached into a calfskin shoulder bag slung over the back of her chair and got out a pack of Marlboro Lights. "You mind?" she asked, lighting up before I could answer.

I wanted to ask her if she knew what lung cancer looked like. Or emphysema. Or congestive heart failure. But no twenty-something wants to hear that from someone my age, who's had friends who smoked themselves to death. Twenty-somethings are invincible. They're going to live forever.

"Somebody told me my friend fell out of a helicopter and that it might've been on approach at the time to the airport," I said. "It's possible the helicopter was based here."

"I wouldn't know anything about that." Kimberleigh turned her head and blew a stream of smoke. "I heard that some guy fell, but that's all I know. I'm really sorry it was your friend, though."

I watched a white Cessna 172 with blue trim grease a perfect landing. The plane was the same make and model as the *Duck*, but much newer—undoubtedly tricked out with a modern glass cockpit and a plush interior that smelled of springtime. I was glad the *Duck* couldn't see me lusting after it.

"What I could use," I said, "is a yenta."

Kimberleigh flicked ash from the tip of her cigarette. "What's a yenta?"

I apologized. I'd been hanging around Mrs. Schmulowitz so long, much of her vocabulary had become mine, too. "They're kibitzers," I said. "They like to kibitz. Stick their nose in other people's business. Every small airport has one. Anybody you know like that around here?"

She took another long drag. "Yeah, you know, when I think about it, there is *one* guy."

His name, Kimberleigh said, was Otto Suggs, a retired air traffic controller known to all as "Skip." He managed the Santa Isabella Airport's small Museum of Flight—when he wasn't cruising the field on his golf cart, eager to chew the fat with anyone willing to humor a doddering pensioner with nothing better to do in retirement than stick his nose in places it didn't belong. If anybody knew anything about a connection between Chocks's murder and a helicopter possibly based at the Santa Isabella Airport, Kimberleigh said, it was Skip Suggs.

―

The museum was housed in a World War II Quonset hut hunkered between a row of T-hangars and a dirt field strewn with weeds. On static display out front, decaying slowly in the sun, was an air force F-4 Phantom jet bearing fading tan-and-green Vietnam-era camouflage. A handwritten sign was duct-taped inside a cracked window of the museum's front door: *Closed, please telephone for appointment.*

I called the number. The geezer who answered sounded like he was from Texas and as old as the Alamo.

"This is Skip."

"Mr. Suggs, my name is—"

"You're gonna have to speak up, ma'am. My ears are shot. Too many years in too many cockpits with no headset."

"My name is Cordell Logan. I—"

"Stand by. Just hold on a minute." There was a long pause. I could hear rustling. This was followed by the sound of something crashing and breaking on the floor, like maybe a ceramic vase. Then he was back. "All right, there we go. Had to get my hearing helpers in. Yes, ma'am, now, how can I help you?"

I told him that I was a pilot and flight instructor from Rancho Bonita, and that I was interested in a tour of the museum. He said he'd have to check his busy schedule, then snorted gleefully at the notion of having *anything* on his schedule. He said he'd meet me outside the museum in eleven minutes. Not ten minutes. Not twelve. Eleven.

Eleven minutes to the second later, a primer gray Oldsmobile Cutlass that probably rolled off the assembly line when LBJ was president pulled into the totally empty parking lot going about five miles an hour. The rear license plate frame read, "Too Close for Missiles, Switching to Guns."

Skip Suggs got out of the car like a pretzel untwisting itself, slowly and with considerable effort. His bald scalp was flamingo pink. His nose belonged on a man three times his size. He wore rimless glasses, a checked flannel shirt, trousers belted well above his navel, and well-loved suede moccasins.

"Thanks for doing this, Mr. Suggs. It's a pleasure to meet you, sir."

He walked with a cane. We shook hands. "So, you're a CFI, are you?"

"Yes, sir. C-F double I, actually. Flew A-10s in the air force before that."

"A Warthog driver. Well, good for you, young fella. I was navy myself before I joined the FAA. Eggbeaters. 'Course, back then, we called 'em whirlybirds. The old H-34s. Pieces of crap. Not like what they're flying today."

He dug a key ring worthy of a medieval jailer out of his front pocket, then devoted the better part of a minute trying one key after another, stooped and squinting, before finally finding the one that fit the dead bolt. He turned back to me before opening the door.

"Admission's free, but we do advise a five-dollar contribution to the museum fund."

I reached for my wallet, then remembered that I'd given all my cash to that girl, Charlotte, in the RV park.

"My apologies, Mr. Suggs. I don't have any cash on me right now. I can go to the bank, if you'd like."

"No, no, no. Don't worry about it. You're here. You can pay me later. Come on in."

He flipped on the lights. The Santa Isabella Airport had been built during the war to train B-25 crews, so it wasn't surprising that the one-room museum was heavy on memorabilia commemorating the famed twin-engine Mitchell bomber. On display was the gutted forward fuselage of a B-25 one could walk through, a Link flight trainer, a plexiglass top gun turret stripped of its machine guns, various old flight instruments, a leather flying jacket donated by a Santa Isabella–area farmer who'd served with the 42nd Bombardment Group, and a five-hundred-pound bomb that Skip assured me had been disarmed. Framed pictures of aircrews who'd long since gone west filled the walls. Toy planes hung from the rafters on fishing line. Everything had a fine layer of dust on it.

"Fascinating collection," I said.

"Tell you what," he said. "How 'bout a souvenir to remember your visit? You can pay me later for that, too, if you want."

"Sure."

I followed him as he shuffled over to a cabinet that passed for the museum's gift shop. The shelves were filled with aviation-themed baseball caps, airplane lapel pins and key chains, plastic model kits of B-25s, and, weirdly enough, a collection of women's lingerie. The old man held up a sexy little nightshirt with spaghetti straps bearing the words, "Remove Before Flight."

"Bet your special gal would enjoy one of these jazzy numbers, eh?" His snowy caterpillar eyebrows danced. "Guaranteed to get you to third base at least."

"I would not take that bet," I said. "She might like one of those little airplane pins, though, if you don't mind me paying you later for it."

"I think we can arrange that."

"This one should do." I picked out a pin that looked like the *Duck*, only in miniature. It cost $7.95. "You mind me asking you a question, Skip?"

"Depends on the question."

"I hear you have your finger on the pulse of this airport."

"Who told you that?"

"An attractive young lady who works over at BillionAir. She thinks very highly of you, by the way."

"A member of my vast harem," Skip said with a wink. "What's your question?"

I asked him about the helicopter. His already wrinkled brow furrowed like an old washboard.

"'Man must rise above the earth,'" he said, "'to the top of the atmosphere and beyond, for only thus will he fully understand the world in which he lives.' Know who said that?"

"Socrates," I said.

"Very good." Skip smiled with teeth the color of old wood, as if I'd passed some unspoken test. "I was gonna ask to see your airman's certificate, just to make sure you're on the up-and-up," he said, "but if you know Socrates, you are definitely the real deal."

On the shelf next to the lingerie was a notepad. Skip picked up a stub of a pencil with a gnarled, arthritic hand, touched the tip of it to his tongue, and wrote down an address. When he was finished, he licked his thumb, carefully tore off the page, folded it in half, folded the half in half, and handed it to me.

"Look for the Greek," Skip said. "Just make sure you take a gun with you."

EIGHTEEN

The marquee out front read, "Santa Isabella Valley Mortuary, a Tradition of Trust." The house looked like it belonged on a cotton plantation in the Deep South, not on the outskirts of a college town in central California, surrounded by vineyards. Back in the late 1800s, when it was built, it had served as the home to some wealthy family. Now it was a home for all eternity—a white three-story Victorian with gray-and-green gingerbread trim, a corner turret, and manicured rose gardens. Hardly the kind of place that screamed, "Just make sure you take a gun with you."

Between the curb and the house, facing the street and flanking either side of the front walkway, were two marble headstones, one gray and the other brown. Neither struck me as necessarily out of place considering it was, after all, a mortuary. Sample products, I figured.

I climbed three wooden steps to the covered wraparound front porch and rang an antique brass bell affixed to the oak front door. The door opened, giving way to a six foot platinum blonde in a white pantsuit who looked to be of retirement age and who bore no resemblance to any undertaker I'd ever seen. Everything about her was fake. Eyelashes. Wig. Breasts. A former Vegas showgirl, trying hard to hang on to what she once had, was my guess. Her citrus-sweet perfume barely masked the smell of formaldehyde.

"Yes?"

"Hello," I said. "Is the Greek here?"

". . . Who?"

"The Greek. Skip Suggs sent me. From the airport."

"And you are . . . ?"

"My name's Logan. I'm following up on a murder that occurred here in Santa Isabella recently."

"Are you a cop?"

"I've been getting that a lot lately." I gave her my best disarming smile and handed her a business card. "I'm actually a private investigator."

"Above the Clouds Aviation. Flight training, whale watching, and aerial charters." She looked up from my card and eyed me skeptically. "Doesn't say anything about a private investigator."

"I just want to talk to the Greek. Is he in?"

"There's no 'the Greek' here," she said.

I double-checked the paper Skip Suggs had given me. I had the right address, the woman said, but she insisted she'd never heard of anyone by that name. Then a man came to the door. He was decked out like he belonged in Las Vegas, too—or what wise guys on the Strip *think* they're supposed to dress like: slicked-back hair, pinky rings, sharkskin suit, and sockless Italian loafers.

"What's going on, Phoebe?"

"This gentleman here says he's looking for somebody named *the Greek*," the woman said.

"Skip Suggs told me to drop by," I said.

"I don't know any Skip Suggs."

"Skip Suggs. He runs the museum out at the airport."

"I just told you. I never heard of him," Mr. Vegas said. "Never heard of no Greek, either."

"My name is—"

"Yeah, I know who you are," he said. "You're that guy who's been running all over town making trouble for law-abiding people that don't need trouble."

A sawed-off shotgun was propped against a wall inside the entryway behind him. "What's with the street sweeper," I said, "if you don't mind me asking?"

"We've had a few break-ins around here," he said. "Dopers, mostly, looking for drugs."

"Dopers looking for . . . *formaldehyde*?"

Mr. Vegas narrowed his eyes. "Is there something I can help you with, pal? Perhaps a prepaid funeral plan. Pay up front, you get ten percent off our best package price. We even throw in the roses. Your choice of colors."

"Sounds tempting," I said, "but I'm afraid I'm not planning on dying anytime soon."

"No one ever does." He pushed his sports coat back and planted his hand on his hip, making sure I saw the pistol holstered on his belt. Chrome finish. Mother-of-pearl grips. A pimp gun if there ever was one.

"Sorry to have wasted your time," I said.

"No problem. Have a wonderful day, Mr. Logan."

Phoebe looked like she wanted to tell me something, but a sidelong glance from Mr. Vegas stopped her short. I headed back to the car.

The guy knew who I was. He knew what I was looking for. But how? Why had Skip Suggs sent me to a funeral parlor and told me to *look for the Greek*? Why would he have warned me to go armed, which I was? Walking past the two headstones flanking the walkway, I glanced down at the one on my right. The epitaph read: Lorraine McCall, *Cherished mother and grandmother*. Then I read the engraving on the headstone to my left:

DEMETRIUS TOMOLONIS

1973–

SHINE WHILE YOU LIVE.

BLAZE BEYOND GRIEF

FOR LIFE IS BRIEF

AND TIME, A THIEF

Look for the Greek, Skip had advised me.

"Well, Skip," I said to myself, "looks like I found him."

I drove on. When I looked in the rearview, I could see Mr. Vegas standing outside the funeral home, watching me through binoculars.

Three blocks to the west of the funeral home was a Chevron mini-mart. I pulled in and parked next to a metallic bronze Volvo station wagon with a crucifix hanging prominently from the rearview mirror. Then I got out my phone and Googled Demetrius Tomolonis. The search produced news articles that portrayed a man whose life was no less mysterious than his death.

Tomolonis—known to his American friends as "the Greek"—had emigrated from Athens as a teenager. Described as rotund and jovial, with a weakness for attractive women and the black mulberry liquor called *mournoraki*, he'd worked his way up from washing dishes at a restaurant in Englewood Cliffs, New Jersey, to managing a used car lot in New Orleans, to working as a low-level line mechanic for Honeywell Aerospace in Phoenix. Along the way, he'd gained US citizenship, learned to fly, collected a wife and three kids, and earned a bachelor's degree in mechanical engineering online from Arizona State. By 2015, he had relocated again, this time to Santa Isabella. There, according to an investigation published by *The Los Angeles Times*, Tomolonis bought a small, financially struggling avionics repair shop located near the airport with the grandiose name of Universal Sky Support. The shop was soon flush with Department of Defense–issued contracts to refurbish what a government spokesman would only describe as "navigational components for tactical military aircraft."

Within a year, Universal Sky Support had inexplicably expanded to a one-hundred-eighty-four-thousand-square-foot warehouse in the same industrial complex where Electrogenics was located. Tomolonis, meanwhile, acquired a handful of other local businesses, bought himself a twin-engine Beechcraft turboprop, and moved his family into a six-thousand-square-foot Santa Isabella mansion with a wine cellar and an infinity pool. He and his wife drove matching Jaguars. Soon, he began flying away on extended business trips, sometimes for weeks. His wife suspected he was having an affair. The FBI suspected something else.

Federal prosecutors in Washington announced they had opened an investigation of several government contractors who'd allegedly peddled sensitive trade secrets to an unnamed foreign government. Universal Sky Support was rumored to be among them. Tomolonis was issued a subpoena to appear before a federal grand jury. He denied any wrongdoing. He told his wife a few days later he was going flying to clear his head.

After making a left downwind departure from Santa Isabella, air traffic controllers tracked his plane headed west until it disappeared off radar somewhere out over the Pacific. Authorities ruled it a suicide.

An unnamed Justice Department source told the *Times* that Tomolonis had negotiated a deal—a reduced sentence in exchange for his testimony against other unnamed conspirators implicated in the case. "We have reason to believe," the Justice source was quoted as saying, "that one or more of those individuals may have threatened the welfare of Mr. Tomolonis's family if he testified, and that he killed himself to protect them."

Skip Suggs had to have known all of that when he sent me off to find "the Greek." I needed to circle back to him and find out what else he knew. Plus, I owed him money.

"Mr. Logan, I thought that was you."

I glanced up from my phone into the pudgy, smiling face of Cyrus Simpson, the clergyman who'd presided over Chocks's memorial service. He was holding a thirty-two-ounce bottle of Pepsi in one hand and a large bag of Doritos in the other.

"What're you doing out this way?" he asked pleasantly.

"Catching up on my reading." I nodded toward the Doritos. "Those things'll kill you."

The pastor grinned. "Junk food. My number one vice. Hey, I'm so glad I ran into you. I'm still interested in taking flying lessons, though I do have to be honest, I'm a little afraid of heights."

"No one's twisting your arm, Pastor. Flying a small plane isn't for everybody."

"This is true. But we must learn to overcome our fears, Mr. Logan. It's the only way we can grow as the good Lord intended all of his children to grow."

He said he was planning a trip the following week to the Del Mar Fairgrounds near San Diego, to watch the Thoroughbreds run and to spend quality time with some good friends who were horse trainers. Playing the ponies, he admitted with a sheepish smile, was his number two vice.

"Maybe I can stop in Rancho Bonita on my way down to Del Mar and take you up on your very gracious offer of an introductory flight?"

"You bet," I said. "Just let me know when works best for you. I gather you work Sundays, so they're out, right?"

Again, he smiled. "Spreading the joy of the gospel is hardly work, Mr. Logan."

We arranged to meet that Saturday morning at eleven o'clock in Rancho Bonita outside Larry Kropf's hangar. Then Pastor Cyrus offered me a Dorito. I hadn't had one in years. It was as addictive as I remembered. There was an ATM inside the mini-mart. I withdrew sixty bucks, leaving less than ten in my checking account, and bought my own bag. Then I went to pay back Skip Suggs what I owed him.

As I approached the airport, I could see the flashing red lights of emergency vehicles clustered on the north end of the field. Drawing closer, I counted an ambulance, an airport police SUV, and two lime-green fire trucks. They were congregated around the Quonset hut that housed the airport's museum.

I pulled into the parking lot and got out as two paramedics wheeled an obviously dead person out of the building. A white sheet covered the body down to its ankles. I recognized Skip Suggs's beat-up suede moccasins.

"What happened?" I asked one of the paramedics as she opened the ambulance's rear doors.

"Are you a relative?"

"A friend."

"Heart attack," she said. "The gentleman expired by the time we got here."

"How do you know it was a heart attack?"

"He called 911 and said he was having one. He said it wasn't his first. Also because he was pushing ninety. So, yeah, we're pretty sure."

I stood aside as the ambulance backed up and drove away. Had I gotten to know Skip Suggs better, I might've grieved his loss. I might've honored the passing of a fellow pilot by quoting the Buddha about life's capriciousness and the inevitability of death. But at that moment, the only thing I felt was frustration. An old man was dead, taking to his grave a tantalizing lead that might've gotten me one step closer to finding Chocks's killer.

Another dead end.

The paramedics had left the museum door unlocked. I walked in and left twenty dollars on the five-hundred-pound bomb to cover my admission and the little airplane pin I'd bought. After that, I dropped off Little Red Riding Hood at BillionAir, fired up the *Duck*, and flew home to Rancho Bonita. I needed time to regroup. I needed some sleep. First, though, I needed to reach out to Layne. My fingers were crossed that in my absence, she'd tapped her sources in the intelligence community and worked up some new investigative angle for me to pursue. But that wasn't to be, either.

"It's not looking good, Logan. I've hit up everybody I can think of. Nobody seems to know much of anything—or, if they do, they're not talking."

"I appreciate you trying, Layne. That's all anybody could ask for."

We were standing on the tiny terrace outside of her new condo, watching the sun setting over the ocean. The clouds blazed with backlit shades of yellow and orange. The sky looked like a celestial bruise. Layne offered to make me dinner. I told her I wasn't hungry.

"I bought you a present," I said.

"You bought me a present?"

"From Santa Isabella. The little airport museum. I thought you might like it. It's no big deal."

I pulled the Cessna pin from the front pocket of my jeans and handed it to her. I would've put it in a little box and gift-wrapped it if I'd had a box or wrapping paper, or if I was any good at that kind of stuff, which I never was.

"It's beautiful," Layne said. "Thank you, Logan. I'll treasure it always."

I couldn't tell whether she meant it or not. Reading women has never been my strong suit. What I did know with certainty was that it felt like something inextricable had shifted in our relationship, like the way the sun feels on your back on that one afternoon when you realize summer is over and autumn has arrived.

Layne leaned on the railing, gazing out at the waves. "Maybe we should just go to bed," she said.

Physical attraction is physical attraction. Sometimes it can be undeniable, even in relationships going down the tubes.

"Sounds like friends with benefits," I said.

Layne didn't respond. I followed her into the bedroom.

We were tangled in each other's arms, both asleep, when my phone rang shortly after two A.M.

"Sorry to be calling so late," the voice on the other end said. "It's Phoebe."

"... *Who?*"

"Phoebe. We met yesterday at the mortuary in Santa Isabella."

It took me a few seconds to clear the cobwebs from my brain. Phoebe. The tall blonde in the white pantsuit. "No worries. What can I do for you, Phoebe?"

"I wanted to warn you. Before it's too late."

Layne turned on the lamp on her nightstand, rubbing her eyes. I put the phone on speaker so she could listen in.

"Must be pretty important, you calling me this late."

"I couldn't sleep, knowing that . . ." Her words trailed off.

"Knowing what, Phoebe?"

She muffled a sob over the phone as she struggled to compose herself. Then she said, "You really have no idea what you've gotten yourself into, do you?"

As it turned out, I didn't.

NINETEEN

Phoebe's boss at the mortuary, the Vegas-looking tough guy in the sharkskin suit, was named Johnny Baylor who, she said, was also her physically and psychologically abusive fiancé. Convicted in Oregon on more than a hundred counts of forging OxyContin prescriptions, he'd the good fortune to serve out his sentence in a low security prison where the warden still believed in rehabilitating inmates, not warehousing them. Baylor had been allowed to learn embalming under close supervision at a funeral home in Grants Pass before returning to his cell each night. Five years after being paroled, he was operating his own funeral home in Santa Isabella and, according to Phoebe, laundering money for a Mexican drug cartel.

"By any chance, that wouldn't be the Pascua cartel, would it?" Layne asked her.

The three of us were sitting in a McDonald's in downtown Rancho Bonita. Phoebe stared at her coffee for several seconds, cupping it with two hands, straw-colored hair uncombed, eyes downcast and bloodshot. "Some things I can tell you," she said, "some things I can't. He'd kill me."

Dawn was still two hours away. I thanked her again for making the long drive to meet with us. I reassured her that whatever she shared with us was in confidence. I'm not sure she heard me.

"If Johnny knew I was here," she said, "they'd never find my body."

"What can you tell us about the Greek," Layne asked gently.

Phoebe sipped her coffee. She said she'd learned by overhearing snippets of Johnny Baylor's phone conversations that the Greek, Demetrius Tomolonis, had sold the mortuary "and a bunch of other businesses" under pressure to Baylor and a confederation of investors, including the Mexican drug dealer whom she refused to identify by name. Another investor, she said, was from Russia. She didn't know his name, only that he owned a small restaurant in Rancho Bonita called Red Square West and claimed to be friends with Russian President Vladimir Putin.

Layne narrowed her eyes. "Putin has no friends."

"I'm just telling you what I heard," Phoebe said.

I asked her about the marble headstone with Tomolonis's name carved on it. "An odd location for a grave marker," I said. "Most people get planted in the cemetery, not outside a funeral home."

Phoebe said it was her understanding that Tomolonis had the headstone engraved and put on display for use as a tax write-off.

"He figured he'd need it someday anyway," Phoebe said, "so why not take advantage of it now, you know? After he sold out, Johnny said let's just leave it. Those things are a bitch to move, you know?"

"He must still be alive, the Greek," I said. "The headstone shows he was born in 1973, but there's no year of death."

"He's still around to my knowledge," Phoebe said, "but I couldn't tell you where for sure."

I leaned closer to her, across the table. "Phoebe, you said when you called me that I didn't know what I was getting into. What did you mean by that?"

She took a deep breath, as if to gather her courage, and let it out slowly. "I was in the office yesterday. Johnny, he—"

A stocky dude in black motorcycle leather strode past our table carrying a tray of eggs and hash browns. Phoebe waited, watching him nervously, until he found a seat on the far side of the dining area.

"Johnny was what, Phoebe?" I asked.

"He got on the phone, all pissed off, after you left yesterday—I mean, like, 'That guy Logan needs to die' kind of pissed. You wanna give Johnny his space when he gets into one of his moods like that. Anyway, I couldn't make out everything he was saying or who he was talking to, but what I did pick up was . . . Remember how I told you how I heard Tomolonis sold him some other businesses?"

I nodded.

"Yeah, well, what I heard," Phoebe said, "was that Johnny and this Russian guy with the restaurant, they're in on some company that's selling some kinda secret stuff to Europe or Asia, somewhere like that. They're worried you're gonna screw it up for them by running around asking too many questions."

"What kind of stuff?" Layne asked before I could.

Phoebe shrugged again. "Like I said, I only caught part of the conversation."

I asked her if she'd heard of Electrogenics, or Ed Millisohn, or Chocks. She shook her head no. She said she'd left Santa Isabella with little more than the clothes she was wearing. She wasn't going back.

"Johnny can be a real sweetheart. He's got a lot of good qualities," she said as her eyes filled with tears, "but playing by the rules isn't one of them. It's taken me a long time to realize that. I'm leaving him. This time for good."

"Where will you go?" Layne asked.

"I'll figure that out when I get there," Phoebe said. Then she looked over at me. "You might want to think about doing that, too, if you know what's good for you."

"Knowing what's good for me has always been my problem," I said.

———

We went back to Layne's condo as twilight gave way to dawn. She took a shower while I opened her laptop and Googled "Red Square West, Ventura."

On its website, the restaurant billed itself as the best eatery between Los Angeles and San Francisco serving authentic Russian food. As far as I could determine, it might've been the *only* restaurant between those two cities offering such fare, which didn't surprise me. After all, how much demand can there really be for borscht outside of Mother Russia? I'd spent enough time operating covertly in Russian-controlled territory to know I was no fan of Slavic cuisine. The thought of liver dumplings and potatoes fried in lard made my stomach churn.

"I'd just as soon go hungry," I heard Layne say.

I turned. She was standing behind me, naked, toweling dry, looking over my shoulder at Red Square West's menu on the computer. Her eyes shone like emeralds in the new morning sun that came filtering through the blinds. Her skin was porcelain. Too much is made of a woman's looks, but it's no exaggeration to say that in that moment, Layne made my blood pulse a little faster.

"Well," I said, "at least we can agree on that."

"I got you something," she said, wrapping the towel around her.

"You got me something?"

"A gift. To reciprocate."

"Is it an airplane pin?"

"Something even better," Layne said. "Do you know who Nikolay Andreev is?"

"Doesn't he play for the Maple Leafs?"

"He owns Red Square West."

"Never heard of him."

"Rancho Bonita is a small town, Logan. I thought you knew everybody."

"Obviously, I don't get out enough."

She disappeared into the bedroom, which doubled as her home office, and returned in a flowered silk robe, carrying a sheet of paper. "This landed in my in-box while I was in the shower. One of my old colleagues at Langley came through."

Printed across the top of the page in boldface were the letters *DORDSUBGRU*, followed by "Priority YELLOW."

"Directorate of Operations, Russia Desk, Sub-group GRU," I said. "Subject deemed of potential midlevel intelligence value."

"Read on," Layne said.

What followed was a three-paragraph summation taken straight from CIA files detailing restaurateur and naturalized American citizen Nikolay Andreev's suspected ties to Russian intelligence. He was believed to have spent more than a decade working undercover in the United States as a recruiter of covert assets for the GRU—the Russian Federation's version of the CIA. Andreev, however, was so good at his job that government investigators could never make a case against him stick.

"So," Layne said, "what do you feel like for lunch?"

"Anything but borscht."

The shadow of a smile crossed her face. "Borscht it is."

Before it was Red Square West, it had been West of Albuquerque, a Tex-Mex restaurant that would've been criminally prosecuted had there been a law on the books against serving felony awful burritos. Before that, it had been a high-end furniture boutique. The sign over the entrance incorporated images of the Kremlin's iconic multicolored spires and an old hammer-and-sickle Soviet flag, along with a slogan: "Just Like Mama Used to Make."

"Not *my* mama," Layne said.

The older gentleman who greeted us at the door had a Cro-Magnon brow and dyed black hair combed to one side. His lumpy pin-striped suit and floral tie were long out of fashion. He looked like an escapee from a gangster movie.

"Anywhere you like," he said in a Slavic accent as thick as, well, borscht.

We were the first customers of the day.

Red walls. Red ceiling. Even the floor was red. I followed Layne to a red table with a street view. We sat. A dour-looking young woman promptly delivered glasses of water and a plastic basket of white bread, sliced thin. She was dressed in a plain white blouse and black skirt and could've been the greeter's granddaughter, given the similarities of their faces.

Our door greeter handed us menus. They were, of course, printed in red.

"First, please permit me to explain the specials of the day," he said. "We have the *varenyky*, also known as pierogi. Dumplings made with fancy fillings such as potatoes and the fried onions. Delicious. You will love it. Also, the cabbage and liver. Also delicious. You will love it."

"Those are Ukrainian recipes," I said, "not Russian."

He stared at me like I'd just caught him stealing from the collection plate at church. "You are correct. Of course, they are Ukrainian. Everyone knows Russian food is crap—well, *most* Russian food. You have been to Russia?"

"Once or twice."

"On holiday?"

"More on business, I'd say . . . Mr. Andreev."

The smile melted from his face as it dawned on him Layne and I weren't there for the cabbage and liver.

"Who are you? From the health department? I do nothing wrong! I pass last inspection no problem. Flying colors. My kitchen is clean as whistle. I am loyal American citizen. I do not appreciate this harassment!"

"Relax, Mr. Andreev," Layne said, "We're not from the health department."

"We're looking into a murder," I said.

"You are FBI?"

"Not FBI, either. I'd say more like concerned citizens."

His eyes seemed to soften. He looked at me as if everything had suddenly become clear.

"You want to know about Peter Hostetler, yes?"

A Russian émigré with purported ties to Moscow's premier intelligence service was admitting without prodding that he knew about my murdered former wingman. I purposely avoided looking over at Layne. I knew that if I did, both of our jaws might hit the floor.

"How did you know Hostetler?" I asked as casually as my elevated pulse would allow.

He was a regular customer, Andreev said. He'd come in

every few weeks and always order the same thing: fried meat known as *sichenyky*.

"Mix with egg. An inconsequential percentage of onion. A dash of garlic. Roll in breadcrumbs. Is delicious."

"Let me guess," I said. "He *loved* it."

Andreev smiled, but there was no warmth behind it. "Is it the menu, my friend, or me you find distasteful?"

What I didn't care for was his smile. It was a distinctly Russian smile. I'd erased a similar one once from the face of an arrogant Kremlin colonel who'd been responsible for paying cash bounties to Taliban fighters who killed American service members stationed in Afghanistan. In appreciation of his highly successful efforts, his commanders had rewarded the colonel with a two-week vacation at a resort spa in Sevastopol, complete with hot-and-cold running hookers. I shot him dead in his hot tub overlooking the Black Sea.

"Mr. Hostetler and I were friends," I told Andreev. "I want to know who killed him and why."

"All I know is what I see on the news," he said. "A tragedy what happen to this man. Terrible."

"When did you start working for the GRU?"

The blood drained from Andreev's cheeks. "*What*? The GRU? You are crazy."

"Mr. Andreev," Layne said, shooting me a disapproving glance for needlessly escalating the situation, "do you happen to recall the last time you saw Mr. Hostetler?"

Andreev kept glaring at me. "Not for many weeks. Therefore, when I see the television, I think, oh my God, I *know* this man. He is good customer. Always leave big tip."

"Who killed him?" I asked.

"You are asking *me*? I know nothing. I own restaurant. This is all. I am loyal American citizen."

"Yeah, I believe you already mentioned that." I peered under the table. "Gee, I hope those aren't rat droppings down there because I sure would hate to call the health department and have this place closed down this afternoon."

"There are no rats! You are threatening me. For no reason."

I could feel Layne's eyes boring into me. "Maybe my partner should go out and feed the parking meter . . . *now*."

I walked out before I could cause any further damage. My anger was irrational. Hardly Zen. I'll admit that. Part of the reason, I suppose, was frustration, my inability to connect the dots linking Chocks's murder, Electrogenics, and those classified radar components. Part of it was the memory Andreev's smug smile evoked of that Black Sea op. We lost two guys that night getting to that Russian colonel. But part of it also was learning that Chocks Hostetler had been a regular visitor to my city for years and that we'd never once crossed paths. I wondered how many other friends I'd similarly let drift away as time plodded inexorably forward.

Layne emerged from the restaurant with her jaw set tight and her eyes smoldering.

"What was *that* all about in there?"

"That was me losing my cool a bit."

"A *bit*? Do you really think you can just bully your way through life, Logan, intimidating people, bending them to your will by sheer brute force? It doesn't work that way anymore. You're like a swamp creature from the Mesozoic era. Times have changed. You either change with them, or I guarantee you, you *will* go extinct."

"I'm sorry, Layne. It won't happen again."

"Please stop saying that, Logan. You know that's not true. It *will* happen again."

Pedestrians on their way to lunch or shopping bypassed

us like we were radioactive. Layne stared down at the sidewalk with her hands on her hips, shaking her head. I offered to give her a ride home, but she turned me down. The walk, she said, would do her good, as would some extended time apart—a "cooling off period," as she put it. There was no use trying to persuade her otherwise. Layne Sterling was her own woman. I had to respect her for that.

"A little advice before I go," she said. "You definitely can catch more flies with honey than vinegar."

"So I've heard."

She told me that after I stomped out of the restaurant, Nikolay Andreev calmed down and passed along a worthwhile tip without any arm-twisting:

Andreev had a regular customer who lived in Santa Isabella County, who frequently stopped off in Rancho Bonita to have dinner at Red Square West whenever he was on his way to or from Los Angeles on business. The customer loved *sichenyky* like nobody Andreev had ever seen. He was married to a Russian beauty queen he'd met online, whose father worked for the old KGB. The man's family hailed from Russia. He was fluent in Russian and Ukrainian and never without a pistol under his jacket. If anybody had ties in California to Russian intelligence, Andreev said, it was that guy.

His name, Layne said, was Thomas Kasparov.

"Small world," I said. "I know a Thomas Kasparov. He's the lead sheriff's detective on Chocks's case."

Layne didn't say anything. She was already walking home.

TWENTY

When I confronted him about his alleged ties to Russian intelligence, Detective Thomas Kasparov laughed. "That," he said a tad too adamantly, "is the biggest bunch of bull I've ever heard in my entire life."

Yes, his father's side of the family hailed from Russia, but they'd emigrated to the US generations ago. Yes, he once spoke Russian, thanks to the sixty-four weeks he spent at the Defense Language Institute in Monterey before the Marine Corps assigned him guard duty at the US embassy in Moscow, but he'd forgotten most of it. And, yes, he was married to a former Russian beauty queen he met online, but her father worked in Volgograd at a tire factory, not for the KGB. The only thing wholly factual that Nikolay Andreev had said about him was that Detective Kasparov did, in fact, love *sichenyky*.

"There's no Russian restaurants within fifty miles of Santa Isabella," he said. "My wife used to make me drive her down to Rancho Bonita whenever she got to jonesing for some borscht. Personally, I can't stand the stuff."

"You and me both," I said.

We were parked down the street from Chocks's house, surveilling it. Kasparov had invited me along. He'd reclined his seat back and was slouched behind the wheel of his unmarked Crown Vic, wearing his aviator shades.

"I can tell you this much," he said. "Her brother didn't kill him."

"Marvin, the pistol-packing jeweler, you mean?"

"Marvin, the respected local merchant, I mean," Kasparov said. "His alibi's solid, Logan. He was at a trade show in Denver the night your buddy Hostetler dropped in unannounced on Mr. and Mrs. Rizzo's mobile home. As far as I'm concerned, your whole Russian theory's a loser, too. The whole thing's preposterous."

"Then, who killed him?"

"My bet's on the poor suffering widow. Why do you think I'm sitting out here, sweating my balls off?"

"To see if she shows up driving a new Ferrari."

"Insurance money makes people do crazy-ass stuff," Kasparov said.

"How do you know it wasn't the cartels, or Ed Millisohn at Electrogenics?"

"Maybe it was them. Maybe it wasn't. Hell, I dunno." Kasparov took off his sunglasses and rubbed his eyes. "You want something to drink?"

"I'm good, thanks."

"Whatever you say."

He pulled out a pint bottle of Jack Daniel's from under his seat and took a hit. We sat in silence, watching the house, waiting to see who came and went, but no one did. Another slug of whiskey was followed by more silence. Then, without prompting, he started telling me all about how his immigrant wife had left him. She'd run off with a roofer and called from Reno to say she wanted a quickie divorce. The only thing Kasparov was good for, he realized in hindsight, was a green card. He'd sensed from the get-go she was using him, but his heart overrode his cop instincts.

"I mean, anybody would've fallen for this piece of tail, am I right?"

He showed me her photo on his phone—Miss Chelyabinsk in high heels and a bikini. She had marble-blue eyes and a goddess's curves. She was also easily twenty years younger than he was.

"Pretty," was all I could think to say in the moment.

The only thing that was getting him out of bed in the morning in the weeks since she'd dumped him, Kasparov said, was his faith in Jesus Christ.

"To each his own," I said.

He asked me if I was born again. I said I was more interested in Buddhism, but that I was a work in progress.

"Why Buddhism?"

"It helps keep a lid on my less gentle impulses. Most of the time, anyway."

"To each his own," Kasparov said, toasting me.

"If you *were* a Russian operative," I said, "your job would be perfect cover, and this would be a great location."

"Oh, yeah?" He looked over at me. "How so?"

"Sleeper cell. You operate under color of civil authority. Vandenberg is just down the road, home to military missile development and sensitive civilian space programs."

"Yeah, well, I don't know anything about missiles, and I'm no spy, OK?"

No spy ever admits he's one. Kasparov was an ex-marine with Russian roots. He'd studied Russian. He'd married a Russian. He'd served in Russia where he'd undoubtedly encountered any number of GRU recruiters bearing briefcases of untraceable American greenbacks. Then there was his taste in pricey jewelry. He wore a lot of it. Jewelry requires disposable income. Most cops working for semirural sheriff's departments have little to spare.

I had my doubts about him.

On the other hand, I knew what a traitor looked like, what they *smelled* like. I'd helped rid the world of a few of them back when I worked for Uncle Sugar, including a civilian defense contractor who sold top-secret blueprints of a stealthy new submarine to China for $5 million. He promptly bought himself a mansion in the Hamptons where, weeks later, he "accidentally" drowned in his swimming pool. Detective Tom Kasparov struck me as nothing like that guy. Still, I had my doubts about him.

"Fair warning," I said. "If I find out you were involved in any way with what happened to my friend, you're gonna wish we never met."

"Threatening a peace officer is a felony, Logan."

"Not a threat, Detective. A promise."

I could see the muscles in his jaw twitching. "I'm gonna tell you for the last time. I had nothing to do with it. You keep pushing it, and *you're* the one who's gonna wish we never met."

"I go where the facts lead me."

"Get out of my car," Kasparov said. "Now."

―――

A wise person once observed that the gods don't deduct from a pilot's lifespan the hours he or she spends flying. You are no mere mortal in those moments. You are untethered, above it all, flirting with the heavens in intimate ways only a pilot can ever know. That sense of privilege is especially profound when the sky is not out to kill you. On days like that, when the ceiling and visibility are unlimited, when the air is cloudless and silken and your ship is tracking trimmed and true, it's easy for a pilot to feel like a god themselves. This was my reality that afternoon returning VFR to Rancho Bonita.

For the first time in days, I wasn't trying to figure out who killed Chocks or what their motives were. I wasn't thinking about Layne and the rocky prospects of our relationship continuing. I was simply *flying*, reveling in my competence at keeping an aging, single-engine Cessna straight and level high above the earth. Below me, waves unfurled on white sand beaches from an ocean the color of cornflowers. I could see all the way south to Point Conception, where the West Coast curved east. Far to my left, the mountains of the central Sierra Nevada jutted up through a thin haze, their peaks dappled with snow. I was relishing the view when air traffic control intruded upon my reverie.

"Cessna Four Charlie Lima, traffic, three miles, eleven o'clock, same altitude, northeast bound. I'm not talking to him. If not in sight, suggest a twenty-degree turn to the right."

It's a big sky. Other small aircraft can be deceptively difficult to spot from the air, especially at the same altitude. But not this time. A metallic glint caught my eye. Immediately, I observed the speck of a helicopter, no larger than a mosquito given its distance, crossing left to right a couple of miles ahead of me.

"Nor-Cal, Cessna Four Charlie Lima has the traffic in sight. A helicopter. No factor."

"Four Charlie Lima, roger; thank you."

We converged swiftly, at right angles. The speck grew from the size of an insect to that of a dinner roll as it streaked past and disappeared under the *Duck*'s right wing—but not before I got a good, clear look at it:

A silver MD 500—the same make, model, and color of helicopter Charlotte Gibbs said she looked up at from her owl-watching duties that night and saw Chocks fall to his death.

My mind started working overtime. Was this *the* helicopter? Was whoever flying it responsible for the murder of my former wingman? If it was, I was going to make him pay.

The helicopter appeared to be navigating in the direction of the little airport at Oceano, on the coast south of San Luis Obispo. I banked the *Duck* steeply and gave chase.

The runway at Oceano was two-thousand-three-hundred-feet long and extremely narrow, bordered on one side by a line of corrugated aluminum hangars, all within walking distance of a state recreational area where off-roading enthusiasts camped and drove around on sand dunes. It was a near-newsworthy event when any out-of-town aircraft landed there, let alone a sleek, million-dollar MD 500. As I turned base-to-final, I could see a crowd of about a dozen people gathered behind a chain-link fence at the edge of the tarmac, watching the helicopter softly touch down. I purposely landed long to cut down my taxiing time. By the time I parked, shut down the engine, and jumped out, the number of spectators behind the fence had more than doubled to include what looked to be professional photographers and a local television news crew. Then, from out of the helicopter, behind a ragged beard and cool-guy sunglasses, stepped a famous movie star whose initials were Brad Pitt. The crowd cheered as he walked over to the fence line to sign autographs.

My first thought was that he was taller in real life than he looked on film. My second thought was that I had just chased a wild goose. The helicopter's pilot was a prematurely balding kid in camouflage fatigue pants and a Led Zeppelin T-shirt.

"Good-looking whirlybird," I told him. "I'll trade you straight across."

He surveyed the *Duck* with a bemused expression. "I'll have to think about it."

His name was Gary. He flew for a charter service based out of Camarillo, where he'd picked up his famous passenger. Pitt was producing a documentary on the plight of a species of rare shorebirds that nested among Oceano's sand dunes. Their native habitat was being destroyed by the four-wheel drivers who regarded the dunes as their own personal playground. The actor wanted to see firsthand the damage being done.

Gary nodded toward him. "He's a super good guy. Not full of himself or anything."

"Must be nice," I said, "having enough dough to make a difference in this world."

I leaned in and looked around inside the helicopter. Other than a few obvious avionic upgrades, it appeared hardly different from the Little Birds I used to ride in.

"How long you been flying this bad boy, Gary?"

"This particular aircraft? First time. It's been down three months for maintenance. Just got out of the shop a couple days ago."

I asked him if his charter service owned any other MD 500s. No, Gary said, every other helicopter in the fleet was a JetRanger.

"You wouldn't happen to know anybody else in the area flying MD 500s, would you, Gary?"

He said he didn't.

I rubbed the frustration from my neck and turned to watch the TV reporter stick a microphone under Pitt's nose. Her smile was that of a starstruck schoolgirl. I toyed with the notion of sticking around for a few minutes and maybe snagging an autograph for Mrs. Schmulowitz, but then Larry called.

The FBI, he said, had just raided my office in his hangar.

TWENTY-ONE

When the headquarters of your international flight school is only slightly more spacious than a walk-in meat locker, furnished with nothing more than an old metal desk, a three-drawer government surplus filing cabinet, and a couple of green plastic lawn chairs, a raid by federal authorities doesn't take long. Larry said a single agent showed up unannounced and was gone within fifteen minutes. The place looked like a Kansas tornado had hit it. Papers were strewn everywhere.

Larry surveyed the damage. "He was looking for memory modules."

I looked over at him. "Memory modules?"

"Scandisks. For those advanced radar components you were asking me questions about. The secret sauce is the modules. Control them, you control the whole radar apparatus."

"How did you know that's what he was looking for?"

"He told me he was."

"Did he show you a search warrant?"

"He was wearing one of those raid jackets with 'FBI' on the

back, and he was carrying a gun. What did you want me to do, Logan? Play Perry Mason?"

"Did he show you his ID?"

"I didn't ask for any."

"FBI agents show ID, Larry. It's standard operating procedure." I started picking up papers off the floor. Larry stood there, watching. "What kind of vehicle was he driving?"

"Didn't see one."

"What did he look like? You could at least tell me that."

"I dunno, he looked like an FBI agent. Khakis, clean-cut, button-down shirt, raid jacket. What did you want me to do, Logan? Check out his Tinder profile?"

"You didn't find it suspicious he was by himself?"

"Why would I find that suspicious?"

"FBI agents typically work in pairs, Larry. They have partners. You've never watched a cop show?"

Larry pulled on his beard the way he always did when he started getting even more agitated than his usual default state. "Why am I getting the third degree? The guy said he was from the FBI. He looked the part. I took him at his word. Believe whatever the hell you want or don't. Doesn't make no never mind to me."

He asked me if I'd given any more thought to taking over for him, running Mrs. Schmulowitz's campaign for city council.

"The short answer," I said, "is no."

"Well, I quit. I'm out. I should've never volunteered to begin with. She's your landlady, Logan, which means it's your problem finding a replacement, not mine."

I exhaled and told him I would talk to her. As if I didn't have anything better to do.

Whoever the guy was who claimed to be from the FBI, at least he didn't trash my apartment. Nothing seemed amiss after I got home that night—a relief given how long it took for me to put everything back together after those three goons from the CIA had turned the place upside down. Kiddiot was perched on the sofa, eyes half hooded, and greeted me with his usual indifference as I walked in. Or was it mild disdain? He'd never been one to wear his emotions on his striped, orange sleeve, unlike Ack-Ack who practically bounced off the walls with happiness on my arrival.

Only there was no Ack-Ack.

"Hey, Ack-Ack, where are you, buddy? C'mon, here, boy."

"He's gone."

I turned to find Mrs. Schmulowitz standing outside my screen door. Even through the mesh, in the dark, I could see tears glinting in her eyes.

"I went to take the trash out," she said, "and he bolted out the back gate like a bullet. I'm yelling, 'Get back here, Snoopy!' but he just kept running. It was just like *The Great Escape*, only if Steve McQueen had been a dog. I've been all over the neighborhood. Twice. I can't find him. I'm sorry, bubby. You got girl troubles. You got work troubles. This is the last thing you need right now."

"These things happen. He's a smart dog. He loves your brisket. He'll be back." I gave her a hug, but Mrs. Schmulowitz would not be consoled.

"How can I be a responsible member of city council when I can't even be a responsible dog-sitter?"

"Don't worry, Mrs. Schmulowitz. It'll be OK."

I got in my truck and went looking for him. Down side streets. Up alleys. Through downtown, the rose garden of the Old Mission, and along the beach. Three hours canvassing the city for one AWOL beagle, and no Ack-Ack.

I called what was once known as the "dogcatcher" before it became Rancho Bonita Animal Control Services, but the recording indicated they were closed for the night. Then I called Layne to let her know the dog was running around and to keep an eye out for him, but there was no answer on her phone. I left a message and drove home, feeling about as low as I'd felt in a long time.

The best psychologist, it's been said, has a fur coat, four legs, and a wet nose. Kiddiot didn't qualify. Much as I normally appreciated his presence, he was a better doorstop than a therapist. I missed that hound.

Mrs. Schmulowitz cooked a brisket for dinner. We ate at her kitchen table. There was applesauce and potato pancakes. For dessert she'd baked a honey cake even though it wasn't Rosh Hashanah.

"Delicious as always, Mrs. Schmulowitz."

"You're too sweet, bubby, but we both know I overcooked the meat and didn't put in enough garlic. Julia Child said the secret ingredient to any meal is love, but she really meant garlic."

I forced a smile, picking at my food.

"You're not eating, bubby."

"I'm sorry, Mrs. Schmulowitz. I'm just not hungry."

She knew I was worried about the dog, and that things weren't going well with my "lady friend." And, while I hadn't shared much with her about Chocks's death, she also sensed my frustration at not making more progress in finding his killer.

"Look, bubby, if it takes any pressure off you, you can forget about taking over for that *meshuggener* Larry as my campaign manager, OK? His heart was never in it to begin with. In fact, you can forget about the campaign, period. I'm dropping out of the race."

A new opinion poll conducted by Rancho Bonita's

fish-wrapper of a local newspaper found her fading in the polls. "As my second husband put it, I'm an acquired taste—may he rest in peace." Mrs. Schmulowitz insisted she didn't take it personally.

"You need to aim higher, Mrs. S.," I said. "Run for president. I'd definitely vote for you."

She took my hand and kissed it.

We were doing the dishes after dinner. Mrs. Schmulowitz was washing; I was drying. She was telling me all about how she once beat Olympic champion Wilma Rudolph in an exhibition two-hundred-meter foot race for charity at Madison Square Garden when I heard a faint scratching sound at the back door. My hand went instinctively to the revolver still tucked under my shirt as my thoughts immediately went to my office in Larry's hangar and the supposed FBI agent who'd ransacked it earlier that afternoon. I wondered if I'd forgotten to lock the back gate.

Mrs. Schmulowitz seemed not to have heard anything. "Next thing you know, she's sobbing. She can't believe it. I'm telling her, 'Wilma, calm down, you lost a race to a nice Jewish girl from Bensonhurst. It's not the end of the world.'"

I walked to the door and opened it, ready to draw.

There sat Ack-Ack, tail wagging.

"Well, look who's back."

Mrs. Schmulowitz's face lit up—"The prodigal son has returned! Mazel tov!"—as the dog trotted over to the trash can, knocked it over like it was his birthright, and started scarfing down table scraps.

"Silly boy must be starving," Mrs. Schmulowitz said, stooping to pet him. "That's why he came back."

Ack-Ack stopped eating only enough to slather wet kisses on the old lady's face before returning to his foraging.

"I can think of another reason," I said.

She shooed him away from the garbage and served him a plate of brisket. Kiddiot had arrived by then and demanded his own plate. Mrs. Schmulowitz was happy to oblige them both.

An hour later found me sitting alone in her parlor, devouring a piece of honey cake the size of a brick and watching the local news on her ancient Magnavox. The room smelled of wax furniture polish and hot cathode-ray tubes. Mrs. Schmulowitz had retired for the evening. The dog was curled asleep at my feet. The cat, meanwhile, was lying on his side in the middle of the floor, the tip of his tail flicking, watching me in that inscrutable feline way.

"No, you are not getting any cake," I told him. "Cake is bad for kitties."

He got up and started sharpening his claws on the upholstered leg of Mrs. Schmulowitz's sofa. I was so busy trying to get him to stop that I almost missed it:

"Meanwhile, in other news, new developments tonight in the investigation of a Santa Isabella man who died earlier this month after falling out of the sky."

I instantly forgot all the cake and Kiddiot and focused on the TV. A male-female anchor pair was tag-teaming the story, both taking turns reading from the teleprompter. It was the female's turn. She barely looked old enough to drive.

"As you may recall, the man's body bizarrely crashed through the roof of a mobile home in the Sun Country Trailer Park near the Santa Isabella Airport, narrowly missing an elderly couple living inside."

The male anchor was a poster boy for Botox and bleached teeth. "Tonight," he said, "law enforcement sources tell *Action*

News that a possible suspect has been identified in the case and is wanted for questioning."

According to the report, the suspect had served in the air force, owned his own small airplane, and ran a flight school in Rancho Bonita.

Kiddiot was eyeing me like he had a sneaking suspicion who they were referring to.

TWENTY-TWO

My phone rang.

"Are you watching this insanity?" Layne asked. "You're all over the news."

"You know what they say," I said. "All publicity is good publicity."

"They're accusing you of murder, Logan. That's not good publicity. That's a ticket to prison."

I assured her there was nothing to worry about. My guess was that Detective Tom Kasparov had planted the story in retaliation for my having intimated the possibility of his involvement in Chocks's death.

"So, you *do* think Kasparov had something to do with it?"

"Everybody's a suspect until they're not," I said.

"You're such a cynic, Logan."

"I prefer disappointed idealist. Ack-Ack came home, by the way. He's fine."

"That's a relief," Layne said. "I'm more concerned about you, though. What if you're being set up?"

"I'll be OK."

"You don't know that."

"Why don't you drive over, and we can work out a plan? Who knows? Maybe in bed."

"I can't, Logan. I'm kind of busy."

"Doing what?"

"Updating my résumé." There was a pause, then she said, "I've been offered a job."

"Congratulations," I said as dispassionately as my disappointment would allow. "Where?"

"McLean."

I assumed at first that she meant she was returning to her former employer, CIA headquarters, in the Langley neighborhood of McLean, in suburban Northern Virginia, but I was wrong. Layne said she'd been approached by Booz Allen Hamilton, a major defense consulting firm whose primary offices also were in McLean. They were tentatively offering her a managerial position in the company's Homeland Security Division. The job came with stock options, free health club membership, the unlimited use of a company car, a matching 401(k) program, and a six-figure salary. She was flying out in the morning for interviews.

"Short notice," I said. "They must want you pretty bad."

"We'll see."

"Just do me a favor?"

"What's that?"

"Stock options. A company car. If you decide to turn it down," I said, "gimme a call. Hell, I'd take that job myself."

My meager attempt to lighten the conversation was met by several seconds of cold silence.

"We have issues, Logan, significant issues. I'm not at all sure you're capable of working on them—or that you're inclined to."

"What if I agreed to go to counseling or we went together? Would you stay?"

A pause. "I'd have to think about." Then another pause. "I'll be back in a few days. Fly safe, Logan."

"You, too."

Click.

Romantic relationships can be uncomfortable. A couple's mutual desire to resolve that discomfort is the very definition of love. So said the Buddha. Layne was uncomfortable living in Mrs. Schmulowitz's garage. She wanted me to move out and move in with her. I was uncomfortable with that idea. She was uncomfortable with who I was at my core. She wanted me to be less reactionary and more deliberate. I saw merit in her vision of that new kind of me, but I was uncomfortable with any notion she may have had of me getting there anytime soon. And so, there we were, each mired in our discomfort with the other, and no easy solutions in sight. I didn't want to lose her, but I knew that, ultimately, I might not have any say in the matter. Mick Jagger was right. You can't always get what you want.

I tried to sleep that night. I couldn't. To get my mind off Layne, I turned my focus on Detective Kasparov. That *I* somehow was responsible for Chocks's murder was beyond preposterous. The more I thought about it, the more convinced I became that Kasparov was behind that news report, and the more chapped I got. I called the sheriff's office's nonemergency number and asked to speak with him. Immediately.

The overnight watch commander was an officious-sounding female sergeant who said her name was Trevino. "Detective Kasparov's gone for the evening. He'll be back on duty tomorrow," she said.

"I need to speak with him tonight."

"Sir, I just told you, he'll be back in the morning."

"Let me put it to you this way, Sergeant," I said. "Either you get Kasparov on the phone for me right now, or I'm going straight to the FBI with some very important information on a big homicide case the detective is handling. And I'm sure I don't need to remind you how much the feds hate stealing credit from local law enforcement."

The sergeant said nothing. I could hear some drunk arrestee in the background screaming about police brutality and constitutional rights.

"You still there, Sarge?"

"Unfortunately." She exhaled like she was blowing out candles on a birthday cake. "Who may I tell him is calling?"

"Cordell Logan."

"And he'll know which case this is about?"

"Tell him it's about Peter Hostetler."

"Lemme see if I can locate him. You mind holding?"

"No."

Ack-Ack climbed up on the couch and fell asleep with his head in my lap as I waited on hold. His long beagle ears were as soft as a whisper. When Kasparov finally got on the line ten minutes later, he sounded sloshed.

"What the hell do you want, Logan?"

"A public apology and a retraction."

"For what?"

"You know what."

Kasparov denied having anything to do with the bogus news report identifying me as a suspect in Chocks's death, so I did what any cop would've done under similar circumstances: I bluffed.

"I have two independent sources with firsthand knowledge that you planted that story, Detective, purposely and maliciously, knowing it was false."

"Why the hell would I want to do that?"

"To stop me from digging any deeper into whether you had anything to do with Pete Hostetler's murder."

"You're a liar, Logan. You got no sources. And I keep telling you: I had nothing, *zero*, to do with what happened to Hostetler."

"Have it your way. You want to play that game? Fine. I'll go to the local newspaper first thing in the morning. It may not be *The New York Times*, but I'm sure they'll be very interested in hearing everything I have to say about your many Russian connections, especially to Nikolay Andreev, a known Russian spy. After that, I'll be going over to the county courthouse to sue your ass for defamation. See you on the front page, Detective. Enjoy the rest of your evening."

"Wait, wait, wait! Wait."

Yeah, OK, he conceded. He *did* happen to have a cousin who worked in production at the only TV station in Santa Isabella, and that he "may have mentioned" something about a flight instructor from Rancho Bonita being a potential person of interest in the Hostetler case.

"But it wasn't like I identified you by name," he said. "And by the way, just so you know, I'd deny saying what I just said."

"Too late," I said.

"What're you talking about?"

"I've got you on tape saying it."

That was a bluff, too. Kasparov went off like a grenade, regardless. "You gotta have two-party consent to record a conversation in California, Logan. You didn't ask for my consent!"

"You're absolutely right, Detective. I didn't ask for your consent. So sue me. By the time your lawsuit gets to court, you'll probably already be in Leavenworth for violations of the Espionage Act."

I hung up and started counting down from ten. My phone rang before I got to five. Kasparov grudgingly agreed to contact his cousin at *Action News* and have them run a follow-up story clearing the unnamed flight instructor from Rancho Bonita of any involvement in Pete Hostetler's murder. I, in turn, I agreed to dispose of my recording of Kasparov's confession, even though I'd made no such recording.

Kasparov belched. I could practically smell the Jack Daniel's over the phone. "Look," he said, "let's just forget all this crap. I wanna close this case as much as you do, and I ain't getting nowhere on it. So you help me, I help you, and we cover ourselves in glory. Whadda you say, Logan?"

"That's what I proposed in the first place, remember?"

"That was then," Kasparov said. "This is now. My supervisor's breathing down my neck. If I don't close this case soon, they're gonna bust me back down to patrol."

I told him it was a helicopter, not an airplane, from which Chocks had taken his fatal plunge. Kasparov said he suspected as much. Two other eyewitnesses who saw what had happened that night had already reached out to the sheriff's office, he said. They, too, had seen a helicopter. What Kasparov didn't know was the helo's tentative make and model. He and his partner, Gregory, had canvassed the Santa Isabella Airport and found that seven helicopters of various designs were based there. Their owners had accounted for each chopper's whereabouts on the night in question.

"Sounds like we're looking for a helicopter based somewhere else," I said.

"Sounds like it," Kasparov said, starting to fall asleep.

I told him I'd keep digging and get back to him with any actionable intelligence I found. He promised to do the same. He offered no apology for having me slandered on local television. I didn't press for one. A public retraction was good enough. Let bygones be bygones. This wasn't about me, after all. It was about Chocks.

Without refueling, the MD 500 has a maximum range of approximately 270 miles, which means its operational radius is half that—135 miles. Prudent pilots, however, never push the ranges of their craft without maintaining a healthy fuel reserve, which usually equates to no less than half an hour of flying time. In an MD 500, that reserve restricted one-way flights to no more than about a hundred miles.

I got out of bed, unfolded an old aeronautical chart covering most of southern and central California, and drew a circle around Santa Isabella extending outward one hundred miles in any direction. Inside the circumference were easily more than thirty public and privately owned airfields. Checking them all in hopes of tracking down one small four-seat helicopter, I realized, could take weeks.

Sleep finally came to me, but even more fitfully than my usual restless night. I was dreaming again about an Iraqi soldier cartwheeling through the air, blown out of the turret of his tank by my heat-seeking missile. One of his legs and his left arm were missing. As I flew past him, I could see sunshine through a gaping hole in his neck.

I awoke to my phone vibrating. Buzz was calling. I squinted at the glow-in-the-dark digital clock on the upturned orange crate that served as my nightstand.

"What the hell, Buzz. It's not even five o'clock."

"Not in Cleveland, *mon ami*. In Cleveland, some of us are already hard at work keeping the world safe for democracy."

My head throbbed. My shoulders ached. I had no problems when I was younger functioning on a couple hours' sleep—or no sleep at all, if need be—but that was then. This getting older thing was no fun.

"When somebody gets a call this early," I said, trying to get my eyes to work, "it's usually to tell them their grandmother has died."

Buzz grunted. "Yeah, well, not this morning, Logan. This morning... Hold on a sec." He cupped a hand over the phone, but I could still hear him barking out his breakfast order at the drive-through of a Burger King—"Gimme two fully loaded, chicken strip croissant sandwiches with eggs, three orders of those potato bites, jumbo coffee, extra cream, extra sugar." Then he was back. "Where was I? Oh, yeah. I got your good news, and I got your bad news. Which one do you want first?"

"Let's get the bad out of the way."

"Boeing's no joy. They don't maintain a master list of MD 500s. The FAA might, but I don't have any juice with those guys."

"I appreciate you trying," I said. "What about the good news?"

"I finally heard back from my guy at NORAD."

Per Buzz's request, his source had harvested classified military satellite data to isolate the georeferenced ground tracks of every aircraft flying over or near Santa Isabella within a two-hour window of Chocks's death. Four targets were identified, though none by their types or tail numbers. Only their cruising altitudes and ground speeds were provided. I quickly disregarded two of the four—commercial airliners—based on how high and fast they were flying. The other two aircraft held potential. Both had overflown the city of Santa Isabella at low VFR altitudes— one at about eighty knots, the other at a hundred and ten. Both had subsequently landed at other airfields in central California. The faster of the two appeared to have terminated its flight at the Santa Ynez Airport, the slower one at a private airstrip, Lindemann Air Park, near New Cuyama, north of Santa Barbara. Either one could've been a helicopter given their respective speeds and cruising altitudes. Both bore further investigation.

I thanked him and told him that breakfast was on me the next time we saw each other in person, but I don't think he heard me. He was already wolfing down breakfast.

Lindemann Air Park was nothing more than a short, narrow runway flanked on one side by a decrepit aluminum hangar and cattle feedlots on the other. Even from thirty-five hundred feet, I could smell the manure. There was no mistaking it for anything other than a private airport. My first clue was that it was marked *(Pvt)* with a circled *R*—for restricted—on the *Duck*'s moving map. Then there were the big white *X*'s painted on both ends of the runway, meaning it was closed. Only in emergencies are general aviation pilots allowed to land at such airfields without prior permission.

So that's what I had—an "emergency."

I pulled the fuel-air mixture to idle cutoff and switched off the ignition. The propeller froze. As I glided in, dead-stick style, Layne for whatever reason popped into my head. She was all about planning and preparing for any contingency while I was all about adapting on the fly and overcoming. Our respective approaches to problem-solving were antithetical to each other. Maybe she and I were fundamentally antithetical to each other, too. I tried not to think about her.

There was a fairly stiff crosswind from the left. I crabbed at the last second, planted the *Duck*'s upwind wheel, and let the rest of the plane settle on. Not my best landing ever, but far from my worst. We hadn't yet come to a stop when some grizzled old cowboy in a red pickup truck came veering onto the runway ahead of the *Duck*. I had to all but stand on the toe brakes to avoid crashing into him head-on. He jumped out of his truck and strode angrily toward my plane. Chaps. Riding boots. A sweat-stained Stetson. He looked for all the world like he'd just stepped out of an old Marlboro cigarette commercial. I was glad he left his deer rifle in the truck's gun rack.

"You can't land here. This strip's private."

"I had no choice," I said, exiting the *Duck* carrying a clipboard. "The engine just quit on me."

He wasn't buying it. "The O-360's the best motor Lycoming ever made. They don't 'just quit.' I seen you turn downwind. Your engine sounded like it was running just fine. But if you're telling me you had an emergency, well, I guess there's nothing I can do about it, can I?"

"Congratulations," I said. "You passed the test."

He gave me a puzzled look. "What test?"

I pretended like I was reading from the clipboard, flipping through papers, angling the board so he couldn't see they were mostly blank. "Federal aviation regulation part 139, section 47134, subsection B: allowance of private airfield use by aircraft in distress. You didn't shoot me after I landed. Hence, you passed."

"You from the FAA?"

"Yessir," I said. "From the Flight Standards District Office, down in Van Nuys. We're conducting periodic ramp checks of privately operated airfields in the area. We just want to make sure everything is up to agency standards. Your runway looks to be in good condition, from what I can see."

"It ought to be," the cowboy said. "I just had it resurfaced last summer. Set me back twenty grand."

"You are . . . Carl Lindemann?" I asked, looking through the pages.

"That's me. I didn't catch your name."

Logan, you idiot. I'd failed to remember the first rule of clandestine operations: nail down every aspect of your cover story before going in. What can I say? I was rusty. "My name?" I had to think about it for a second. "It's Paul Horvath. Do you have any aircraft currently on the field, Mr. Lindemann?"

"Just the one. Parked over there in my hangar."

"Let's go take a look at it, shall we?"

"I don't know if you really want to do that, sir."

"No, Mr. Lindemann, actually, I do."

"All right, then. Suit yourself."

That's the thing about clipboards. They convey an air of authority. Football coaches have clipboards. So do public health officials. Carry one and most people will assume you are who you claim to be. Carl Lindemann never even asked to see my ID.

As we approached his hangar, he said, "You don't want to go in there, sir. Honestly, you don't."

"And why is that, Mr. Lindemann?"

He stopped and cleared his throat nervously. "I'll tell you why," he said, tipping his cowboy hat back. "Because it smells like death warmed over in there."

TWENTY-THREE

Cattle rancher Carl Lindemann stepped into the hangar through a side entrance and pushed a button while I waited outside under a relentless sun, waiting as the big hangar door folded up. He was right. The stench of death that emanated from inside the hangar was instant and overpowering.

Lindemann undid the sweat-soaked bandanna wrapped around his neck and covered his mouth with it. "It was dark," he said. "My landing light was burned out. I didn't see him until it was too late."

The "him" referred to a cow that he said had escaped its enclosure and wandered out onto his runway. Lindemann hit it after touching down in his plane, a blue-and-white Piper Malibu, that was parked inside the hangar. Pieces of dried beef and cowhide were fused to the cowling and propeller. Blood streaked the crumpled leading edge of the airplane's left wing.

"Quite a mess," I said.

"Most folks got no idea how many innards a cow has got," he said. "Even your smaller cows."

"Where were you coming in from when it happened?"

"Stockman's Association meeting, up in Sacramento."

"There was an incident involving another aircraft that same night," I said. "A gentleman fell out of a helicopter over Santa Isabella. Or was pushed. We're not sure. He landed on a trailer. Nearly killed the elderly couple living inside."

"Yeah, I heard something about it on the radio. I don't really follow the news all that much these days," Lindemann said. "Too much fake news. All I mostly care about is how hot it's gonna get tomorrow and when's it gonna rain again."

"I've seen and smelled enough," I said.

He pushed the button and joined me outside. The hangar door started coming down, unfolding slowly.

"I would've cleaned her up and gotten her fixed sooner," he said, "but we had a vibriosis scare come through here last week. Had to get the whole herd vaccinated. I probably should've called it in to you folks. I'm sorry I didn't. The last thing I need is trouble with the FAA."

"You're not in trouble, Mr. Lindemann. These things happen."

He pumped my hand in appreciation and offered me a side of fresh-cut beef. "Best T-bones you'll ever eat in your entire life," he said.

I declined. Much as I enjoyed a good steak occasionally (sorry, Buddha), his offer smacked of a bribe. Paul Horvath of the FAA was too ethical to accept a payoff from anyone. So was I.

To my feigned surprise, the *Duck*'s engine fired up with no problem. Carl Lindemann watched me taxi out and waved as I lifted off.

———

The Santa Ynez Airport was twenty-seven miles to the south, nestled amid vineyards, multimillion-dollar horse properties, and an ever-expanding Native American gaming casino where washed-up musical acts that were big in the sixties performed nightly to crowds of geezers. With a solid tailwind, the flight required all of sixteen minutes. It would've taken less time, but I had to extend my downwind leg to avoid a Pawnee towing a sailplane.

I tied down at transient parking, east of the self-service fuel pumps. The breeze was out of the east, not quite a desert wind but close. One of those dry, cloudless California afternoons where anything and everything feels possible, for better or worse.

Resting on a slight rise above the flight line was what had once been a modest wood-frame house with an asphalt-shingle roof that now served as the airport's administrative office. The door was unlocked. The walls were covered with artfully photographed airplanes. Nobody was inside. I helped myself to a cup of water from the office cooler, picked up a three-year-old copy of *Flying* magazine, sat down behind the front desk, and waited. A few minutes passed before a small man with a bad comb-over and a painfully contorted face came limping in. One of his legs was noticeably shorter than the other. He was wearing steel-rim glasses and carrying a greasy paper sack bearing what smelled like a hamburger and French fries. A professional-grade Nikon camera was slung around his neck.

"Can I help you?" His tone suggested helping me was the last thing he inclined to do.

"I'm looking for the airport manager."

"You're sitting in his chair," the man said.

"Excuse me."

I vacated his seat. He sat down, removed the camera from around his neck, put it on his desk, and dropped the magazine I'd been reading into the trash can like it was contaminated. There was a brass nameplate on the desk: "Sherman T. Javer-nick."

"Are you Sherman?"

"Yeah."

"You took all these pictures on the walls?"

"Yeah."

"Nice. They're beautiful."

If he was flattered, he didn't show it. He got out bottle of spray cleaner, a roll of paper towels, and started wiping down anything I may have touched.

"I'm looking for a helicopter, possibly based here in Santa Ynez," I said.

"What for?" he responded tersely.

Being truthful would've gotten me nowhere. I'd started off on the wrong foot, making the mistake of sitting on his throne. I told him the helicopter had been involved in an accident in which someone on the ground had been injured. The pilot had flown away before witnesses could identify the tail number. A lawsuit was pending. I was working as an investigator for the plaintiff's attorney, I said, trying to identify the helicopter's owner. Whoever helped me find him would receive a handsome finder's fee.

"Define 'handsome'?"

"It means you'd never have to work another day in your life."

He ate like a hyena ripping into an antelope carcass. Ketchup and pieces of bun cascaded down the front of his shirt.

"I don't know anything about anybody getting hit by any helicopter," he said. "And I know everything that goes on around here."

"Maybe I'm confused," I said. "Maybe it was another airport. You would've remembered the helicopter. Beautiful bird."

"What kind of helicopter?" he asked, his mouth full of fries.

"A McDonnell Douglas 500. Silver."

"We don't have any MD 500s based here," he said. "One comes in to fuel once in a while. But it's gray, not silver."

Gray and silver are easily confused, especially at night. I could feel my adrenaline kick in. "Then you must have copies of fuel orders, credit card charges, that sort of thing."

He picked a piece of hamburger off his chest and nibbled it with beaver-like front teeth. "The guy always pays cash."

"When was the last time he came in?"

"I dunno. A couple weeks ago."

"You wouldn't happen to have the tail number handy, would you?"

"We don't write down tail numbers on fuel orders when they pay cash."

"What about the pilot?"

"What about him?"

"What did he look like?"

"I don't remember."

"You don't remember? It was two weeks ago, Sherm, not two years."

He looked up at me from behind his desk with the angry eyes of a man who for all I knew had been bullied as a kid.

"Somehow, I don't believe you," he said.

Did I remind him of his childhood tormentors, or was he just pissed off about the chair? I didn't know and I really didn't care. I was out of options with nothing to lose. I told him the truth about why I was there, about Chocks, about how he'd saved my life in Iraq.

Sherman T. Javernick wiped away a gob of ketchup from his chin with a paper napkin and leaned back in his chair like he couldn't have cared less. "I don't know what else to tell you," he said.

I left my business card on his desk and asked him to call the next time the gray helicopter came in. He said he'd think about it.

"But don't hold your breath."

Outside, I watched a yellow Pitts aerobatic plane coming in to land. The pilot's approach was perfect. His touchdown was anything but. The little biplane bounced three times before finally settling onto the runway while I settled into an Adirondack chair in the shade of an oak tree overlooking the airstrip. There certainly were worse places to pass the time.

I pondered what the weird little airport manager had told me. That a gray MD 500 helicopter landed once in a while in Santa Ynez to refuel. The pilot always paid cash. Aviation go-juice isn't cheap. Filling up can cost several hundred dollars, depending how big your tanks are. Few pilots carry that kind of money. Who was this one flying for? A narcotics cartel did not seem beyond the realm of possibility.

I spent the rest of the afternoon lounging in that chair, hoping against hope that a gray MD 500 helicopter might show up.

None did.

I needed some burrito therapy to refuel my own tanks and clear my head. There's nothing like black beans, Spanish rice, and slow-cooked pork cocooned in a warm, homemade tortilla to make you forget for the moment your lack of progress in identifying who murdered your former wingman.

Lupita Reyes was the owner, waitress, and head chef of Lupita's, the best hole-in-the-wall Mexican restaurant in Rancho Bonita. She flipped the sign in the front window from *Abierto* to *Cerrado*, locked the door, and sat down at my table. I was her last customer of the night.

"More salsa, *mijo?*"

"I'm good, Lupita, thanks."

A TV hung on the wall next to a handwritten sign that said, "Today's Special: NOT Chimichangas." The late local news was on. The blonde anchorwoman reminded me of the prom queen in my high school who never gave me the time of day.

"Following up on a story we brought you last night," she said, "authorities now say that the Rancho Bonita flight instructor, initially identified as a person of interest in the murder of a Santa Isabella businessman who authorities believe was thrown from an aircraft, has been formally cleared of any wrongdoing."

Lupita nodded toward the television. "That was you they're talking about?"

"It would seem so."

She shook her head. "Hard for me to imagine you hurting anybody, Logan. You don't seem the type."

"My former self," I said, sopping up the last bit of chile verde with a scrap of tortilla.

She'd been a model growing up in Mexico City. Framed photos of her strutting fashion show runways in Europe graced the ocher-colored walls of her tiny restaurant. Lupita was no longer the looker she once was, but she was still lovely. Then as now, she was never without a fresh white hibiscus in the curl of her swept-up raven hair.

"You didn't bring your lady in tonight," she said. "Everything OK?"

"We're going through some stuff right now."

"Stuff, huh?"

I nodded.

"That doesn't sound too good," Lupita said.

I stared at my plate. "It is what it is."

Her busboy started stacking chairs on tables. Closing time. I apologized for coming in so late. She told me to forget it. Then she said, "*Agua que no has de beber, déjala correr.*"

"Don't drink bad water?"

"A saying my mother used to tell me. It means water that is not drinkable, let it run." Lupita's eyes were sad but kind. "If it's not working, Logan, you must let her go."

Mrs. Schmulowitz had fed the pets, but they still looked at me after I got home like they hadn't eaten in weeks, so I fed them again. Kiddiot did his usual thing, turning up his nose at the can of fish and shrimp I opened for him. The can of wild-caught salmon produced the same result. He walked away flicking his tail like I'd insulted him. Ack-Ack was only too happy to demolish both cans of food.

I sat down at the computer and checked my emails. Only the usual miracle toenail fungus cures, male enhancement drugs, and a Nigerian banker who wanted to transfer his multimillion-dollar fortune to me. All he needed was my bank account number.

Nothing from Layne.

I was about to call it a night when a new email appeared—from Sherman T. Javernick, manager of the Santa Ynez Airport. The content of the subject line was all of one word: "Apologies." I opened the email.

> I was having a bad day. Glad you appreciated my photography.

A photo was attached to the email. It showed a gray MD 500 parked near the airport's fuel pumps. Plainly visible on the boom was the helicopter's tail number:

N72BO.

Call it karma. Call it fate. I now had a viable lead.

TWENTY-FOUR

The helicopter's registration was public record.

Seven-two Bravo Oscar, according to the FAA's online aircraft registry, was operated by Tranquil Air, a London-based aviation brokerage and air charter service with twenty-eight outlets scattered across six continents. The company claimed to either own or have access to more than fifty thousand aircraft worldwide, including luxury private jets, cargo carriers, and helicopters. One of its offices was located in Camarillo, ninety-eight miles south of Santa Isabella—well within an MD 500's round-trip operating range.

I stared at the computer. Some days, I couldn't remember what I'd had for dinner the night before, yet I could recollect in vivid detail virtually every Alpha mission in which I ever participated. Right then, some synaptic cells must've fired deep in that part of my brain where memories live, and it all came flooding back:

We'd been hunting a wealthy Arab industrialist, Asad el-Sahli (not his real name), following NSA intercepts that he'd helped finance the suicide attack on the USS *Cole* while the navy destroyer was taking on fuel in the Yemeni port of Aden. The explosion killed seventeen American sailors. Our contacts with Israeli Mossad let us know that el-Sahli chartered Tranquil Air jets regularly, rather than flying commercially, to cover his tracks. We finally located him in a five-thousand-dollar-a-night villa on Italy's Amalfi Coast. I killed his bodyguard while Buzz double-tapped el-Sahli in the back of the head with a suppressor-equipped .22. Pressured by the White House, the Italian government told reporters that members of a street gang had killed both men in a robbery attempt gone bad.

But there was *something* relevant, some hazy connection between Chocks's death and Tranquil Air, that I couldn't quite put my finger on. The recollection floated tantalizingly but elusively just below the surface of my near-distant past. The harder I tried to retrieve it, though, the more it eluded me, and the more my frustration grew.

I went outside and lay down on Mrs. Schmulowitz's hammock, watching the moon play hide-and-seek behind the clouds, hoping the night air might refresh my memory, but it didn't.

Maybe Buzz will remember.

It was half past three in the morning in Cleveland. I phoned him anyway.

"Don't worry about it, Logan," he said after I apologized for calling so late. "I've been back and forth to the head six times already tonight. Amnesia or insomnia. Take your pick."

I asked him how much he remembered of the el-Sahli mission.

"How much do I remember?" Buzz chuckled. It sounded like rocks in a food processor. "All of it. Like it was yesterday. One of our better efforts. Why? What's up?"

"Do you remember the name of the air charter service he used?"

"Do I remember? How could I forget? 'Get High on Tranquil Air.' Worst slogan in history. Might as well call it, 'Stoner Air.'"

"There was something hinky about that company," I said. "For the life of me, though, I just can't remember what it was."

"They were Russkies," Buzz said. "I remember that much."

The hair stood up on the back of my neck. In every hunt, there was always that one fulfilling moment when you realized you were closing in on your prey. Buzz was famous for uttering various nonsensical but no less colorful idioms on such occasions. "Sweet sassy molassy" was a crowd favorite. So was, "Get out the checkbook and pay Granddaddy for a rubdown."

"Well, I'll be a monkey's uncle," I said, borrowing another one of Buzz's signature phrases.

There it was. *The Russian connection.* It all came back to me in crystalline detail—everything our analysts had briefed us on as we geared up to make Asad el-Sahli pay for having slaughtered our sailors.

Tranquil Air was a subsidiary of a Moscow-based conglomerate called Spacestorm. Spacestorm was owned by a billionaire Russian oligarch whose name I couldn't recall, but Buzz did— Yevgenity Rasim Sokolov.

"Sokolov and Putin go fishing together all the time," Buzz said. "They're related by marriage, if I remember right. I'm gathering this has something to do with your buddy falling out of that chopper?"

I told him how the helicopter appeared to be registered to Tranquil Air, and about Detective Tom Kasparov's possible ties to Russian intelligence. I laid out my theory that Chocks had been murdered after uncovering a nefarious connection between Moscow, DARPA, and Chocks's former employer, Electrogenics.

"They make animatronic toys for kids," I said, "but it's really a false front. They're assembling classified radar components and selling at least some of them to the Russians. That's my theory, anyway."

"That's some crazy-ass shit," Buzz said. "What's your next move?"

"I'll let you know when I figure it out. Thanks for the walk down memory lane. Good times. Get some sleep."

"Easier said than done. I'll probably just stay up watching TV down in the den. Don't wanna wake up the Mrs. She puts up with enough from me already."

"You're a saint, Buzz."

"Tell it to my wife." He yawned over the phone. "Hang in there, Logan. Try not to get dead."

Ack-Ack trotted out from the garage, jumped up on the hammock, and promptly went to sleep at my feet. I lay there, gazing up at the stars, careful not to shift my weight lest I disturb the dog's beauty rest. I kept thinking about what Gervasio Pascua had wanted me to know about Chocks, how he'd died *trying to do the right thing*. Pascua, among so many others I'd made contact with, obviously knew more than what he'd revealed to me. I needed to talk with him again, to press him harder for answers. First, though, what I desperately needed was sleep myself. I was fading. An hour or two and I'd be good to go again. I closed my eyes. When I opened them, Ack-Ack was standing on my chest, barking and wagging his tail. Layne Sterling was leaning over me, silhouetted against the sun.

"Good morning," she said.

"'Morning."

The dog could barely contain his excitement at seeing her. He jumped off the hammock and circled Layne's legs, squealing. She knelt to stroke his ears. "And good morning to you, too, sweet puppy."

"How'd your trip go?"

"They want me to start next week," Layne said.

I rubbed the sleep from my eyes. "They're fortunate to have you."

She had no right to look as fine as she did so early in the morning, especially when I looked as bad as I probably did after spending the night on Mrs. Schmulowitz's hammock. Layne's face had a glow about it, like she'd been on vacation. Being apart for a couple of days seemed to have done wonders for her.

"I just came by to pick up some of my things," she said, "unless you feel like talking this out."

"I don't know what more there is to talk about," I said. "You've already made up your mind. You've accepted the job, and you're moving back East. End of discussion is what it sounds like to me."

"Not necessarily."

"What does that mean, Layne? You might reconsider?"

"Possibly," she said.

"What would it take to get you to stay?"

Layne looked over at the garage where I'd lived for more than a decade like it needed to be condemned and torn down. "You know what it would take, Logan."

"It's not just that," I said. "You want me to move out. I don't want to do that, at least right now. You expect me to change who I am. You set a high bar, Layne. To tell you the truth, I'm not sure I would ever be able to reach it."

"Why do you always have to be so stubborn, Logan?"

"I'd ask you the same question."

The sadness in her eyes was unmistakable. She stood there, waiting for me to say something more. When I didn't, she turned without a word and strode inside. Ack-Ack followed her with his tail waving like a conductor's baton. She returned less than a minute later carrying some of her clothes and books.

"Any progress on the case?"

I told her about Sokolov, the Russian oligarch. Layne knew who he was. His name had crossed her desk when she worked at the CIA. Sokolov, she said, was a sociopathic sadist rumored to enjoy torturing his enemies to death.

"The guy's dangerous as hell, Logan. Even if he were tangentially responsible for what happened to Chocks, I'd be careful. You have no idea who he knows and what he's capable of. Besides, what with Putin, the guy's untouchable. And it's not like we have an extradition treaty with Russia."

"Duly noted."

The corners of Layne's exquisite mouth narrowed, and her eyebrows gathered like storm clouds. "Well," she said bitterly, "I'd say we're done here."

I should've been more gracious. Nobody, however, likes getting dumped. And now here she was, effectively killing the fledging investigative agency we'd started together while expressing her concern for my safety. I appreciated her regard for my welfare. Honestly, I did. But I could've done without her unsolicited advice on my need to stand down in the face of potential danger.

"I thought we had something special, Logan. I really did."

"Likewise."

Her chin quivered. She squared her jaw, fighting back tears. "I fly back this weekend," she said. "Should you reconsider."

I didn't say anything.

Then she was gone.

A true Buddhist seeks unattachment from all earthly objects, including romantic partners. I knew I would need to work on that in the weeks and months to come.

"You doing OK over there, bubby?" Mrs. Schmulowitz stepped out onto her back porch, wiping her hands on a dish towel. She was wearing a white cooking apron over a plum-colored tracksuit.

"All good, Mrs. S."

"Not from what I just happened to overhear—not to be a yenta or anything. Come on, come inside; I'll make you a nice plate of eggs and onions. Promise you won't tell anybody, and I'll even throw in some bacon. You know what they say about bacon, right?"

"What's that?"

"The average life expectancy in this country would grow exponentially if veggies smelled like bacon."

It was hard to argue with the truth.

Mrs. Schmulowitz was a force of nature and a port in a storm. Who was I to say no?

Gervasio Pascua was not an easy man to get in touch with. No surprise there. International drug dealers tend not to post their telephone numbers online. But while I had no way of contacting him directly, I did have a number for his personal assistant, Armando Berganza. A recording, however, indicated the number was no longer in service. I dialed it again and got the same result.

Time for plan B.

The Cessna Latitude Berganza had flown in on when I'd met him at the Rancho Bonita Airport was registered in Mexico. The jet's tail number—XA-BYOB—was easy to remember given my long personal history with liquor bottles. When I'd met with Pascua in Mexico, he'd mentioned that he no longer owned his own private jet; he chartered them. On a hunch, I found a telephone number online for the offices of Tranquil Air in Mexico

City and called. The young woman who answered the phone couldn't have been more pleasant.

"*Servicio* Tranquil Air Charter," she said. "*¿Cómo puedo ayudarle?*"

"*Buenos días.* Please tell me you speak English because my Spanish is *no bueno.*"

Her English was perfect. "Yes, sir. How may I help you?"

I explained that I'd recently been a passenger on a Tranquil Air jet of Mexican registry, and that I'd inadvertently left a personal item on the plane that I was hoping to retrieve.

"It would be great," I said, "if you could forward a message to my friends who'd chartered the plane."

"Would you happen to know the aircraft's tail number, sir?"

"Yes, it's X-ray Alpha Bravo Yankee Oscar Bravo."

I could hear the clicking of her computer keystrokes.

"Yes, sir," she said. "That is one of our aircraft. May I inquire as to the nature of the item you'd like back?"

"A stiletto."

"Excuse me?"

"It's a type of knife."

"I see. And do you recall, sir, the specific date of the flight on which you left behind your . . . stiletto?"

"It was last week."

She asked if I minded while she put me briefly on hold so she could look into the matter further. Not at all, I said. Take your time. And thank you.

"My pleasure, sir."

I waited, digesting my bacon and eggs. When the woman returned to the phone, gone was her *My pleasure, sir* pleasantries. She was now all business.

"I double-checked," she said. "The aircraft you referred to is not in our inventory."

"That's not what you told me two minutes ago."

"I was mistaken, unfortunately. Is there anything else I can help you with today, sir?"

"There is. Please pass along a message to Gervasio Pascua. Tell him that if he doesn't call me back in the next hour, I *will* be contacting authorities here in the United States to hand over a tape recording I made surreptitiously of our meeting in the back room of a certain cantina in Ensenada, during which time Mr. Pascua shot a man he believed to be a DEA informant in the neck."

The young woman sounded completely unnerved. "Thank you for calling Tranquil Air," she said. "Have a good day." I'm sure others had been listening in.

My phone rang fifteen minutes later. Armando Berganza, Gervasio Pascua's personal assistant, could not have sounded more charming, in a menacing kind of way.

TWENTY-FIVE

Berganza was laughing over the phone. Not in the way one does, though, when they're mildly amused. No, this was bent-over, hands-on-knees, barely-able-to-breathe chortling. The punchline was my "preposterous notion" that a successful international businessman like his boss, Gervasio Pascua, would be associated even remotely with *any* kind of criminal activity. Berganza sounded like he was convinced the feds had wiretapped the line.

"I can assure you, Mr. Logan, Mr. Pascua has never and would never harm so much as a flea. And we both know you're bluffing. There is no such recording."

"If that's how you want to play it, Armando, I'll see you in district court after the indictments are issued."

I hung up and counted down from ten. He called me back before I got to seven. He was no longer laughing.

"The line's not tapped," I said.

"What do you want, Logan?"

"Another meeting with Pascua. Face-to-face."

"For purposes of what?"

"You told me he said my friend died trying to do the right

thing. I want to know what he meant by that. If he's straight up with me, no playing games, then what happened in Ensenada stays in Ensenada."

"As I'm sure you can imagine," Armando Berganza said, "Mr. Pascua is a very busy man. I'll have to discuss this with him and get back to you."

"Tell him he has until noon today, Pacific time," I said, "or I'm going to the feds with the tape."

"You're making a mistake, Logan. A serious mistake."

"It wouldn't be the first time," I said as I hung up.

I kept myself busy and tried not to look at the clock. I washed out Kiddiot's food bowl. I knocked out a hundred push-ups and a hundred sit-ups. I filled in my pilot's logbook with details of my most recent flights, one line per flight—what the wind conditions were like that day, the visibility, the specific instrument approaches I'd shot. By eleven o'clock, I was beginning to wonder if I'd hear back from Berganza or Pascua. By eleven-thirty, I was certain I wouldn't. My bluff had failed.

Then, at exactly one minute before noon, my phone rang. Caller ID showed 000-000-0000.

"This is Logan."

"You'll be receiving an email shortly," Berganza said. "Make sure you come alone."

The line went dead.

Thirty-five minutes later, an email arrived from an encrypted server under the username 6DHhjs6Gn@77&MaLEwUDu. I was familiar with encryption services. They work by generating two pairs of coded keys, one public and one private. The sender exchanges a public key with the recipient. The recipient can then decrypt the sender's email using their mutual private key. In this way, the sender can ensure that only the designated recipient receives the message. I established an account, chose my security keys, then tapped the box marked, "See new messages." There was only one. It read:

7 Pacific, L78

The FAA assigns big airports three-letter identifying codes—LAX for Los Angeles, MIA for Miami, and so forth. Smaller airports get codes that typically include one letter and two numbers. Aeronautical charts showed that L78 corresponded to the Jacumba Airport, east of San Diego and immediately north of the US-Mexico border. Gervasio Pascua had arranged to meet me there at seven P.M.

"Well, whadda you know," I said to the cat and dog who were stretched out together on the sofa. "It worked."

I tore an old T-shirt into rags, then fieldstripped and cleaned the .357 I'd liberated from Chocks's brother-in-law. Both pets got up and went outside in a hurry as the eye-watering stink of Hoppe's No. 9 solvent filled the garage. I couldn't much blame them, but the revolver was grimy and needed cleaning. A Mexican drug lord had agreed to meet with me after I'd threatened to blackmail him. I would've been nuts to show up unarmed.

I filed no flight plan and turned off both my transponder and radios minutes after taking off from Rancho Bonita. No use making it easier for anyone to track where I was going. My route took me north and east of Los Angeles as I picked my way through noncontrolled airspace. Two hours and seven minutes after departing, I entered the pattern and touched down in the waning light of the day on a lonely strip of asphalt otherwise known as the Jacumba Airport.

Desolate was the word that came to mind. A few small, sun-baked metal sheds near the runway. A couple of dust-covered, beat-up pickup trucks parked on the other side of a chain-link fence. No sound beyond the hiss of the wind. The place was as empty of airplanes as it was people. The *Duck* and I were alone.

Some two hundred meters south of the runway was the US-Mexico border, demarked by a wall constructed of slatted steel posts topped with razor wire, each as tall as a three-story building. The wall came to an abrupt end a half mile beyond the airport, giving way to open scrubland and unobstructed access to anyone who wanted to enter the United States or leave it.

Weird.

My phone showed no new voice messages or emails. It also showed I had no cell service. I sat and watched the sun begin its fiery exit from the day behind the Laguna Mountains to the west, and waited.

Soon, I spotted a bicyclist pedaling slowly toward the airport on a two-lane road parallel to the runway. As he got closer, I could see that his bike was as creaky and old as he was. A grizzled desert-dweller in shorts and sandals, a battered straw sombrero, and a T-shirt advertising Corona beer. His foot-long chin whiskers could've challenged ZZ Top to a beard-growing contest and won.

I stuffed the revolver under my shirt and stepped out onto the tarmac.

"You Logan?"

"I am."

The old man ran a hand over the *Duck*'s propeller. His leathery face and forearms were mottled with skin cancer scars. "How old is this old airplane, anyway?"

"Old enough to know better," I said.

His grin reminded me of a "before" picture for cosmetic dentistry. "You're supposed to go to the bar," he said.

"Which bar?"

"Ain't like there's more than one bar around these parts, amigo." He aimed a crooked finger west. "'Bout a mile that way, toward town. Look for the spa. You can't miss it."

"The spa. Got it. Thanks."

"Easiest fifty bucks I ever made," he said. Then he turned around on his bicycle and pedaled off in the direction from which he came.

I made sure the *Duck*'s doors were locked and started walking.

Abandoned mobile homes and ranch houses, their caved-in, graffiti-covered walls a testament to economic collapse, marked the way into town. The landscape was parched. An occasional car or pickup truck whizzed past. Nobody stopped to offer me a lift, which was just as well. I didn't have to explain what I was doing there or, worse, lie about it.

Jacumba itself was little more than one flashing stoplight and a handful of weathered wooden storefronts flanking the road. The "spa," otherwise known as the Jacumba Hot Springs Resort, wasn't hard to spot given the sign out front. It was flat-roofed and single-story, built in the style of roadside motels circa 1950, with a grandiose, stuccoed Spanish façade that evoked images of the Alamo. The sign said the place served breakfast, lunch, and dinner daily. Parked out front was a black showroom-new Nissan Armada, with tinted windows, all-terrain tires, and Mexican license plates. The SUV was massive in size and stood out in the parking lot like a fly on a wedding cake.

Waiting for me inside the bar, Gervasio Pascua and his bodyguards stood out even more.

He was sitting by himself at a corner table facing the door

and nodded at me in a friendly way behind his cool-guy sunglasses when I walked in. Two badass bodyguards were stationed on either side of the front door. Two others covered the back door with access to the patio. One of them had his iPhone pressed to his ear. The only other people in the bar were the bartender and the barmaid, who went about their business, trying hard not to look freaked out by the presence of a notorious narco.

"You must be thirsty after your walk," Pascua said. "May I buy you a drink?"

I nodded toward the glass he was holding in his left hand. "What are you having?"

"The house special," Pascua said. "Vodka, gin, rum, tequila, blue curaçao, peach schnapps, and triple sec, topped off with a can of Red Bull. They call it an Irish Trash. Very refreshing."

"Much as I wish I could, I'll stick with water for now."

"You really don't know what you're missing," Pascua said.

"Actually, I think I do."

He gestured toward the barmaid. She hustled over, a middle-aged redhead in a pink tank top with a dragon tattoo on her right shoulder.

"Ice water for my friend," Pascua said, "with a slice of fresh lemon."

"Sorry, we ran out of lemons this morning."

Pascua took off his sunglasses and looked up at her slowly. "You're telling me you have no *lemon*?"

The barmaid's face was a mask of dread. "Please. I—"

"Don't worry about it," I said. "I don't need any lemon. Thanks."

She stood there, frozen with fear.

"You heard the man," Pascua said.

"Yes, sir. Right away."

He watched her hurry back to the bar, then asked if I was armed.

"Wouldn't you be?"

"Absolutely."

He tilted his head like he wanted me to look under the table. I did. He was holding a gold-plated .45, aimed at my crotch. The hammer was back.

"Good-looking pistol," I said. "Those grips are what, ivory?"

"Mother-of-pearl," Pascua said. "Everyone knows ivory is illegal."

I tilted my head in the same manner. Now it was his turn to look under the table. When he did, he saw my revolver aimed at his crotch, obscured from his bodyguards' view by my legs. He sat back up and nodded approvingly. Then he rested his gun on the table. Slowly, as not to alarm his bodyguards, I did the same.

The barmaid returned with a glass of ice water and set it down in front of me with a trembling hand, pretending not to notice either weapon.

"Will there be anything else?"

Pascua peeled off two crisp one-hundred-dollar bills from a sterling silver money clip. "One for you," he said, handing her the money, "and one for the excellent mixologist over there."

"Thank you *so* much. This is really just so generous of you. I—"

"Leave us."

"Yes, sir."

Away she went.

"The going rate for a few minutes of privacy used to be fifty dollars," Pascua said. "Now it's a hundred."

"Everything's gotten more expensive these days," I said. "I went to the grocery store the other day to buy a steak, and the butcher offered to finance it for me."

A smile stretched slowly across Pascua's lean, hawk-like face.

"Threatening me. Demanding to meet. You possess some major cojones, hombre."

"So did Pete Hostetler."

"Indeed he did."

"You said he died trying to do the right thing," I said. "I need to know what you meant by that."

"Not before we discuss this supposed recording you made of our meeting in the Baja. You can appreciate my concern, Mr. Logan, if something of that nature was to fall into the wrong hands."

"There is no recording. I lied."

"As I suspected." Pascua calmly sipped his drink. "How do I know you're not wearing a wire now?"

I hiked up my shirt to show him I wasn't, then stood while one of his bodyguards patted me down. After he was finished, he nodded to Pascua that I was clean. I returned to my seat.

"Are you sure you don't want to come work for me? I pay my people very well."

"I didn't come down here looking for a job, Mr. Pascua. I'm here looking for some answers."

He took another sip of his drink. "In my line of work, Mr. Logan, discretion and stealth are everything."

"You mean not getting caught smuggling narcotics."

"You can call it that. I prefer to call it *moving inventory*. We—" He paused midsentence. Heads turned as two guys in motorcycle leathers walked in. They took one look at Pascua's bodyguards and at the firearms on our table, turned around, and walked out in a big hurry. Pascua continued:

"As I was saying, in my line of work, we are always looking for an edge, Mr. Logan. An acquaintance in your defense industry mentioned a company in California that he heard was producing a military cloaking device designed to confuse radar.

I was keenly interested, for obvious reasons, in equipping my transport aircraft with such a device."

"So, Pete Hostetler comes along and now you're good to go."

"It was hardly that simple. As I explained when we first met, I was looking to hire a replacement for my personal pilot. One of my people found Mr. Hostetler's résumé on a job website. His credentials were impressive, so we arranged an interview. When he indicated he was working for the same company manufacturing these cloaking devices, and that he was looking for a change of pace, to get back into flying, I immediately offered him the position. Unfortunately, he didn't stay that long."

"Why would he go to work for a drug dealer? No offense."

"None taken." Pascua sat back with his hands folded placidly in his lap. "Had he known the full extent of what we do, the nature of our work, he probably would've turned me down. But as far as he was aware, I was nothing more than a businessman with a family and a busy flight schedule. If he suspected anything, he never let on."

"Pete always saw the good in people," I said, "never the not-so-good."

"That was certainly my impression," Pascua said. "I do know that his work at Electrogenics—before he came to work for me, kept him up at night. He was troubled by what he saw there."

"How do you know that?" I asked.

"Because he told me. Things were not as they appeared at the company. He would never get into specifics, though." Pascua drained his drink and signaled to the bartender for another. "I tried, subtly of course, to get him to tell me about these devices they supposedly were manufacturing. He'd merely smile and insist Electrogenics was in the business of making children's toys. So, of course, I had my people hack his phone."

Pascua got out his own phone. He showed me a brief email Chocks had sent to the FBI's field office in Los Angeles, accusing Electrogenics's chief executive officer, Ed Millisohn, of doing business with foreign governments hostile to the United States. There was no mention in the email of radar-defeating equipment.

"Your friend was planning to meet with the FBI," Pascua said. "He was murdered before he could."

"In other words," I said, "doing the right thing."

Pascua nodded solemnly. The barmaid arrived with a fresh cocktail. He slipped her another two one-hundred-dollar bills. I waited until she moved off.

"Which governments?" I asked.

"That I do not know, nor do I particularly care," Pascua said, stirring his drink. "I'm not interested in international politics, Mr. Logan. Only profits."

He reiterated how much he'd admired Chocks for his piloting skills and personal integrity, and how saddened he was to learn of his death. He looked me in the eyes when he said it, and I believed him. Then one of his bodyguards who'd been standing near the back door with a phone to his ear walked over and whispered something in Spanish to him. The urgency in the bodyguard's tone required no translation. Pascua stood, grabbing his .45 off the table and shoving it in his waistband.

"I'm afraid we'll have to leave the discussion of your potential employment for a future date, Mr. Logan. Good hunting. I mean that sincerely."

We shook hands. His men quickly followed him out into the parking lot. The second the last was out the door, the bartender grabbed his phone and punched in 911 while the barmaid sat down on a stool like her knees were about to quit on her and fired up a cigarette. I, meanwhile, ducked out the patio door.

I was about a quarter mile down the road when three green-and-white Border Patrol SUVs came racing by, headed for the Jacumba Hot Springs Resort.

None of them noticed me walking back to the airport.

TWENTY-SIX

I called Detective Tom Kasparov at the Santa Isabella Sheriff's Office the next morning. Whoever answered his phone said he was away and wouldn't be back for two days. She put me through to Kasparov's partner, Lloyd Gregory, who groused about my having interrupted his breakfast. I told him I now had a specific reason for why Pete Hostetler had been murdered, and that it had nothing to do with the Mexican drug trade.

"He got killed before he could go to the FBI with what he knew about what's going on at Electrogenics."

"What about Electrogenics?" Gregory demanded.

"The CEO's selling radar components to foreign buyers."

"Where'd you get that?"

"I can't say."

"You can't say, or you *won't* say?"

"I can't say."

"You don't know what the hell you're talking about," Gregory said. "What happened to Hostetler had nothing to do with whatever this crap is you're peddling."

"Then set me straight. Who killed him?"

"This is an ongoing law enforcement investigation, Logan, an *official* investigation. I don't need to tell you anything. But I *will* tell you, because the victim happened to be your friend, that we're close to making an arrest."

"Who?"

"Forget it. You'll just have to wait until it's on the news, like every other civilian."

"Lemme talk to Kasparov."

"You can talk to me."

"I'm just trying to help, Detective."

Gregory cleared his throat over the phone. "You just don't get it, do you, Logan? We don't need your help. You keep getting in our way, and I guarantee you, you *will* be arrested for obstructing an investigation. You feel me?"

"I'd prefer not to."

I hung up on him.

My next call was to the FBI field office in Los Angeles. The woman who answered the phone said no agents were available to talk to me. I left my number. Nobody ever called back.

The cat and dog were sitting together on the kitchen floor, looking up at me like they were waiting for my next move.

It hit me like a bus.

"Hang on to your pelts, boys," I said. "This one's gonna be a mind-blower—*if* she goes along with it."

"A *honeypot?*" Layne stared at me with her mouth open as if I'd just asked her to help me rob a bank. "Forget it, Logan. No way."

"It's not a honeypot, Layne. It's . . . an inducement."

"Please dispense with the semantics, Logan, OK? Inducement, entrapment. It's the same thing. A honeypot. And the answer is still no. Besides, unless I'm mistaken, I thought you and I were history."

"Can we please talk about this somewhere other than with me standing outside your front door?"

"What is there to talk about? I already told you. No."

"Please, Layne."

She blew some air through her mouth like she knew she was making a mistake, turned on her heel, and walked back inside. I followed her into the kitchen.

"It's the only way," I said, watching her get out a basket of strawberries from a stainless steel refrigerator that made the hand-me-down icebox that came with my apartment look ancient by comparison.

"You're asking me to seduce the chief executive officer of Electrogenics."

"To establish evidence, Layne. To prove he's doing covert business with the Russians or the Iranians or whoever else he's selling these things to. To extract a confession so I don't have to beat one out of him."

She dumped the berries into a blender along with some yogurt and a banana. "How do you know Gervasio Pascau isn't blowing smoke up your skirt? How do you know he isn't trying to misdirect you?"

"Why would he do that?"

"Gee, I dunno, Logan. Could it possibly be because Chocks was gonna go to the FBI about what he knew of Pascua's activities? Smuggling routes? Aircraft capabilities? Chocks worked for the guy!"

"Pascua showed me the email, Layne."

"He could've manufactured the email."

I took a deep breath and let it out slowly. "Layne, listen to me. Chocks was going to the FBI because Ed Millisohn's company is dealing highly sensitive radar components under the table to God knows where, components intended for use by the United States military."

She shook her head like I'd lost my mind and pushed a button on the blender. She wasn't wrong about me playing semantics. Inducement. Entrapment. Sexual seduction was a mainstay of spy craft, as old as the Philistines who exploited Delilah's feminine charms to coax Samson into revealing his one true vulnerability.

"All I'm asking you to do is stroke the guy's ego over a couple of cocktails," I said over the whirring of the blender. "Gain his trust. Get him to tell you who he's selling to, brag about how much money he's making. I've worked a hundred dirtbags like him, Layne. So have you. I guarantee, you pump a couple of drinks into him, show him a little skin, he'll be only too eager to step on his own meat."

Her back was turned to me. The blender sounded like a tornado.

"You want a smoothie?" she asked.

I'm not the smoothie type. But when you're trying to persuade a former CIA case officer and your soon-to-be ex-lover to work a covert op that she's plainly opposed to, the only obvious response is, "Yes, I'd love a smoothie."

Layne poured the pink concoction into two glasses. It looked like something a space creature might've regurgitated, but it smelled OK, and I had to admit, it didn't taste bad.

"Why won't you do this, Layne? A couple of hours, then you're off to DC. Forever."

"Why? Because it's degrading, Logan, that's why. It's the classic male objectification of women. You're being used. You can take a two-hour shower when it's over and you still can't get the stink of humiliation off your skin."

She said she'd been forced to play undercover seducer in

a handful of CIA-orchestrated honeypots early in her career, before she'd accrued enough seniority to say no. One assignment involved an intelligence analyst suspected of spying for the Cuban government. Another involved a clerk at Langley who'd been passing classified data to an intelligence officer with the Ghanaian Provisional National Defence Council. Both men spilled their guts after Layne lured them with the promise of sex. Both ended up in federal prison.

"I knew I was doing the Lord's work," she said, "but all I felt was cheap and manipulated. I told myself the last time that I'd never do it again. And now here I am. Again."

"I wouldn't ask you," I said, "but Millisohn's dirty. I can *feel* it. And this is Chocks we're talking about, Layne. My academy classmate. My wingman. I'm alive today because of him. I owe him my life. I owe him this. You have to help me. Please. Not for me. For Chocks. Please."

We sipped our smoothies. Seagulls glided past the windows. The air smelled of sea salt, and I could hear children laughing out by the beach.

"OK, I'll do it," Layne said finally, "but under one condition."

"Anything."

"That you'll do the Buddhist thing, not just talk the talk. That you'll think twice before automatically resorting to violence."

"Fair trade," I said. "All I can do is try."

"No, Logan. Not try. *Do.*"

Her eyes held steadily on mine. They were the most alluring shade of green I'd ever seen.

"I'll need a wig," she said.

I bought a spoof card online. For the low price of $9.95, I got forty-five minutes of talk time during which I could override caller ID, change my phone number to any number I desired, and electronically disguise my voice in the same manner. I chose to sound like a woman with a New Zealand accent whose number corresponded to the New Zealand Chamber of Commerce. Then I called Electrogenics and asked to speak with Ed Millisohn. "Good day, my name is Susan Stewart. I'm calling from the Business Chamber in Auckland, New Zealand. I'm trying to reach Mr. Millisohn. Is he in, please?"

His assistant sounded like Minnie Mouse with a cold. "Mr. Millisohn is gone for the day. Is there something I can help you with, miss?"

"Yes, as a matter of fact, there is."

I told her how prominent members of the Auckland business community had grown "insanely perturbed" over Electrogenics's successful marketing of cuddly Australian animatronic animals while completely disregarding New Zealand's no-less-lovable national bird, the kiwi. A wealthy consortium of New Zealanders was prepared to pay Electrogenics a hefty sum to remedy the disparity.

"As it happens," I said, "a representative from our organization is in California today on a goodwill tour. She's leaving early tomorrow. I realize it's quite short notice, but if Mr. Millisohn could spare a few minutes this afternoon, I'm sure he would find what she has to offer extremely worthwhile."

"Let me check with him. Can you hold?"

"Bully."

I wanted to kick myself. Who the hell says "bully" other than some dumb American who *thinks* that's how people from New Zealand speak? But if Ms. Minnie Mouse was at all suspicious, she didn't sound it. I sat on hold, listening to the same singsong kiddie tune I'd endured while waiting for Millisohn in the company's lobby. Then she was back:

"Thank you for waiting."

"Righto."

"Mr. Millisohn is playing golf today at the Torito Canyon Country Club. He asked if your representative can meet him in the clubhouse at one thirty."

"She shall be there," I said.

Right then, a raven-haired, stunningly gorgeous seductress floated into the kitchen in five-inch slingback heels, cream-colored hip-huggers, and a low-cut black satin blouse. Gold gypsy hoops hung from her earlobes. A tear-shaped jade pendant dangled from a gold necklace between her breasts. Her lips were painted sinfully red, as were her fingernails. It took me a second to realize I was looking at Layne Sterling.

"And who should I tell Mr. Millisohn he'll be meeting with?" the assistant asked.

Stunned as I was by Layne's transformation, I could think of only one name.

"Aphrodite . . ." I said. "Aphrodite . . . Williams."

"I'll let him know. You're all set. Thank you for calling Electrogenics."

"Thank *you*." I hung up.

Layne shook her head scornfully. "*Aphrodite*, Logan? Really?"

Comparing her to the Greek goddess of beauty was intended as a compliment, I said. She didn't seem to take it that way.

Bob's Copy Shop in downtown Rancho Bonita offered fifty custom-printed business cards in twenty minutes or less. I placed an order online for "Aphrodite Williams, Associate Director of

Marketing, Auckland Business Chamber." I assumed Ed Millisohn would be blinded by Layne's good looks, and that would do much, if anything, to confirm her identity. But, as they say, better safe than sorry. Handing him a business card with Aphrodite's name on it couldn't help but cement her credibility.

We picked up the cards on our way out of town. Millisohn had seen my truck, so we took Layne's Camry. I drove while she practiced a Kiwi accent. By the time we got to Santa Isabella, she sounded fairly convincing.

My plan called for her to drop me off at the Santa Isabella Public Library where I could lay low while she proceeded to the Torito Canyon County Club to do her Samson-and-Delilah thing with Ed Millisohn.

"Just don't say 'bully,'" I cautioned as I pulled over outside the library.

"Thanks for the advice, Teddy Roosevelt."

We got out and switched seats.

"I appreciate you doing this, Layne. I know you'll knock 'em dead. Have fun."

"*Fun*? You must be kidding me."

I leaned down to give her a kiss for luck, but the look on her face said don't even try.

The library was closed. A notice posted on the front door stated, "Plumbing issues. Our apologies for any inconvenience"—only *plumbing* was spelled *pluming*. When librarians no longer know proper spelling, civilization is in trouble.

Around the corner from the library was a used bookshop—as good an alternative as any to hang out in until Layne returned. Hundreds of books were heaped in one big, disorganized pile on a long table out front. I was perusing titles when the shopkeeper, a pear-shaped older man in farmer-friendly bib overalls emerged with an armload of even more books and dumped them on the table.

"Must be exhausting," I said, "carrying all these in every night and out every morning."

What hair he lacked atop his head, he more than made up for with his wispy, white, out-of-control sideburns. "Why would I do that?" he asked.

"You're not worried about people stealing your inventory?"

"Readers don't steal," he said, "and thieves don't read. So, no, I'm not worried."

I followed him inside. The place looked like an episode of *Hoarders*, jammed floor to ceiling with precariously stacked, pile upon pile, and shelf upon shelf of books arranged in no apparent order. The place smelled like rotting wood.

"Anything in particular you're looking for?" the shopkeeper asked.

I almost laughed. Amid such a disaster zone, how could anyone possibly remember where *anything in particular* was?

"Do you have any books on Buddhism?" I asked.

"Come with me."

Making your way through his shop was like navigating a jungle on your own. I followed him as he shoved aside cardboard boxes overloaded with paperback novels and squeezed through towering stacks of hardbacks that teetered precariously with our passing. Sitting on the floor in the back was an old steamer trunk plastered with stickers from places like Niagara Falls and Miami Beach. He opened it. Crammed inside were dozens upon dozens of books on the Buddha and Buddhism.

"We're open 'til six," he said. Then he turned and headed

back through the jungle to his tiny, cluttered desk near the entrance.

I read sitting on the trunk. The Buddha's words were tonic for the soul. One proverb stood out: "The way is not in the sky. The way is in the heart. What we think, we become." A solid hour flew by in a flash, and I hadn't thought at all about Chocks. For sixty minutes, give or take, I felt better about my fellow man. Less in conflict. More at peace. The feeling wouldn't last.

My phone buzzed. A new text message from Layne. "On my way," it read. I texted her back to let her know where I was.

The shopkeeper was engrossed in a biography of Alexander Hamilton. I carried three books to the front desk—*Siddhartha*, *The Light of Asia*, and *Zen for Americans*.

"I'll take these," I said. "How much do I owe you?"

"Five bucks," he said, not looking up from his reading.

"For each one?"

"Total."

What a deal.

"I've been in for an hour," I said. "You've had no other customers. How do you manage to stay in business?"

He quoted the Buddha. "Money's the worst discovery of human life," he said, "but it's the most trusted material to test human nature."

I gave him twenty bucks, told him to keep the change, and left.

Layne was waiting for me out front. I got in on the passenger side.

"How'd it go?"

"A lot of ambient noise," she said. "Light conditions were so-so."

"I'm sure you did the best you could," I said.

Layne gazed straight ahead. A thousand-yard stare, like she'd been to war. Her slacks were speckled with blood. Hers or somebody else's, I couldn't tell.

"You OK?"

"He gave me his card. With his personal number." She handed it to me.

"Did he talk?"

"Yeah. He talked. You were right, Logan. The asshole would've said anything to get laid."

"So, what did he say?"

"I just want to drive. Decompress for a while, OK?"

"Sure. Whatever you want."

We drove on, turning frequently, checking the mirrors to make sure we weren't being followed. On the west side of Santa Isabella was a public park with a playground. Children were swinging on swings and sliding down the slide, shrieking gleefully, as mothers stood and chatted. Layne parked at the far end of the lot where there were no other cars. After she switched off the ignition, she unclasped the jade pendant from her necklace, turned the pendant over in her palm, and pried off its false back, revealing the miniature video camera and audio receiver inside. I watched as she plugged one end of a USB cable into the pendant and the other end into her iPhone.

"It's uploading to the cloud," she said.

I nodded like the cloud and I were on a first-name basis. The cloud didn't exist when I was with Alpha. Neither did artificial intelligence, 3D printing, or datafication. We relied on wiretaps, paid informants, extraordinary rendition, and our Tier One Ultra authorization to terminate anyone our command staff deemed deserving of termination. The good old days.

"All I want to know," I said, "is whether Millisohn admitted he had anything to do with what happened to Chocks."

Layne handed me her phone. Anyone could see she was emotionally spent.

"Watch the tape," is all she said.

TWENTY-SEVEN

Layne leaned her head back against the seat and closed her eyes. She didn't feel like providing me an executive summary or a blow-by-blow of what Millisohn revealed. She'd done what I'd asked her to do, and that, she said, was enough.

"Just watch the tape," she repeated.

The video was grainy, the sound quality sketchy. But there was no disputing that the man her tiny pendant camera secretly recorded was Ed Millisohn, the CEO of Electrogenics. And there was no denying that what came out of Millisohn's mouth amounted to a criminal confession which probably would've been admissible in court had it been lawfully obtained.

The recording began with Layne approaching Millisohn as he held court in the clubhouse bar of his country club, trading jokes with other members. Other men turned to look at her. How could they not?

"Mr. Millisohn? Aphrodite Williams, Auckland Business Chamber," she said in her fake New Zealand accent over the laughter of golfers enjoying their gin and tonics after a day on the links. "Thank you so much for agreeing to see me."

And see her Millisohn did. The video resolution was hardly high-quality, but I could plainly see his smile go wide in the way of all lounge lizards as he turned and undressed her with his eyes.

"Well, hello there, Aphrodite Williams. Love your accent, by the way. Please. Call me Eddie." He dug a business card out of the pocket of his aloha shirt and handed it to her. "Got my private number on there. Feel free to call anytime."

"Thank you, Eddie. Shall we trade?" She handed him her fake business card. He didn't even look at it. The stool next to him was vacant. Layne sat.

"What's your pleasure?—drink-wise, I mean." He said it with a sly wink.

"I'll have what you're having," Layne said.

"Jimbo!" Millisohn yelled, holding up his half-empty glass so the bartender could see it. "The lady from Down Under would like an extra dry vodka martini. Stirred, never shaken. And while you're at it, another one for me, s'il vous plaît." He sounded like he'd already had more than a few drinks.

"Thank you, Eddie," Layne said. "I think I like you already."

"The feeling is definitely mutual." Millisohn tried not to stare at her breasts. "So, I understand you folks are interested in investing in Electrogenics."

She wasted no time explaining how wealthy investors in Auckland were impressed with the quality of his company's animatronic toy animals. "Very lifelike," she said, "yet so cuddly. We could make a fortune marketing little kiwis. They're so cute to begin with. A 'piece of piss,' as we like to say where I'm from."

He gulped down his martini and made quick work of two more, hardly listening to what she had to say and getting progressively more sloshed, while Layne proposed a joint operating agreement that promised huge profits.

"I don't know the first thing about these birds, and I really don't care." He leaned closer to her. "What I'm really interested in is you, Aphrodite. Great name, by the way."

"Glad you like it."

"You mind me asking you a personal question, Aphrodite?"

"Not at all," Layne said.

"I'm not seeing any wedding ring. You married?"

"Not presently, no."

"Boyfriend?"

Layne leaned closer to him. You could see her setting the hook. "No boyfriend, either," she said. "What about you, Eddie? Are you married?"

"Not so's you'd notice," Millisohn said, cracking himself up.

Layne laughed, too, playing along.

"Hey, I got an idea," Millisohn said. "How 'bout you and me go somewhere else not so loud. Get to know each other better. Negotiate a deal. Whadda you say?"

"Sounds delightful," Layne said.

I looked over at her. "I know how difficult this must've been for you," I said.

"No, you don't, Logan. You have no idea. Let's just get to the money shot."

I fast-forwarded. I didn't need to watch Millisohn walking drunkenly from the clubhouse to the parking lot and Layne getting into his Tesla with him, or how he was instantly all over her, pawing her and trying to force his tongue down her throat. She rebuffed his advances gently but forcefully. Even sober, he would've been no match for her.

"Let's just take it slow," Layne told him. "We can play later."

"Whatever you want, baby. But let's not take it *too* slow. You're busy. I'm busy. It's not like we both got all day, right?"

"Tell me more about your company."

"What do you want to know? Our debt-to-equity ratios?

Operating cash flow?" Millisohn stroked her shoulder. "All that sexy stuff?"

"Actually," Layne said, "what I'm more interested in is your accounts receivable."

"My what?"

"Who you do business with."

Millisohn grinned. "Hell, girl, we do business with every major toy wholesaler in North America. Canada and Mexico, too. They freakin' *love* us in Mexico."

"What about internationally?"

"Hell yeah. Internationally, too." Millisohn leaned closer to the camera, whispering, "And not all of our contracts involve animatronics, either. Let's just say we do some pretty high-level stuff, if you catch my drift."

"An international man of mystery," Layne cooed. "Tell me more."

"Between you and me?"

"Cross my heart and hope to die."

Millisohn sat back with a smug look on his face. "Let's just say we happen to be at the forefront of what's called 'proprietary defense technology.' You wouldn't believe some of the countries that wanna do business with us."

"Which ones?"

"If I told you, I'd have to kill you. And that's the last thing I wanna do with a sweet little thing like you, believe me."

Layne stroked his thigh. "Why can't you tell me which countries, Eddie?"

"Because it's secret, that's why," Millisohn said. "*Top*-secret."

Her long, elegant fingers inched toward his crotch. "It isn't Italy, is it? I love Italy. So much culture."

"*Italy?*" He laughed. "No, not Italy."

I couldn't see where her hand went next given the camera's

angle, but I didn't have to. Millisohn began panting like a pervert at a peep show.

"Is it Croatia?" Layne asked.

"Not Croatia, either."

"How about Russia? They're always in the market for things."

"A definite possibility," Millisohn moaned.

"Don't tell me you're selling classified technology to the Russians?"

"Hey, it's not like they don't have plenty already," Millisohn said, enjoying whatever she was doing to him below his equator. "All we're doing is leveling the playing field a little bit, that's all."

"Your government must know about this?"

"Sure. Absolutely. They're pretty much cool with whatever we do. As long as the right palms get greased."

"Greased palms?" Layne faked a laugh. "You Americans and your silly expressions."

"It means you gotta pay to play," Millisohn said. "It's how the world works, the *real* world, not the animatronic world. Probably even in the land of wonder, the land down under, right?"

"What can you tell me about Peter Hostetler, Eddie?" Layne asked, dropping the accent.

"Who?"

"Peter Hostetler. You remember him. Went by 'Chocks.' He used to work for you before he got thrown out of a helicopter. Was it because he found out you were selling radar components to Moscow?"

Millisohn sat upright and sobered up in an instant. "Who the hell *are* you?"

"Answer the question. What happened to Hostetler? Did you pay to have him killed?"

Millisohn panicked. He reached to grab Layne by her hair

across the Tesla's center console. She elbowed him in the throat, knocking him back against the door. Gasping and gagging, he tried to slap her. Layne blocked his hand with a forearm and drove her palm up, into his nose. Blood flowed.

"Bruce Lee couldn't have done it any better," I told her.

"Millisohn was never going to admit to being directly involved in a murder," Layne said, "so, I got what I could and got the hell out of there." She reached over and took back her phone. "His admitting to doing business with the Russians was coerced under false pretenses. It's worthless. Any competent defense attorney would have it tossed out in a heartbeat."

"It was worth it anyway," I said.

"Worth it anyway?" Layne looked over at me with fire in her eyes. "Then what was the point? Because, unless I missed something, Logan, you didn't go in there. I did."

"I needed you to provoke him, Layne. To soften him up. He's not done talking, I guarantee you that."

"You *used* me, Logan. Don't you understand that?"

I more than understood, I said, and I apologized to her. But sometimes, I told her, the ends do in fact justify the means. That's when she stormed out of the car and started walking.

"Where are you going, Layne?"

"I'll take the bus home."

"Layne, I'm sorry. Forget what I said. I'll drive you home."

"You had your chance. Multiple chances," she said without looking back. "We're done."

"What about your car?"

"You wreck it, you pay for it."

"I owe you, Layne. Big time. Chocks does, too."

"Go to hell, Logan."

I had asked too much of her. We were finally, irrevocably finished. Of that I was certain.

Way to go, Logan. When will you ever learn?

I made a few phone calls. Then I picked up Millisohn's card and dialed his private number.

———

The three smokestacks jutted into the sky over the deserted power plant at Big Rock Bay like giant concrete fingers. Millisohn proposed meeting there that afternoon. "Look for a sally port on the plant's north side," he said. "Come alone."

The drive from downtown Santa Isabella took ten minutes. Millisohn's Tesla was parked outside the plant's main gates. The gates were unchained.

He was waiting for me inside the plant's gutted control room. The walls were scrawled with gang graffiti. Broken window glass and spent syringes littered the floor.

"Where's your gun?" I asked him.

"No guns. I was hoping we could do this civilly."

I trusted him about as much as a gas station hot dog. Layne definitely had done a number on him. Bandages and surgical tape covered his broken nose. Both eyes were blackened.

"You look like you just went three rounds with George Foreman," I said.

"I should've known that bitch was a setup," Millisohn said. "And I should've known you were behind it. But let's dispense with the foreplay, Logan, shall we? You give me the video she shot, I tell you what I know about Hostetler."

"We'll get to all that," I said. "First you tell me about your little side hustle with the Russians."

He repeated what he'd told Layne. That it was no big deal. That Russian engineers had already developed their own phase-coherent klystron transmitters. Electrogenics was merely providing Moscow a "few minor improvements" that in no way influenced the global balance of power.

"They were gonna produce the refinements eventually on their own anyway. It was only a matter of time," Millisohn said. "So why not make a few bucks in the interim? It's called capitalism, Logan. The American Way."

"It's also called treason," I said.

His eyes were as dark and flat as river stones. "I didn't kill Peter Hostetler, Logan. You can believe me or not."

"I don't."

"I'm telling you the truth."

"OK, if you didn't, then who did?"

"If I knew, I would tell you."

"See you in court, Ed."

I turned to go.

"OK, wait. Wait!" He ran his hand over his nose, forgetting it was broken, and winced in pain. "There's a huge market for radar components all over the world. I've got customers everywhere. Governments. Maybe it was one of them, I really don't know. That's the God's honest truth."

"Which governments?"

He shook his head. "Not until you give me the video."

"Which governments, Ed?"

"Give me the video, Logan. Or else."

"Or else what?"

As if on cue, one of the burly security guards I'd encountered when I first visited Electrogenics stepped out from the shadows across the room with his submachine gun leveled at me.

"You really didn't think I'd come alone, did you?" Millisohn started to smile, then stopped himself, in pain. "The video, Logan. *Now.*"

"Look," I said, "far be it from me to lecture a techno-whizbang like you on I-T stuff, but it's my understanding, Ed, that there's this new thing you may have heard of. It's called 'the cloud.' You can pretty much upload anything you want including—let's say, for example—a confession from an American CEO who's been colluding with the Russians. Then, guess what? It floats around up there, wherever the cloud is, or *what*ever it is, for all to see, forever and ever."

"You think I'm an idiot? I know how the goddamn cloud works, Logan. Gimme the password to the account the video was uploaded to, so I can erase it."

The building began to shake like a small earthquake, followed by the rumble of an incoming helicopter.

"Forget it, Ed. I'm not scratching your back until you scratch mine."

I started toward the door.

"Logan! We're not done talking! You come back here!"

The shaking intensified as the sound of the helicopter became a thunderous roar. Millisohn's bodyguard walked over to an empty window, realized what was outside, and headed for the exit, like his beard was on fire—only to be confronted by incoming SWAT cops with their own submachine guns, yelling, "Drop your weapon!" and "Get on the ground!" He kissed the cement floor. So did Electrogenics's stunned chief executive officer. Both were handcuffed on their bellies with their wrists behind their backs. I leaned down, close enough that Millisohn could see my face.

"You didn't really think I'd come alone, either, did you, Ed?"

He turned his head away and said nothing. That's when Detectives Tom Kasparov and Lloyd Gregory came strolling in like it was just another day at the office.

"Took you long enough," I said.

"Rush-hour traffic," Gregory said. "Might as well be living back in New York."

I unbuttoned my shirt, peeled off the wire they'd taped to my chest after Layne left and I phoned him. "You get all that?"

"Every beautiful word," Kasparov said.

The SWAT team hauled Millisohn to his feet. Kasparov told him he was under arrest for violating the Espionage Act and various export control regulations, then read him his rights.

"Those are federal laws," Millisohn seethed. "You guys aren't the feds!"

"A matter of paperwork," Gregory said.

"This is bullshit!" Millisohn shouted as two SWAT guys hauled him outside to a waiting patrol unit. "I didn't do anything!"

"The guy admits to being in cahoots with Putin and he didn't do anything?" Gregory rolled his eyes the way only a native New Yorker can. "The world is filled with dickweeds."

"Agreed." I handed Kasparov the wire.

"My apologies if we were dickweeds, Logan," he said. "You done good."

"You as well," I said.

We shook hands.

I still didn't know who killed Chocks. What I did know, if only to assuage my own feelings of guilt, was that I needed to try one last time to save whatever it was Layne Sterling and I once had.

I couldn't have known then that doing so would nearly cost me my life.

TWENTY-EIGHT

We ate at Captain Ahab's on the wharf. The restaurant was a nautically themed, overpriced tourist trap, its walls adorned with commercial fishing nets and stuffed trophy fish, but the one-hundred-and-eighty-degree view of Rancho Bonita's harbor was unmatched. So were the captain's eggs Benedict.

"Thank you for letting me take you to breakfast," I said. "I didn't think you would."

"I needed my car back," Layne said, sipping orange juice and looking at anything but me.

"How was the Greyhound?"

"Fine."

She was still upset with me. That much was obvious. I couldn't blame her. I would've been, too, had I been in her shoes.

"Look, Layne, I know words are cheap, but for what it's worth, I'm truly, deeply, sorry, for everything. What you did went above and beyond. It produced results."

She gave me the silent treatment from across the table, gazing out at a kayaker rowing toward the breakwater. I could hear waves lapping against the wharf's pilings below us. A formation of pelicans glided past the restaurant's windows. In the morning sun, the ocean glittered like gemstones.

"Another perfect day in paradise," I said. "Not too many mornings like this in DC. Back there, you bake in the summer and freeze in the winter. But, I guess you knew that already."

More silence.

"OK, look," I said, "what about this? What if we went to counseling?"

She looked over at me in earnest for the first time since we'd sat down. "You're only saying that because you think it's what I want to hear."

"That's not true, Layne."

"Be honest, Logan. Not just with me. Yourself. You don't mean it. You know you don't."

"I *do* mean it. It's just . . ."

". . . Just what?"

I took a breath and let it out. "What's wrong with just trying to be more accepting of each other's faults? Everybody's human, Layne. Everybody makes mistakes. Seems to me like that would be way more convenient and a lot more affordable than having to sit in some shrink's office, navel-gazing at two hundred bucks an hour."

Her eyes locked on mine, like she was trying to peer straight through me. Then her eyebrows arched almost imperceptibly, and I knew she had.

"You're afraid," she said. "That's it, isn't it? You're afraid of being forced to take a hard look inside yourself, frightened by what you might find."

I smiled to cover the lie that followed it. "I'm comfortable in my own skin, Layne. Except when it's super humid."

"Not everything has to be a yuk, Logan," she said.

She was right, of course. Not everything was a joke. Only

most things. Because the minute you stop laughing at life is the minute you start moaning about it. I wanted to tell her that, but then our waitress, who looked old enough to have dated Captain Ahab herself, arrived with our meals.

"Eggs Benedict, hash browns extra crispy, extra hollandaise?"

I raised my hand. She plopped the plate down in front of me.

"And for the lady, egg white scramble, tomatoes on the side. Enjoy."

We ate without speaking. The hollandaise had an odd aftertaste, but I didn't think much of it at the time. I hadn't eaten much since the day before and I was starving. Layne, meanwhile, barely touched her food.

The hostess walked past us, shepherding a young couple to their table with two little kids in tow, a boy and a girl, both wearing Halloween costumes. He was Batman. She was Wonder Woman.

"I don't get it," I said. "Why does every superhero wear their underwear *outside* their clothes?"

Layne's gaze was downcast, her thoughts clearly far away. "Breakfast was a bad idea," is all she said.

I suggested that we retire to our respective corners and take the day to see where we both stood, then maybe reconvene that evening if she were willing for a beach walk at sunset. To my surprise, she agreed. We set a specific time and place to meet.

"I'm not ready to give up on us, Layne," I said as we were leaving the restaurant. "Not yet."

Layne stared down at her shoes. "I frankly don't know what I'm ready to do right now, Logan."

She said that if I was truly serious about counseling, the ball was in my court to find a psychologist willing to meet with us on short notice. Fair enough, I told her, only it would have to wait until the following day. I was scheduled that afternoon to give a two-hour introductory flight lesson to a prospective student. I hadn't had one of those in a while.

"My very first member of the cloth."

Layne looked at me like she didn't understand.

"Cyrus Simpson. The pastor who officiated at Chocks's funeral. I thought I mentioned him after I got home that night."

"Maybe you did. I don't remember."

She asked me if I wanted a ride back to my place. I took it as a good sign, but I didn't want to press my luck with her any more than I already had. I told her I was happy to walk home. I needed the exercise anyway.

Clear skies. Light winds. Visibility unlimited. An ideal afternoon for flight, and for a mini vacation from my issues with Layne. For a couple of hours anyway, I could also escape the mind-bending, still-unresolved enigma of my late wingman's murder. I was looking forward to getting back in the air. But as I drove to the airport, I started feeling queasy. By the time I got there, I was full-on sick to my stomach. The strange-tasting hollandaise sauce on my eggs that morning. Food poisoning. Had to be.

A giddy Cyrus Simpson was waiting for me in the parking lot outside Larry's hangar like a kid counting down the minutes before Disneyland opened. He'd exchanged his clerical collar for cargo pants, hiking boots, an Oakland A's baseball cap, and a Shasta Bible College T-shirt. A green daypack was slung over his right shoulder.

"I can't tell you how much I've been looking forward to this," he said. "I've never been in a small plane before. I barely slept a wink last night."

"Makes two of us, Pastor," I said.

"The Lord gave me the day off. Please call me Cyrus."

"Cyrus it is."

He'd driven almost two hours to experience for the first time what it felt like to be a pilot, the thrill of flight. I didn't want to disappoint him. I tried to convince myself that I wasn't sick, and that it was all in my head. Mind over matter. But my roiling intestines insisted otherwise.

Our footsteps echoed through the hangar as we walked past airplanes in various states of repair to my office. His head was on a swivel, taking it all in.

"Is this *your* hangar?"

"It's my mechanic's, but it looks like he went home early for the day."

"So, which one is your plane?"

"It's out on the flight line," I said. "We'll get out there in a couple of minutes. We need to get some preliminary paperwork out of the way first."

The paperwork was a standard waiver of liability. It said that if Pastor Simpson was injured or killed going up with me in the *Duck*—or *down*, as would more likely be the case—he couldn't sue me, nor could his survivors.

"The chances of anything happening," I assured him, "are astronomically remote."

"I'm sure you're an excellent pilot," he said, signing the waiver without hesitation. "I'm so excited about this, you have no idea."

A wave of nausea washed over me. I had to steady myself against my desk.

"You look a little green around the gills, Mr. Logan," Simpson said. "Are you OK?"

"I'll be fine. Stomach's a little upset, that's all. And you can save the 'mister.' It's just Logan."

"Logan it is."

I pulled a trash can over and chucked half my breakfast into it.

"You're in luck," Cyrus said. "I'm prone to airsickness myself. It used to happen every time I flew back to Kansas to visit my parents. That was before I got prescribed this stuff." He pulled a prescription bottle out of his backpack. "I was worried I might be a little queasy today, so I already took one. Trust me. Take two and you'll be good as new in no time."

I didn't ask what they were. I would've taken virtually anything at that point to settle my stomach. He shook out a couple white tablets, and I gulped them down with water from a gallon jug on my file cabinet. I started feeling better instantly.

"The miracle of modern medicine," I said. "Thank you, Cyrus."

"Don't thank me. Thank the good Lord. And thank *you*. This is the thrill of a lifetime. I can't wait."

We walked out of the hangar and onto the flight line.

"That's my airplane right over there," I said.

If Simpson was disappointed by the *Duck*'s faded looks, or by the prospect of challenging gravity in a flying machine more than a half century old, he didn't express it.

"What a darling little airplane," he said. "It's *so* cute."

"I call him the *Ruptured Duck*."

"The *Ruptured Duck*? A rather odd name for an airplane."

"You'll just have to look it up," I said.

I showed him how to conduct a thorough preflight inspection. We examined the control surfaces for signs of possible damage, checked the oil level, scrutinized the propeller blades for nicks or cracks, and drained a small amount of fuel from both wings to make sure no rainwater had leaked in. Then we stowed his pack in the cargo compartment, and I had him strap into the left seat. He marveled at the flight instruments.

"Boy, so much to learn," he said. "You've really gotta know what you're doing."

"It's like anything else," I said. "The more you do it, the easier it becomes. But it's important to always remember the first rule of being a pilot."

"What's that?"

"If you're not paying constant attention to what it's doing, an airplane will kill you faster than anything."

Cyrus Simpson's breath caught in his throat and his eyes went a little wide. "Good to know," he said.

The *Duck* was cranky that day. I had to prime the heck out of the engine and pump the throttle several times before I got it to go. Everything appeared normal after that. All instruments in the green.

Up we went into the wild blue.

Just as I had done with dozens of other student pilots, I assured him that taking off is easy. I let him do it himself. The goal of any introductory flight is not to overwhelm the student, but to leave them believing, "I can *do* this." It was evident to me, though, from the panicky sheen on his fleshy face, to his lack of hand-eye coordination, that Cyrus Simpson was no pilot. He seemed relieved to relinquish the controls.

"I'm so sorry," he said. "I didn't think I'd be this nervous. How embarrassing."

"Don't be embarrassed, Cyrus. Learning to fly can be seem a little challenging at first. But I promise, the more you practice, the less daunting it gets. You want to give it another try?"

"Good God no."

"Understood. Maybe we should head back."

The pastor shook his head. "Not just yet. I'm not nervous at all with *you* flying. I'd just like to stay up here for a while, if it's all the same to you, and admire the view. I mean, c'mon, wow, what a beautiful day."

That it was. The ocean and sky were mirrored so seamlessly that, looking out at the horizon, it was all but impossible to discern where one ended and the other began. Behind us, as clear as I'd ever seen it, the coastline of California curved west before ambling northward toward Point Conception, and out toward infinity.

"God in all his glory," Cyrus said.

"Roger that."

I had just established a standard-rate turn to the south when I started feeling that something wasn't right—not with the *Duck*, but with me. Without warning, my heart began revving like a motorcycle engine. Then the gauges on the instrument panel went fuzzy.

What the hell was happening?

I blinked and my field of vision cleared, but only for a moment. The altimeter, the airspeed indicator, the attitude indicator—all of them blurred. I swallowed down the panic that rose up inside of me like a wave crashing on the shore.

Just fly the airplane, Logan. That's all you've gotta do right now. You can figure out what's wrong later. Just fly the plane.

"Are you OK, Logan?"

I could barely make out the horizon.

"We have a problem, Cyrus," I said with as much calm as I could muster. "I need your help."

"Yes, of course, anything!" I could hear the fear in his voice.

"There's a long, narrow box mounted just below the radios. It's black. Rectangular. It's showing four numbers. Do you see it?"

"Yes."

"Good. That's our transponder. It helps air traffic control see us more easily on radar. I need you to change the numbers to seven, seven, zero, zero. You think you could do that?"

Silence.

"Cyrus, please, I need you to change the numbers."

"Seventy-seven hundred is the code for an in-flight emergency," he said. "We're not going to do that right now." In an instant, his tone had changed. Gone was the terrified clergyman. In its place was a confident man who sounded fully in control of his circumstances.

I thumbed the mic button on my yoke, struggling impulsively to keep the *Duck*'s wings level and fighting the not-unpleasant sensation that I was about to lose consciousness any second.

"Mayday. Mayday. Mayday. This is Four Charlie Lima. We're—"

The radio went dead in my earphones as Simpson turned off the avionics master switch.

"I have the airplane," he said like he didn't have a care in the world.

If a turn is perfectly coordinated in the air, the only force you'll feel in the cockpit is a slight pressure straight down in your seat. Mastering that kind of coordination requires considerable training. I couldn't see the *Duck*'s flight instruments—or anything else, for that matter—but I could tell by how the turn felt that it was flawlessly executed, and that Simpson knew exactly what he was doing.

The pastor is a pilot.

That's the last thing I remember thinking before everything dissolved to nothing—that and wishing I'd brought a gun.

TWENTY-NINE

My skull pounded. My guts felt like they were lined with glass shards. The first thing I saw when I persuaded my eyes to unseal was a huge green man standing over me with arms held high, like he was surrendering. I blinked a couple of times before my vision cleared and I realized I was staring up at a saguaro cactus.

Both doors were open. I was still sitting in the copilot seat, but the *Duck* and I were no longer in the air. I'd flown through Death Valley enough to recognize the desertscape surrounding me and the lunar-like mountains of the Panamint Range to the north. We were somewhere south of Twentynine Palms, having landed on what barely amounted to a game trail. I saw no houses. No power lines or fences. No nothing. It might not have been the end of the earth, as the old saw goes, but you could see it from there.

To my left, a shirtless Cyrus Simpson was sweating and digging what looked like a grave—my grave—with a short-handled collapsible shovel. A pistol was wedged in his belt. He must have stowed the gun and shovel in his backpack before we took off from Rancho Bonita, along with the duct tape that now bound my wrists tightly behind my back.

He paused his labors and gulped water from a plastic bottle. The desert sun was a blowtorch. My mouth was as dry as raw cotton.

"Man," I said, "it's a scorcher out here today."

Simpson glanced over, wiping his mouth with the back of his hand. "Gracious. You're awake."

I nodded toward his water. "You think I could get some of that if it's not too much trouble?"

He walked over and held the bottle to my lips. The water was warm but it felt good going down.

"I'm surprised you regained consciousness," Simpson said. "Then again, I was surprised when Hostetler did, too. I should've upped the doses."

". . . Doses?"

"Ketamine. More than enough to kill both of you outright. Or so I thought."

A light bulb went off in my head. "Horse tranquilizer. From your friends at the racetrack in Del Mar. Very resourceful, Cyrus."

Simpson shrugged like a man pleased with himself. "I was going to dump him out over the ocean. But then he woke up and tried to fight me. I kicked the door open and out he went. Those poor, sweet old folks in that trailer. I'm glad they weren't hurt."

"You have a helicopter rating, huh?"

"Helicopter. Multi. Instrument. Commercial. By the way, Logan, the *Ruptured Duck* is a worn-out piece of crap. I've flown bricks with better handling characteristics."

"Insult the pilot," I said, "never his airplane."

Granted, the *Duck* was tired and slow and not particularly easy on the eyes, but he'd always gotten me where I needed to go and back again in one piece. I'd grown accustomed to his limitations and his looks. I now set about trying to take advantage of one of his infirmities:

The copilot's seat cushion was threadbare. The padding had collapsed long ago, leaving little more than fabric covering a broken section of metal tubing where the seat bottom met the seat back. If you shifted your weight the wrong way, it felt like your tailbone was being stabbed with a dull knife. I had never bothered replacing the cushion or having the framing fixed because I could never afford to. Also, when I flew as an instructor, it was always from the right seat, so that my students would not be subjected to such torture. I calculated that if I could keep the good pastor talking long enough, distracting his attention, I might have enough time to use the edge of the broken seat framing and subtly saw through the tape before he killed me.

"I have a question," I said.

"You want to know if God really exists. The good news is, you're going to find out very shortly."

He picked up the shovel and went back to digging my grave. I continued working the duct tape back and forth against the seat.

"You told me *how* you killed him, Pastor, but you didn't say *why*."

"You wouldn't understand."

"Try me."

He stopped shoveling long enough to mop the sweat from his brow. "Where does it say I owe you any explanations? I've already told you enough."

"He was my wingman. I owed him my life. I have a right to know."

"You have no rights, Logan. Not here. Not after the anxiety you've caused me, running around asking questions, sticking your nose in places it doesn't belong. But I am a pious man, a man of deep religious conviction, so I will tell you this much: I had no choice."

"Charles Manson said the same thing."

Simpson's nostrils flared. "You think I'm deranged. I'm not. What I did—what I'm doing—I do in defense of my people against Western imperialism."

"What people would those be, Cyrus?"

"The Russian people."

"Really? That's surprising. You don't exactly strike me as Russian."

He proudly shared how, when he was a toddler, his father, Colonel Nikolai Shiskin of the Soviet air force, stole a transport plane, loaded up his wife and children, and flew to Japan. They eventually made their way to the United States. Colonel Shiskin legally changed his surname to Simpson and went to work for the CIA, where he eventually found himself caught up in the Iran–Contra scandal. One foggy night, papa flew into a six-thousand-foot mountain in Nicaragua.

Cyrus Simpson gulped down another slug of water. "Washington called it an accident, a tragedy. It wasn't. He'd threatened to go to the press with what he knew about the scandal, so they killed him. Sabotaged his plane. He was an excellent pilot. He taught me everything about flying."

"Hopefully with the exception of slamming into mountains under IFR conditions."

"Are you mocking me, Logan?"

"I'm just trying to understand why my friend died, Cyrus, that's all."

I was stalling for time, grinding my wrists against the seat frame as subtly but determinedly as I could.

"He died, Logan, because America is an immoral wasteland.

Rome in decline. It must be burned to the ground and cleansed of its filth. All I'm doing is helping accelerate the process."

"So, he found out you were trying to secure military-grade radar components from Electrogenics for your 'people,' and he was going to go to the FBI, but you couldn't let that happen, could you, Pastor?"

He said nothing. He didn't have to. His deranged little half smile said it all.

"One thing I don't understand," I said. "How'd you managed to get a guy as big as Pete Hostetler into that helicopter?"

"He told me he'd never flown one. He was interested in learning. I drugged him. End of story. Enough with the questions. Get out of the plane."

"I'd love to, Pastor, but that sun is brutal. I burn like a fried egg."

"I said get out."

"I'd just as soon stay in here, if it's all the same to you."

I could feel the duct tape starting to give way. All I needed was a few more seconds.

"As you prefer," Simpson said. "Then I suppose I'll just have to clean up your brains before I fly this bucket down to Mexico and sell it. The Lord giveth, the Lord taketh away. Goodbye, Logan."

He pulled his pistol. It looked like an old Makarov, standard Soviet issue.

"Listen," I said, "before you do anything more stupid than what you've already done, you might want to take a look right behind you. You squeeze that trigger, and I guarantee you the discharge will spook that snake. He'll have you for supper."

Simpson smirked. "You don't really expect me to fall for that, do you?"

"It's your funeral," I said.

The sober expression on my face convinced him I wasn't bluffing. He turned to find himself staring into the eyes of a Mojave green rattlesnake coiled and ready to strike three feet from where he was standing.

Blam! Blam! Blam!

I freed my wrists and grabbed the fire extinguisher tucked under the *Duck*'s pilot seat while Cyrus Simpson blasted away at the snake. As he turned back to shoot me, I pulled the extinguisher's safety pin and nailed him with a full blast of potassium bicarbonate.

I heard the gun go off again and knew I'd been hit, but I felt no pain. What I remembered most was the sensation of falling.

No darkness compares to the darkness of the Mojave Desert on a moonless night. When I came to, I found myself cocooned in blackness so complete, I literally could not see my hand in front of my face. At first, I wasn't certain I was alive. Then I heard a commercial jetliner flying high overhead and confirmed that I was still sitting in the *Duck*'s copilot seat. The right side of my face was sticky with blood. I was aware that I'd been shot in the head, but I had no way of gauging the severity of the wound. I knew it couldn't have been that bad because I still had feeling in all four of my limbs—or thought I did. Stepping out of the plane, my right leg gave way like it was made of Jell-O. I sprawled onto the ground, coming to rest on my back. Somewhere not too far away, a pack of coyotes was howling in celebration of a fresh kill.

I crawled back toward the *Duck*, dragging my useless Jell-O leg behind me and inching my way through in the darkness until I reached the landing-gear strut and pulled myself up, back into the cockpit. Inside the plane's glove box was an emergency flashlight. Hobbled but able to stand, I surveyed my surroundings in its halogen beam:

Cyrus Simpson lay sprawled in the dirt with his arms spread wide, pistol still in hand, his lifeless eyes staring up at the stars. Blood oozed from two small puncture wounds on the right side of his chest, just below the nipple. There was no trace of the rattlesnake that bit him. Simpson's aim had been off; the snake's had not. As the Buddha said, "Don't take revenge. Let karma do all the work.".

Simpson may have been a deranged killer, but I had to admire his piloting skills. He'd set the *Duck* down on an impossibly short, narrow piece of ground. Taking off from the same strip in the dark of night, hoping we didn't clip a cactus or some big rock before we got airborne, would've been tempting fate. Add to that a gunshot wound to the head and virtually no feeling in one leg, and I knew I was in no shape to fly.

I couldn't find my phone to call for help. Simpson's phone was still in his pants pocket, but I couldn't get any service. Plan B was to turn on the *Duck*'s battery and broadcast a Mayday. But when I hit the avionics master switch, nothing happened. No lights on the instrument panel. Either the battery was dead, there was a wiring issue somewhere, or the *Duck* was simply being ornery, as senior citizens are sometimes inclined. Recycling the switch produced the same result. Bubkes. Nothing.

I still had one card left to play, though.

The emergency locator transmitter, built to trigger automatically in a crash, was mounted through a narrow opening in the aft fuselage behind the baggage compartment. If I could get to it, I might be able to manually activate the transmitter to send an emergency distress signal.

The newest transmitters broadcast their signals directly to

communication satellites in geostationary and low-earth orbit. Search and rescue personnel use those signals to swiftly pinpoint a downed pilot's precise location. My airplane lacked such a transmitter, namely because I never had the money to buy one. The *Duck*'s ELT was as old as the *Duck* itself and transmitted on the universal emergency frequency of 121.5 MHz. That meant the signal would only be heard by pilots actively monitoring that frequency while flying over the immediate area.

No one had to tell me they were long odds.

More modern planes are equipped with cockpit switches that allow pilots to activate an emergency signal remotely. The *Duck* had no such switch. I would have to crawl into the aft fuselage through the baggage door and trigger the transmitter manually.

With my malfunctioning leg and blood loss from my head wound, getting there wasn't easy, especially after my flashlight batteries died. Getting the door open and climbing in blindly, in complete darkness, took nearly every ounce of energy I had. I groped my way inch by inch, cutting my hands repeatedly on sheet-metal screws. It took what seemed like forever before I found the transmitter and triggered it.

By the time I wriggled back out of the plane and fell to the ground, I had nothing left. Snakes or no snakes, I slept on the ground.

I awoke to hurricane-force winds tattooing my skin with blowing dirt. It was morning. A helicopter was hovering a hundred feet directly above me. A guy in a tan military-style jumpsuit and white crash helmet was leaning out the door, waving.

I gave him a weak thumbs-up.

The helicopter banked steeply away before settling gracefully onto the desert floor not far away, kicking up even more dirt. "San Bernardino County Sheriff" was painted in black on the chopper's boom. The guy in the helmet who'd been waving at me jumped out even before the skids touched the ground and ran toward me carrying a first aid box.

"Are you Cordell Logan?" he yelled over the wind and howling of the helicopter's turbine engine.

I nodded as he snapped open the box and got out a stethoscope. His bushy moustache looked like it was made from horsehair. The winged patch on his flight suit read, "Deputy Scott Weiner."

"You doing OK?" he asked me.

"Better now," I said.

He listened to my heart. "Looks like you got yourself a nice little gunshot wound there."

"Feels like it."

He glanced over at Simpson's body. "That's the guy who shot you?"

I nodded.

"Did you shoot him?"

"Snake got him."

"Hard way to go," Weiner said. "Think you can walk?"

"Negative. My leg's in-op."

"Copy that. We'll let the hospital deal with it. Any other injuries I need to know about right now?"

"Not to my knowledge."

"Good deal. OK, sit tight. I'll go grab my partner and the litter. We'll get you stabilized and out of here."

"Sounds like a plan."

They strapped me to the litter, loaded me into the helicopter, an Airbus H125, and transported me to a trauma center in

Loma Linda. Weiner pasted a bunch of electrodes to my chest while we were en route and monitored my vitals. It might've only been a grazing wound, but my skull felt like someone had taken a sledgehammer to it.

"You must be pretty special," Weiner said as he started a saline drip in my arm.

"How's that?"

"Everybody in the state's been out looking for you since last night. They even called in the Air Guard. Order came directly out of Washington. That's what we heard anyway."

I had assumed that my rescue had come courtesy of the *Duck*'s antiquated but apparently still functional ELT.

I was wrong.

THIRTY

The neurologist looked like one of those bearded opera singers partial to pasta Alfredo. "Dr. Santiago Broca" was stitched over the breast pocket of his starched white lab coat that smelled of industrial-strength disinfectant.

"You appear to have crural monoplegia," he said in a pleasant Castilian accent, standing beside my hospital bed, tapping on an iPad.

"In English, Doc. I don't speak med school."

"Crural monoplegia. This can occur from a limited lesion or bruising of the cortex—as with a grazing bullet wound. Here, let me show you." He flipped the iPad around so that I could see the screen. "Notice here, and here," he said, pointing out several small spots on an MRI image of my brain. "There. You see? Hopefully nothing to worry about. They should heal over time."

"How long will I be stuck in here?"

"Two or three days, depending how you progress. I'd like to run a few more tests."

"When has one of you guys ever *not* wanted to run a few more tests?"

The doctor chuckled. "Point taken."

"What about my leg?" I asked.

"What about it?"

"When will I regain full function?"

The neurologist raised both palms. "The human brain, despite all we know about it, remains largely a mystery, Mr. Logan. Your leg may return to normal soon, or not at all. Only time will tell."

"The wonders of modern science," I said. "Not so wondrous in this case, are they?"

"Get some rest, Mr. Logan," the doctor said as he walked out. "Rest is always the best medicine."

My room was semiprivate. My roommate was hooked up to a ventilator and so many wires, tubes, and monitors, I couldn't see his face. I didn't need an MD after my name to know he wasn't long for this world. Whatever feelings of self-pity I might have had in that moment passed quickly. At least I wasn't *that* guy.

Lunch was watery chicken soup, a veggie panini that tasted like cardboard, and a gluten-free, sugar-free blob of something yellow masquerading as cheesecake. "Heart-healthy," the hospital called it. I would've killed for a burrito and a couple of doughnuts.

I was doing my best to choke down the panini when Layne Sterling walked in.

"Thank God," she said. "You had me worried."

"What would life be without a little excitement now and then," I said.

She leaned down and gave me a hug that felt like an embrace

from a friend rather than a lover. And when she kissed me on the cheek, it left no doubt where things stood between us.

"The cops told me the only reason they found me as fast as they did was because somebody pulled a few strings in Washington."

"I made a few calls," Layne said. "No big deal."

She'd grown concerned after I failed to show up for our sunset beach walk. Then she remembered me saying I was going flying with Pastor Cyrus Simpson. "Unusual name," she said. "I knew I'd heard it somewhere before. I just couldn't remember where."

It bothered her, not being able to remember. She made a call to a friend in McLean. The friends checked classified records and discovered that Simpson had long-standing ties to Russia's Foreign Intelligence Service, the SVR. Layne then traced the *Duck*'s ground track online using open-source databases until it came to an abrupt end, apparently where Simpson turned off the plane's transponder.

"Your last known heading showed you tracking a direct line toward the Mojave. I called my new boss and told him who you were and what the situation was. He was the one who called out the cavalry, not me."

"What you're saying is, if you hadn't taken this new job, I might still be out there."

"Oh, come on. Resourceful guy like you? You would've probably figured a way out yourself. Eventually." She smiled.

The Mojave is forty-eight thousand square miles of some of the most remote, inhospitable turf on the planet. Locating a small plane amid its vastness can make finding Waldo look like child's play.

"I didn't tell Mrs. Schmulowitz what happened," Layne said. "No use her getting all worried, too."

"Agreed. She's probably having too much fun pet-sitting anyway."

"Probably."

An uneasy silence passed between us. We were two very different people, both aware that our time together was coming to a permanent, incontrovertible end. As the Buddha said, some things are never meant to be. Happiness can only be achieved by trading expectation for acceptance.

"I'm grateful to you, Layne," I said. "For everything."

"Same." Layne cleared her throat, barely able to get the word out. "Is there anything you need?"

I couldn't think of anything else to tell her but the truth. "You," I said.

"You don't need me, Logan. You need somebody who won't come unglued every time you go flying off by the seat of your pants, convinced who dares wins."

I reached out and took her hand. She let me hold it, but not for long.

"Wherever you are," she said, "you'll always be in my heart."

I forced a smile, the kind you offer your opponent after losing a game. "Wow," I said, "you know it's time to turn off the lights when the person you're saying goodbye to starts quoting Gandhi."

"Be well, Logan."

"Blue skies, Layne."

I lay in my perfectly adjusted hospital bed the rest of that afternoon and watched TV, when I wasn't gazing out at the snow-dusted peaks of the San Gabriel Mountains. A nurse came in every hour on the hour to check my vitals. I welcomed the intrusions. They helped distract me from my throbbing head, nonworking leg, and the realization that I would never see Layne Sterling again.

The lead story on the KTLA evening news was about an eagle-eyed helicopter crew from the San Bernardino County Sheriff's Department rescuing a private pilot after his single-engine plane went missing in the desert. The deputies who found him were hailed as heroes. No mention was made of Cyrus Simpson or Russian intelligence or classified radar components. Nor was my name mentioned. I was thankful for that.

Shortly after midnight, I awoke to the beeping alarms of an EKG. Two nurses and a physician came rushing in. They all looked like they'd been rousted from sleep. One of the nurses pulled a curtain partitioning me from my roommate. For the next half hour they tried to revive him before ultimately covering his face with a sheet. Relish the good times, I reminded myself as they wheeled his body away. In life there are no do-overs, only memories.

"Stupendous" and "amazing" is how Dr. Broca described my recovery. My head still ached, and my leg strength was not yet a hundred percent, but four days after being airlifted out of the desert, I was deemed healthy enough to be discharged. Deputy Scott Weiner and his pilot, Sergeant Lalo Zuniga, took me to their favorite Mexican food truck in Rialto. They told me that among his other misdeeds, Cyrus Simpson had been passing himself off as an FBI agent. The Bureau doesn't take too kindly to that.

"He had to have been the same guy who showed up in Rancho Bonita and tossed my office looking for radar modules," I said.

"Sounds like that snake did the taxpayers a favor," Weiner said.

I couldn't disagree.

We ate over the hood of their cruiser. The shrimp tacos were so good, I almost lost my burrito addiction. Almost. Then we drove to the sheriff's heliport and flew back into the desert to retrieve my airplane.

I preflighted the *Duck*, taking my time, checking every control surface and rivet, before thanking them both for saving my hide.

"It's what we do," Weiner said.

We all bro-hugged, and I invited them to come see me sometime in Rancho Bonita. I'd take them to my favorite burrito joint. They promised to take me up on my offer.

"You sure you don't have a density altitude issue out here, Logan?" Zuniga asked. "You got a short strip to work with, and it's already hotter than hell. Why don't you wait until tomorrow morning, first thing, when it's cooler? We can bring you back out then."

"I've got a dog and cat waiting for me back home—well, I know the dog is, anyway. If I don't get back this afternoon, my landlady's gonna have a mutiny on her hands. I think I'll be OK."

"Famous last words," Zuniga said. "More pilots die from get-home-itis than anything else."

"What do you figure the elevation is out here?" I asked him.

"Slightly more than three thousand feet."

"Temperature?"

"Low nineties."

"Who dares wins," I said.

I climbed in and went through the start-engine checklist. Simpson had been considerate enough to leave the key in the ignition. The fuel selector valve was set to both tanks. Avionics switch off. Electrical equipment switches off. All circuit breakers in. Brakes set. Mixture set to full rich. Carb head cold. Master switch on. Beacon light on. Throttle cracked open an eighth of an inch.

"Clear prop!" I yelled out the window, then engaged the starter.

The *Duck*'s mood had improved significantly from the last time I tried to start the engine. Two sluggish rotations of the propeller were all it took before the four-cylinder Lycoming thrummed to life. Oil pressure and engine temperature rose swiftly into the green as I back-taxied, with the two cops looking on, shaking their heads like I was a suicide about happen.

The higher the temperature and field elevation, the more runway and headwind an airplane needs to take off, especially on a dirt strip. The Mojave was baking. The wind was listless, a barely discernible breeze out of the west. With the fuel tanks half-full, I estimated I'd need about sixteen hundred feet of runway to get off the ground. The narrow trail on which Simpson had set the *Duck* down looked to be barely that long. Once again, I had to grudgingly admire his airmanship. The pastor may have been a murderous traitor to the nation that gave him and his family shelter, but he was a skilled pilot.

I stood on the right toe brake and advanced the throttle, kicking up dust and pivoting the *Duck* until the nose of the plane was aligned with the trail. A wall of rocks some three stories tall loomed unavoidably at the far end. Cactus and Joshua trees flanked either side of my makeshift airstrip, affording no more than a foot of clearance from either wingtip. I'd have to avoid those obstacles, get the nosewheel off the ground as quickly as possible, immediately establish the *Duck*'s best angle of climb, and gain as much altitude as I could in the shortest distance to avoid flying straight into those rocks.

Had I been the religious type, I might've prayed for a more

powerful engine or a longer runway. I didn't need either as it turned out. As if by some occult hand, the wind began picking up—a headwind. It would gust erratically, strong enough to rock the *Duck*'s wings, then subside, only to kick up again seconds later. The trick would be to coincide my takeoff with those bursts if I hoped to clear the rocks.

I held both toe brakes firmly to the floor while advancing the throttle all the way to the firewall. The *Duck* strained to go like a racehorse at the starting gate. A gust came. A gust went.

Here we go!

I released the brakes.

Rolling. Rolling. Rolling. It seemed to take forever before the airspeed needle came alive. With each passing foot, the rock wall at the far end of the strip seemed to loom higher. At sixty knots, I pulled the nosewheel off the ground and pitched the plane up at the steepest possible angle of attack, ignoring the stall warning horn moaning in my ears.

C'mon, Duck, climb!

The rocks towered dead ahead. I couldn't climb over them, not without first establishing sufficient airspeed, and I couldn't turn, not without stalling.

We're not gonna make it.

A calm came over me, a resignation. Call it acceptance. I was about to crash and burn, and there wasn't a damn thing I could do about it. I closed my eyes. This was it.

Only it wasn't.

Suddenly, we were climbing—steeply. I opened my eyes and watched the vertical airspeed needle jumping past fifteen hundred feet a minute. A powerful updraft had lifted the *Duck* over the rocks. We'd cleared the ridge by no more than a couple of feet, if that.

Who dares wins.

I yelped. I whooped. I slapped the top of the instrument panel the way a jockey does his trusty steed. Banking around, I could see Weiner and Zuniga still standing next to their helicopter. They were pumping their fists in the air.

I made one low pass over them, rocking the *Duck*'s wings, before turning for home.

Teaching Kiddiot algebra would've been less difficult than training Ack-Ack how to fetch. Every time I tossed him the tennis ball across my landlady's backyard, he'd go running after it, then quickly become distracted by some new scent trail. He was a hound, obviously, not a retriever. I had all but given up on him when Mrs. Schmulowitz leaned out her kitchen window.

"Hey, bubby, get in here! They're talking about you on the tube!"

The TV was tuned to the five o'clock news. Assistant US Attorney Robert Poverly for the Southern District of California, an owlish fellow with round glasses and a snowy beard, was standing behind a lectern bristling with news media microphones to announce that his office was prosecuting Theodore Millisohn, age fifty-three, chief executive officer of Electrogenics, Inc. Millisohn was being charged with violating 18 US Code 798—disclosure of classified information. Conviction carried a ten-year prison sentence. He was being held without bond.

"Again, in closing," Poverly said, "this office would like to extend its appreciation to the Santa Isabella County Sheriff's Office, and to Mr. Cordell Logan of Rancho Bonita, without whose assistance and patriotism this case would not have been possible."

Mrs. Schmulowitz gave me the stink eye. "What crazy nonsense have you been up to this time?"

"Just doing my thing," I said.

"That 'thing' is gonna get you killed someday, bubby. You know that, right?"

"You don't need to worry about me, Mrs. Schmulowitz. It's true what they say. Only the good die young."

"That's what I'm afraid of," she said.

The next morning broke gray and misty. Visibility at the airport was less than two miles with a six-hundred-foot ceiling. I requested tower-in-route clearance to Santa Isabella and was airborne by 0900. A cloud layer persisted along the entire route of flight. The *Duck* and I were sandwiched between an unbroken layer of solid white below us and blue sky above. The air was mirror-smooth. I felt unshackled, liberated from the concerns of mere mortals. A feeling only a pilot can understand.

The tower gave me vectors to the final approach course. I established inbound on the localizer, pegged the glideslope, and rode the needles on my omni-bearing indicator down through the clouds. At three hundred feet, the layer gave way and there was the runway, right where it was supposed to be. My landing was a thing of beauty.

Booyah.

Kimberleigh was on duty behind the front counter at BillionAir. She smiled as I walked in.

"They were talking about you on the news last night," she said. "I didn't know you were a hero."

"I didn't know millennials watched TV news," I said.

"*Millennials?*" She tucked her chin, feigning insult. "How dare you? I believe you meant Gen Z."

"My bad," I said, as if I knew the difference between the two. "Is your crew car still available?"

"Right where you left it the last time," Kimberleigh said.

She asked me if I liked French food. An unusual question, especially out of context, I thought, but I played along. I preferred Mexican food, I told her, but that I was known to eat just about anything. She jotted her number along with a tiny heart on a pink Post-it note and handed it to me over the counter.

"I make a mean coq au vin," she said. "Give me a call sometime. We can discuss your favorite memories of Walter Cronkite."

I was flattered. I was also twice her age. I told her I'd give it some thought and walked out.

The last time I set foot in a liquor store . . . well, I couldn't remember the last time.

The clerk was scruffy in a counterculture kind of way. He greeted me from behind the cash register with all the enthusiasm one might expect from an embittered, minimum-wage slave.

"Help you find something?"

"Chivas Regal?"

"Second aisle, third shelf on your left."

"Thank you."

Gray clouds drifted across the treetops and the air smelled of rain. Chocks's grave was an unmarked rectangle of wet dirt. No grass yet. No headstone. He hadn't been in the ground long enough.

I stood there for what felt like a long time, struggling to tell him what I was feeling. How I could never begin to repay him for saving my life that day in Iraq. How I always admired him as a football player, a classmate, and a pilot. And how I would never understand how he could have fallen so far from grace. But the words were lost on me.

"Maybe if I'd kept boozing it up, you'd be the one standing here, not me," I said. "But this isn't about me, though, is it? It's about you, Chocks. I don't know where it all started going south, brother. I only wish I could've been there for you when it did."

I pulled the bottle of Chivas Regal from the pocket of my rain jacket and unscrewed the cap. The smell of twelve-year-old scotch flooded my brain with the echoed memories of daring missions and the drinking marathons that invariably followed them, of Chocks and I laughing so hard that neither of us could breathe.

I thought about what his wife had said, how he'd abused her. I thought about how he'd become involved with a narcotics dealer. None of that squared with the fearless fighter pilot I was honored to have flown with, the sky knight who always had my back. That was the man I chose to remember. A true hero.

"The sky may be the limit," I said, "but for guys like us, the sky is home. I'll see you up there someday, buddy. Hopefully not too soon, though."

Chocks loved Chivas. I tipped the bottle and watched the whiskey seep slowly into the raw soil marking his final resting place. When the last drop was done, I reached into my pocket and took out the medallion I found on the rooftop of Walt and Lena Rizzo's trailer—the same one Chocks had worn flying into harm's way. St. Joseph of Cupertino, patron saint of aviators.

I knelt and placed it on his grave.

Are we reunited in the Great Beyond with those we loved and admired during our allotted time on this rock? Are we rewarded eternal grace for a life well led? Or, as the Buddha believed, are we reborn again and again, consigned to an endless cycle in which there is no soul and no self? I have no proof that either contention is real. Anybody who says they do is lying. All I know is that on that gray, gloomy afternoon, alone in that cemetery, something compelled me to raise my eyes toward the sky. The clouds parted. A patch of blue emerged. And for one fleeting moment, I swore I saw a rainbow.